To Hallie,
Enjoy !
Kelly Kelly

Cursed by the Fountain of Youth

By Holly Kelly

Published by Clean Paranormal

Other Books by Holly Kelly
Rising (book 1 in The Rising Series)
Descending (book 2 in The Rising Series)
Avenging (book 3 in The Rising Series)
Raging (book 4, final book in The Rising Series)
Coming Soon:
Beauty and the Horseman's Head (An Unnatural
States of America Book)

Cursed by the Fountain of Youth

Copyright © 2017 by: Holly Kelly
ISBN: 978-1542764421

Edited by: Tamara Hart Heiner
Cover Design by: James Kelly

Clean Paranormal
P.O. Box 1057
Spanish Fork, Utah 84660

AuthorHollyKelly.com

Cursed by the Fountain of Youth

Prologue

Brigitte stumbled over a moss-covered log and quickly regained her footing as she raced to keep up with the pregnant woman—the one she needed to kill. Why she was there in the first place, Brigitte had no idea. She certainly hoped it wasn't what she feared.

The woman stopped, hunching over and groaning as she held her stomach. Brigitte skidded to a halt and held her breath as she attempted to blend into the bayou. Her mind raced. They'd never trained for this situation. Oh sure, she'd prepared herself to slit the throat of an old man or even an old woman. But a pregnant woman?

How could she end the life of a woman with a baby growing inside her? Perhaps she should call for backup. Emeric would show no hesitation at killing her. He'd kill his own mother if the society asked him to. But he was the last person she wanted to call.

The woman sped off again—running under a canopy of trees, stumbling over foliage, and splashing through puddles as she heaved air in and out of her lungs. Desperation rolled off the laboring mother.

The most terrifying thing of all in this situation— this stranger seemed to know exactly where she was going.

About a minute later, she stopped again, groaning in pain.

Brigitte slipped her dagger from its sheath. Perhaps she could kill her and cut the baby out. The child couldn't possibly remember this location. It should be safe to let it—

The mother ran once again, this time faster, more desperate. Brigitte could hear her sobbing. The shimmer of the fountain sparkled through the trees.

Could she do it? Could she really kill this woman?

Yes.

She had to. She'd sworn to protect the fountain. But she'd wait until the woman reached the water's edge. Running behind, she prepared to confront the mother as soon as she stopped.

Brigitte gasped when the woman didn't stop. She didn't slow a bit as she splashed into the pool of water—her figure a pale silhouette against the rocky mound that rose from the center, bubbling with life-giving water.

Ripping out her phone, Brigitte considered who she should call. Lafayette. Yes! He would be level-headed enough to know what to do.

"What is it?" he said when he picked up.

"There's a woman in the fountain," she answered and then bit her lip.

"How did she get that far?" Brigitte held the phone away from her ear as he shouted.

"I..." she couldn't continue, ashamed of her answer.

"You what?" he snarled.

"She's pregnant," she said, "and she's in labor."

He swore. "You're worthless, Brigitte."

She bit back a retort. "Just get here."

"We're already coming."

"We?"

"Emeric is with me."

Brigitte's heart sank. Emeric—just the man she didn't want to call. As head of the guardians, he had very little tolerance for those who didn't enforce the rules. Brigitte began to tremble when she considered her punishment.

She had allowed a person near the waters. Not just that, she allowed a woman to bathe in them. Looking at the woman, she already looked healthier— more vibrant.

Until the next contraction hit.

An ear-piercing scream tore from the woman's lips. And then she sank down lower in the water, the ripples lapping against her neck. The water took on a red tinge. A few minutes later, a baby's head broke the surface. The mother bellowed in a mixture of laughter and cries as she held the infant up above the water. Brigitte's heart sank at the sight.

The baby was beautiful—pink and bald. With a healthy cry, she greeted the first day of her life.

And likely her last.

There was a strong possibility they would kill her along with her mother. Brigitte looked at the innocent, young child.

"This is heresy!" a deep voice roared from behind her. Lafayette and Emeric burst through the trees and stomped passed her. They stopped at the water's edge with their sacred daggers raised.

"What are you doing here?" Emeric shouted at the startled mother.

"I..." The mother's face blanched white as she pulled her child close and clutched her to her chest. She looked down at her baby and said, "It called to me."

"Impossible," Emeric growled.

The woman backed away as her eyes darted around, probably searching for an escape.

There would be no escape for her.

"Please don't hurt my little girl," she sobbed.

"Tell me how you found it," his voice boomed, making the mother jump.

She looked around. "I don't understand."

"Tell...me...how...you...found...it."

"Found what?"

"You know exactly what I'm talking about."

She shook her head. "I don't."

"The Fountain of Youth." He glared down at her. "Now, get out of its waters. No one is allowed to bathe there."

She took a step back.

"Get out, or I'll come in after you and slit both your and your baby's throats."

He was bluffing. He wouldn't dare touch those waters, but the woman had no way of knowing that.

The mother broke down in tears. "No. Please. I'll do anything. Just don't harm her."

"Get. Out," he snarled.

The woman took a hesitant step forward, and then another. As she stepped onto shore, Brigitte could see the mother's legs were shaking so hard that she looked as if she might fall. When she stepped completely out of the water, Brigitte could see water mixed with blood flowing from beneath her skirt and pooling on the ground beneath her—evidence of her recent delivery. Emeric walked up to her, towering above her.

She put her head down. "Please," she whispered, her breathing ragged.

Lafayette stepped toward Emeric, his eyes conflicted. "Let's not act rashly. Why don't we just—"

Emeric thrust his knife into the woman's stomach. She gasped as her eyes opened wide.

"There's no debate," Emeric said, as the mother—now gasping for breath—sagged against him. He pushed her away and jerked his knife from her belly. "There is no leniency." She fell, to the ground, still clutching the child to her chest. "You know our sacred calling."

Lafayette lowered his head. "Yes."

Brigitte turned away. Tears streamed down her cheeks as she stepped behind a tree. Was this really her calling? She thought to protect the fountain was a sacred, holy duty. But what were they, really? Nothing but murderers?

"What are you doing?" Emeric's voice growled in desperation. "Get away from there."

Brigitte looked back to see the mother kneeling at the water's edge. Emeric lunged toward her, as she flung her child with all her might. The baby splashed into the water and sank below the surface.

Both Emeric and Lafayette rushed forward and stood above the water. They searched for any sign of the infant.

"She's killed her," Lafayette gasped. "Her own child."

"You stupid woman." Emeric turned on the woman who had collapsed on the ground. "Why did you do it?"

But the woman didn't answer. She lay still, at the water's edge.

Lafayette knelt beside her and pressed his fingers against her throat. Moments passed before he spoke. "She's dead."

"Her behavior makes no sense," Emeric said.

"I know," Lafayette said, "and we can't go in after the child. The law forbids it."

"Yes," Emeric said somberly. "It's for the best. Who knows what effects those waters would have had on that child? We'd have to kill it anyway." The two men stepped away from the body of the woman.

"Shouldn't we move her?" Lafayette asked as he looked back at her.

"She's not touching the water," Emeric said. "She'll be fine where she is. Let Gerard handle it."

They stepped into the trees. "Where's Brigitte?" Lafayette asked, his voice fading as they strolled away. Brigitte backed behind a tree and held her breath.

"She probably couldn't stomach all this," she could hear Emeric say. "Either that, or she's afraid to face punishment. I'm sure we'll find her back at camp eventually."

They continued on, and soon they disappeared into the woods.

Brigitte inched around the tree and stepped into the scene. Swallowing bile, she crept forward. The young mother lay on her back at the water's edge. Blinking back tears, she leaned over to see the woman's face. She didn't know what she'd find. She'd never seen a dead person before, but she didn't expect the expression she found. She looked at peace.

"Why did you fight so hard to protect your baby, and then toss her into the water to drown?" Brigitte

7

looked back at the glassy-smooth surface of the water.
That poor child floated down there somewhere—
probably dead by now.

She sighed. Her heart felt like lead in her chest.

She turned away and started back toward camp.
Just as she reached the edge of the trees, she heard
the most curious thing—the sound of a baby crying.

Chapter 1

Twenty-two years later

Fae slipped on her short-sleeved jacket to cover her bare shoulders. She should have insisted on being dropped off somewhere else. This neighborhood didn't look so good. Hopefully, she wouldn't die just because she didn't want to inconvenience her previous ride.

She stepped out and jabbed her thumb in the air at the next passing sedan.

A dark-haired man who appeared old enough to be her father pulled up to the curb. "Hey, sweet thing. You need a ride?" He looked her up and down, practically salivating.

"Um, no thank you," she said, her stomach souring.

His smile turned into a scowl as he mumbled a vulgar insult and drove away.

Fae swallowed the lump in her throat. She'd had very little contact with people in her lifetime. If this was how city folks acted, maybe she hadn't really missed much. She took a deep breath, shook off the insult, and put her thumb back in the air. She really hoped she survived the trip to St. Augustine.

The next three cars were also a bust. The insults even started to lose their sting. Did she really look like a prostitute? Her shorts were nearly to her knees, her shoulders were covered, and she wasn't even showing any cleavage.

It was probably her body shape. She couldn't help being well endowed. If she had the choice, she would have chosen a more conservative shape.

Another car approached. This one looked more promising. A white-haired old woman peered over the steering wheel.

"You should be ashamed of yourself," the old woman said as she glowered at her from a Buick the size of an aircraft carrier. "A pretty thing like you—"

"It's not what it looks like," Fae said quickly. "I'm a college student. I'm just trying to get to campus."

The lady looked her over, obviously attempting to see if she were lying. Fae gave her most innocent expression.

"Okay," the woman said, "get in. But don't try anything. I have a gun in my purse and I know how to use it."

"I wouldn't think of it," Fae said as she retrieved her suitcase from behind a bush.

The woman eyed the luggage and unlocked the doors. Fae put her case in the back and got it the front seat.

"My name is Eleanor," the woman said. "What's yours?"

"Fae."

"Oh, I have a good friend named Fay."

Fae wasn't surprised; her name was painfully old-fashioned. "That's nice."

"Are you from around here?"

Fae nodded. "Um, yeah, but farther south." She didn't mention exactly where. It was such a tiny place it wasn't even on a map. None of the places she'd lived in had been. Brigitte had been very careful choosing where they'd lived. Inconspicuous was her middle name.

"Why didn't your parents give you a ride to campus?"

Fae sighed. "They can't."

The old lady nodded as if she knew exactly what Fae meant. She couldn't possibly guess why Fae's parents were unavailable.

Eleanor chatted on and on about this and that—how much St. Augustine had changed over the years, what hadn't changed, what should change...

Fae's lids were drooping when the familiar campus came into view.

"Wow," Fae said, her sleepiness shaken off by sudden awe. "It's even more beautiful than I remembered."

"How long have you been gone?" Eleanor asked.

"I was here a few weeks ago, but this is my first semester attending." She turned to the old woman. "Thank you so much for the ride."

"No problem, sweetie. Just...try to be safe. A girl like you should never hitchhike. You don't know what kind of crazies are out there."

Fae swallowed her first response and said, "Don't worry, I won't."

Eleanor jabbed her pointer finger at her. "You'd better not." She nodded toward the school. "Good luck."

"Thanks." Fae gave a genuine smile as she got out of the car.

She pulled the strap of her bag over her shoulder and looked across campus. Taking a deep breath, she attempted to calm her pounding heart. She could do this. She wasn't that old. A twenty-two-year-old freshman was not unheard of, right?

Putting her feet to the pavement, she marched toward the dorms trying to look confident. She'd get settled in, and then she would see admissions to confirm that nothing remained undone.

Walking under the arched entryway, Fae was once again amazed at the campus. History and elegance shone through the columns and grand fountain inside the courtyard. It really didn't look like a college at all, more like a resort. She'd walked into a fairy tale.

Glancing down at her second-hand clothes, she felt out of place. When she purchased them, she'd fallen in love with them. They were the nicest clothes she'd ever owned. But she couldn't help but think that everyone could see through her façade. People like her didn't go to colleges like this. Or college at all, for that matter. But Fae had always loved learning new things and immersed herself in every book she could get a hold of—fiction and non-fiction. Still, reading books did not replace a formal education. And in that area, Fae was grossly lacking. Pushing back her thoughts, she swallowed her doubts. She could do this!

She approached student housing, took a deep breath, and walked inside the building. She nearly jumped out of her skin when someone screamed. Looking down the hall, she could see two girls bouncing like jackrabbits and squealing.

Fae had no idea what they were so excited about, but the act seemed juvenile. Perhaps living in freshmen housing was a bad move. She was practically an old woman compared to these girls.

"Hello, my dear." A white-haired woman stood and shuffled toward her. "You look a bit lost."

"I was just looking to um, check in."

"Sure thing, sweetie." The old woman smiled warmly. "I'm Mrs. Albrecht, and you are...?"

"Fae Miller."

"Fae, what a lovely name."

"It's actually short for Fontaine."

"Ah, a French name. Are you native to Florida?" the woman said as she ruffled through some files.

"Um, I think so."

"You don't know?"

Fae sighed. "I don't know who my birth parents are."

"Well, your adoptive parents—"

"No, I...listen, I'm really tired, and I'd like to get settled in."

"Sure thing, sweetie. I didn't mean to pry." Mrs. Albrecht looked down, her face flushed.

"No, it's all right," Fae said, wanting to reassure the poor woman. She didn't know her simple questions were sore spots.

"Okay." Mrs. Albrecht looked up, her face brighter. She pulled out a file and opened it. "It looks like you're rooming with Morgan. She's a sweetheart. I'm sure you'll get along swimmingly."

Fae cracked a smile.

"You're in room one seventy-nine." She glanced behind Fae and pointed. "Just down that hall, dearie."

Fae made her way, avoiding curious eyes. She always drew attention wherever she went—though she tried her best not to. Her platinum blonde hair and icy-blue eyes made her stand out. There wasn't much she could do about her eyes, but she'd tried dying her hair brunette once. It ended in a disaster and took a painfully long time to grow out enough to cut off. Since then, she'd given up on it.

Stepping up to the door, she debated whether to knock. No. This was her room too. She didn't need to ask permission to go inside. Clutching the knob, she turned it.

A cheerful smile from a young girl greeted her.

"Hey roomie!" The girl bounced off the bottom mattress of a bunk bed and stood, grinning widely.

"Morgan, right?" Fae asked.

"Yeah," she answered. Fae didn't think her smile could get any wider, but somehow Morgan accomplished it. "Wow, is that your natural eye color?"

"Um, yeah," Fae said, brushing a curl behind her ear.

"That's seriously amazing!"

"Thanks. I'm Fae."

"Oh, sweet!" Morgan turned around and plopped down on her bed again. "Fae," she said, as if she were giving her name a test drive on her tongue. "That totally fits you."

"Really?" Fae had always hated her name. But it was better than Fontaine. Seriously, who names a girl Fontaine?

"Yeah," Morgan answered, her head bobbing up and down. "With your wickedly awesome blond hair and amazing eyes, you almost look like a fairy. Did your parents drop you off? My mom and dad followed me everywhere around campus when we first got here. It was so embarrassing." She huffed and threw herself back against the bed.

"No, um." Fae dropped her bag down and looked up at the top bunk. "I came here by myself."

Morgan scrunched her eyebrows in confusion. "You're a freshman, right?"

Fae nodded.

"So, your parents—"

"No," Fae interrupted. "I don't have any parents."

Morgan sat up, her eyes wide. "Really?"

"Yeah," she answered as she walked over to a dresser. "Is this one empty?"

Morgan nodded and said, "That's sad. What happened to them?"

The question caught Fae off guard. Most people didn't ask such personal questions of strangers. Should she answer her? Maybe if she only answered the bare minimum. "I never met them." She pulled a drawer open and started filling it with clothes.

"Then who raised you?" Morgan asked.

Fae sighed. "I was raised by a woman who knew my mom." *Sort of.*

"Oh," Morgan said with her brows creased together in confusion. "What's her name?"

"Brigitte."

"Well, where is she?"

"She's in jail." Fae didn't bother with neatness as she stuffed the rest of her bag into her drawers. She'd have to organize it later. She had a sudden desire to leave the awkwardness of the conversation. "Listen, I'm going to look around campus."

Morgan jumped up, smiling once again. "Do you need a tour?"

Is this girl for real? She just told her the woman who raised her was in jail, and now she wanted to give her a tour? Fae cracked a grin. "Uh, yeah. I guess so."

Morgan shoved her feet into her shoes and stood.

"You're not freaked out about my..." Fae began.

When she hesitated, Morgan said, "Foster mom being in jail? Nah, my uncle's in prison. The big one. He got mad at his girlfriend for cheating on him and ran her down with his oversized truck. Killed her on the spot. I heard it was pretty gory. But he was always nice to me," she said with a shrug.

Fae found herself shaking her head and suppressing a smile at Morgan's candid talk about something so horrific. Fae knew she shouldn't be amused about a murder, but still, Morgan was quite a unique character. Fae liked her already. Maybe this year would be a good one, after all.

Fae followed Morgan into the hall.

"Candice and Brie are our next-door neighbors on this side." She pointed to the door on the right. "They're pretty nice. And the bathroom and showers are on the other side." She pointed to the door on the left. "We're really lucky. It's the only bathroom on this floor. If you like to shower in the morning, you'd better do it early. There's no hot water by seven o'clock. So, what are you majoring in?" Morgan opened the door to the outside, and Fae followed her out.

"Criminal justice."

"Really? Is it because of your foster mother?"

"Partly." Fae looked at her new friend. "What's your major?"

"Art," she answered enthusiastically. "I adore sketching, painting, sculpting, and do you know what?" Morgan didn't give her a chance to answer before she blurted, "They use nude models here." Morgan smiled with her eyebrow raised. "Seriously, they're totally in the buff! And if you're lucky, they are buff. But they stress that models and students are not allowed to talk to each other, much less date. My mom told me I couldn't take figure drawing because of it. But I'm an adult. I don't even have to tell her what I'm taking. Do you get to learn to shoot?"

"What?" Fae asked, confused at the turn in the conversation.

"In your criminal justice classes. I'm assuming you're learning to fight crime."

Fae shook her head. "My focus is purely on investigation."

"Yeah, but even detectives have to carry a gun."

"They don't allow guns on campus," Fae said.

"Oh, right," Morgan said. "Maybe they'll have you shoot somewhere off campus, like at a police shooting range."

"I doubt it." Fae didn't mention she was already very adept at handling guns.

"Huh." Morgan shrugged, and then continued to chatter nonstop. This girl's mind ran a mile a minute.

Morgan stopped in front of a building. "And here we are at the criminal justice building—at least where they have most of the classes."

Fae looked up at the imposing structure. Well, it was imposing to her. She'd never been to public school. She'd actually had little formal education—until this past year. Thank heavens she learned fast. And her unique situation led to a full-ride scholarship. So now, here she was, in college...and it was seriously starting to freak her out.

"Do you have any classes here tomorrow?" Morgan asked.

Someone brushed by Fae, nearly knocking her over. A man ran toward the building. He glanced over his shoulder and flashed a smile. "Sorry."

Fae found herself suddenly breathless. That man was seriously hot—tall, muscular, with a tan you only got from being outside a lot.

"Do you think that's a student?" Fae asked.

"Gawd, I hope so," Morgan said, fanning herself. She whipped her head around, facing Fae. "What do you say we find out?"

"What?"

19

"Your criminal justice education starts now," she said, pulling Fae toward the door. "Let's investigate."

Fae resisted. "I don't think that's a good idea."

"Oh, come on," Morgan said. "Live a little. This is college. We're supposed to do stupid things."

Fae sighed and said, "Oh, all right."

They glimpsed him just as he dashed up the stairs. "Let's go," Morgan said, and then whispered, "Quietly."

They stepped up to a dark hallway and heard voices down the hall. "Looks like most of the professors are gone for the day," Morgan whispered.

"There's no good place to hide," Fae whispered back.

"If he comes out, we'll just act natural."

"Act natural?" Fae repeated.

"Yeah," she answered confidently. "If he asks, we'll say we were figuring out where all your classes are. Do you have any classes around here?"

Fae pulled out her map and found she did have a class here. In fact, she did, in this exact room. "Yes," she whispered, and gestured to the door. "In there."

"Sweet." Morgan smiled broadly and then put her ear to the door.

Fae followed.

"I *have* a job," a deep voice said.

"It's only one class," another man's voice responded. "Two times a week. And it pays well."

"And how much is that?"

"Considering the hours, twice what you're making with the FBI."

Morgan's eyes widened, and she mouthed, "FBI?"

"How do you know how much I make?" the voice answered.

"I did my homework."

"I don't know if I can swing it."

"I've already cleared it with your boss. She thinks it's great for public relations."

There was silence. Fae jumped when Morgan whispered, "I wonder which one's which?"

Fae shrugged.

"It's only Introduction to the Criminal Justice System," he said, "Tuesdays and Thursdays at seven o'clock a.m."

"Oh, my gosh," Fae said. "That's my class."

Morgan turned to her, her mouth dropping wide open. "If the hottie ends up teaching your class, I'll seriously consider changing my major."

"You could teach that class in your sleep," the man continued.

"I just don't think I can find the time," the FBI guy said. "They have me putting in extra hours to wrap up an investigation."

"Well, just think about it. But think fast. Class starts tomorrow."

"Thanks for not giving me any pressure. I gotta go. I'll let you know tonight."

"Thanks, Nick." Footsteps indicated they were approaching.

"Oh, no," Fae said.

"Shh!" Morgan whispered. "Remember, we're just finding your class."

"Right," she said as the door opened.

"Whoa," the hottie said as he stopped in his tracks. "You girls lost?"

"Nope," Morgan said, cheerful. "We're just looking for my roommate's classes. She has Introduction to the Criminal Justice System tomorrow at seven."

He gave Morgan a passing glance, then locked eyes with Fae and raised his eyebrows. "Does she, now?"

Fae looked down, avoiding his gaze.

"Well," he said, "it so happens I'll be the teacher for that class."

"Professor." Another man stepped from behind him.

"Right. Professor."

Fae glanced up and caught him watching her. His intense blue eyes made her tingle all over. He looked even better up close!

The other man took the professor by the arm and said, "Sorry we can't stay and chat, girls. Professor Chase has a lot of paperwork and policies to sign—including that all-important 'no-fraternizing-with-your-students' policy."

Nick blinked and turned to him. "Right. Student/teacher relationship stuff."

The moment they were out of sight, Morgan exclaimed, "Holy wow! He seriously has the hots for you."

"No, he doesn't," Fae said as heat filled her cheeks.

"Oh yeah, he totally does," she said. "He couldn't take his eyes off you. And he's even freakin' taking the teaching job because of you."

"I seriously doubt that." Fae shook her head. "It doesn't matter. He's a professor, I'm a student. We can't date."

"Huh," she huffed, frowning. "Well, that stinks. But...you can date him next term. Though, that is four months from now." Her excitement deflated as she spoke. "Oh well, let's see where your other classes are."

Chapter 2

Nick slouched down into the chair across from Anthony's desk.

"I've half a mind to rescind my offer," Anthony said, scowling down at him.

"What? You offered, and I accepted." Nick raised an eyebrow. "I thought you were desperate."

"And I'm sure you'll tell me that you accepting the job had nothing to do with the student you just met?"

Nick shrugged. "It's just coincidence."

"Right," Anthony said, drawing out the word. "How long has it been since you've seen a woman that beautiful?"

"She's not my type," Nick said.

"Not your type?" Anthony repeated, doubt ringing loudly in his voice.

"Yeah."

"She'd better not be," Anthony said. "Because if I find out you're sleeping with her or any of your other students, I'll personally fire you and report the act to your superiors at the FBI. We have to maintain a professional environment, and that does not include fraternizing with the students."

"Understood," Nick said as he tried to wipe her face from his mind. It wasn't as easy as it seemed. Her eyes haunted him even now—that was one downside to having a photographic memory. Images tended to replay in his mind. Getting involved with that woman would not be good for his career. He could take or leave the teaching job, but the bureau was his life.

Despite knowing that he should turn down the job, he found himself filling out paperwork. About five minutes into it, his phone vibrated.

"Hey, Don," Nick said.

"Hey, back," Don said. "I'm sorry to be the bearer of bad news, but Young wants you to finish up the Petersen file and have it to her by ten o'clock tomorrow morning."

"Oh, yeah?" Nick frowned. "You might want to remind her about her recommendation for me to teach at a certain local college. Apparently, she said it would be good for public relations."

"You. Teach college?" Nick could hear the smile in Don's voice.

"Do you have an issue with that?"

Don laughed. "I knew you in college. You're the last person I'd ever picture teaching there."

"I graduated at the top of my class," Nick said.

"It's not the grades I'm talking about. I'm talking about your...behavior. Need I remind you what happened with the cheerleading squad?"

"Oh no, you just had to bring that up. I was young and I was drunk."

"Apparently not drunk enough."

"Oh, shut up." Nick rubbed his temples. A headache built behind his eyes. "Listen, I've got a lot of work to do. Lesson plans to make."

"You'd better add the Petersen file to your workload because Young wasn't kidding."

Nick swore. "Yeah, I'll have it to her by ten." He hung up and sighed. *It looks like he'll need some coffee—about a gallon of it.*

Nick walked into his classroom with papers under his arm and about an hour's worth of sleep under his belt. At least he finished the Petersen case. Perhaps he could actually get in a full eight hours tonight. Why did he even accept this job? It wasn't like he had lots of extra time.

Looking down at the class list, he wondered which name belonged to the girl from yesterday. They never did introduce themselves. No. He chided himself. She was a student taking a lower-level undergraduate class. Probably a freshman, barely out of high school— much too young for someone his age.

Young men started filing in and taking seats. Fifteen students later, there was yet to be a girl in the class, much less the girl he wanted to see. From the looks of the roll, there were only five women in a class of a thirty. And here was one. A dark, short-haired girl with thick glasses entered first. No one even glanced her way. Of course, she wasn't trying to get anyone's attention. She kept her head down and her eyes on the floor. She'd have to learn to be more observant of her environment if she wanted to go into law enforcement.

Ten more boys and three more girls entered. That was everyone but one student. Glancing at the clock, there were only seconds before class started.

And there she was with a can of Coke in one hand and a stack of books in the other. All eyes were on her as she rushed through the door just as the second-hand passed over the twelve.

"Just in time, Ms...Thomas?"

She shook her head. "Miller," she answered breathlessly. "Fae Miller."

"Miller?" he asked, worried she'd made a mistake and wasn't in his class after all.

"I registered late," she said, setting her soda down, pulling out a creased yellow paper, and unfolding it for him. Relieved, he signed it and handed it back.

"Are you a transfer student?" he asked, wondering at her age. She seriously didn't look like she'd just graduated from high school. "You don't look young enough to be a freshman," he said. He needed to know how old she was. If she were eighteen, or heaven forbid, seventeen, he'd have to whip himself for lusting after a child.

"I *am* a freshman," she said as a blush rose in her cheeks. "But I got a late start in college. I just turned twenty-two."

He felt bad for embarrassing her in front of the class. But at the same time, he was relieved. A twenty-two-year-old woman was perfectly fine to lust after. Now if only she weren't his student.

"How soon you start college doesn't matter," he said. "It's finishing that's important." His statement earned a smile from her that warmed her icy-cool eyes. His heart missed a beat. He'd never seen a more beautiful woman. And the way she blushed so easily made her seem sweet, innocent—nothing like any other girl he'd dated. She definitely wasn't what he'd consider his "type."

She took her seat and he turned to address the students. "My name is Professor Chase, and I'll be teaching Introduction to the Criminal Justice System. You might ask yourself why a young guy like me is qualified to teach this class. Well, I'm also known as Special Agent Chase of the FBI."

That earned him some "oohs" and "aahs" from the class and some whispers between the students.

"My specialty is Missing Person's Investigation. I look for people who are lost, kidnapped, or have just turned up missing."

Several hands went up. Nick looked around, considering calling on someone when he noticed Fae with her hand high in the air and excitement in her eyes. He stopped himself from smiling.

"Ms. Miller," he said professionally, and nodded toward her. "Do you have a question?"

"Yes. How good are you?"

Her question caught him off guard. "At finding people?"

She nodded and said, "Let's say, an abandoned baby turns up with no sign of who her mother and father are. Do you think you can figure out who she belongs to?"

Nick raised an eyebrow. This was not some random question she pulled out of the air. "It depends."

"On?" she asked.

"Whether her parents left any clues." He shrugged.

"Let's say they didn't."

"Well," he said, "you could have the child's DNA tested and see if her parents or any of her relatives turn up in the database."

"And what if they don't?"

"I'm sorry. It's hard for me to tell you how to find them without knowing more about the situation. Like, where was she found? What kinds of clothes was she wearing? Does anyone remember seeing anything unusual?"

"I'm sorry. I...I didn't mean to—"

"No," he interrupted. "You gave us a situation that caused us to think. And that is the most important thing about investigation. You need to use your brain along with your eyes. The smallest, most insignificant detail can be the key to solving a case."

He turned back and retrieved the syllabi from off his desk and started passing them around. "This is what we are going to cover throughout the year. And if you noticed, we have a field trip planned in which you can see firsthand what kind of career you are getting yourself into."

As he expected, there were smiles all around. It didn't matter if you were in first grade, high school, or college. Everyone loved a field trip. And there was no better place to learn than in the field.

The following hour and a half went by smoothly, and he found teaching this basic class was a cinch. Besides, it gave him an excuse to share the success stories he'd seen and been a part of. They were what made his job worthwhile. He frowned when he thought about the failures he'd experienced. They were an inevitable part of the job—one his students should know about before deciding to commit to this life. Some people couldn't handle it. He could barely handle it.

When he ended the class, the students began to pack up their books and tablets. He wanted to find an excuse to talk to Fae again but squelched the idea. He really needed to back down. She was his student, and he was her teacher. He swallowed down his regret.

Chapter 3

Fae's head felt like it was going to explode. The day had been enlightening, filled with information, and completely draining. She gave Mrs. Albrecht a passing grin and headed straight for her room.

She hadn't been assigned any real homework yet—just introductions to the class and a get-to-know-me worksheet where she was supposed to bear her soul to her psychology professor—as if that would ever happen.

Fae wished she could plop onto her bed and sleep the rest of the day, but she had zero funds and needed a job in a big way. Instead, she dropped her bag on her desk and headed back across campus to the employment center.

Her heart dropped when the saw the sparse listings. Coming in and trying to find a job so late in the game, she may have a hard time getting one.

Cafeteria server...minimum wage. That was no surprise.

Landscape worker...minimum wage and morning work. Yeah, that wouldn't work with her schedule.

Custodial work...minimum wage and late night work. That was a possibility.

Model, working with the Art department...well above minimum wage and the hours vary. Must be willing to pose nude. Nope. Forget it. Not a possibility.

Her eyes remained glued to the per-hour figure. She wouldn't have to work as many hours if she did that job. She'd have more time to study.

No, who was she fooling? She absolutely couldn't do it!

She forced herself to look at the next entry.

Custodial work...bathroom maintenance...minimum wage and late-night work. Bathroom maintenance? What in the world did that mean? Probably plunging stopped up toilets. Ugh!

The rest of the listings were no more appealing than the first.

Fae jotted down the numbers to contact on several possibilities. As a last-minute impulse, she also jotted down the modeling number. Of course, she wouldn't do it. But if all the other jobs didn't pan out...

No! She'd work off campus if she had to. Of course, that may be difficult with no car.

Wandering back to her dorm room, exhaustion nearly overwhelmed her as financial worries plagued her mind. Her thoughts derailed when she approached the door to her room. Water pooled from underneath and inched its way down the hall.

"Hey, Fae!" Morgan smiled as she sauntered up. "Wow, 'hey' rhymes with 'Fae.'" Her smile widened. She slipped in the puddle, and Fae caught her by the arm before shc could fall.

Fae frowned. "Looks like our room is flooded."

Morgan's eyes turned to the floor, widening slowly. "Oh, no," she said as she yanked open the door. She splashed through a half an inch of water to get to a large leather case lying on the floor under her bed. "Oh, please don't be wet," she said as she put in on her bed and unzipped it.

"Is that your portfolio?" Fae asked, looking around. Water covered the entire floor. Part of the wall looked soggy, and the paint peeled in a patch where the wall met the ceiling. Looked like a broken pipe. Thank heavens she didn't leave any of her things on the floor.

Her eyes returned to Morgan's, now brimming with tears.

Fae stepped up behind her and put a hand on her shoulder.

"Are you all right?"

Morgan shook her head. "They're ruined. Every drawing and painting I've saved clear back from junior high until now. They're all soaked."

"I'm really sorry," Fae said.

Morgan was too choked up to talk.

"Maybe we can save some," Fae said. "Is there a way to dry them?"

"You mean like hanging them up on a clothesline?"

Fae shrugged.

"It might work. They'd never be perfect again, but maybe..." Morgan's voice trailed off.

"Maybe once you dry them and put them in a frame, you won't be able to tell they'd ever gotten wet."

Morgan's eyes lit with hope. "Maybe."

"Oh dear," Mrs. Albrecht cried out. "What happened?" She stepped to the edge of the advancing water. "Oh, poor Morgan," Mrs. Albrecht looked at her soaked pictures. "Is there anything I can do to help?"

"Is there someplace I can hang these up?" Morgan asked.

"I'm sure we can figure something out, dear." She turned to Fae. "Are your things okay, sweetie?"

"I think so," Fae answered.

"Oh, good," Mrs. Albrecht said. "Now let's move you girls and I'll call maintenance."

An hour later, Fae stepped out of the door into the hall. She'd just gotten settled in her new room. It didn't seem new, though. All the rooms looked identical. Morgan didn't mention the fact they were as far away from the bathroom as you could get. Perhaps it was better that way. It was likely a bathroom pipe that burst.

Morgan oversaw her artwork that hung in rows behind the check-in desk. She'd had several admirers ask about them and offer to pay her money to paint pictures for their rooms.

"Hey, Fae!" Morgan called out, once again cheerful. "Do you want some company?"

Fae shook her head. "I'm just going to take a swim."

"Are you a swimmer?" Her eyebrows rose.

"Um, not really. I swim for fun. It helps me relax." She didn't mention the fact she'd never actually swam in a swimming pool. She usually frequented watering holes.

"Cool. You'll have to navigate the crowds to get there. There's some kind of celebration going on."

"I'll be careful," Fae said, smiling.

Morgan wasn't kidding. Fae stepped outside the dorm to see a crowd of partying college students in the courtyard. Chaos surrounded her, and the roar of music, shouting, and mayhem filled her ears. Looking around, she could identify a clear division. There were the jocks on the left, mixed with cheerleaders and admiring fans, and then there were normal-looking people talking and slipping peeks at the jocks and cheerleaders. And then there were school officials running booths, sitting in dunk tanks, and mingling with students on both sides of the social divide.

"Hey, beautiful," someone shouted.

Fae looked over to see a big jock approaching her—probably a linebacker. *Was he talking to me?*

"Um, hi," Fae answered as she clutched her towel to her chest. She really wished she'd worn more than a wrap around over her hips. At least she didn't wear her bikini. She already felt half naked. *And I thought I could pose nude. As if!*

As he got closer, she could see that he was seriously good looking, for a football player. And she guessed he was an upperclassman. He looked too old to be fresh out of high school. A frown settled on his face. It looked like he didn't think she was so beautiful up close.

"You're not a freshman, are you?"

"Actually," she said. "I am."

"Really?" His face lit up. "It's my lucky day."

She puzzled over what he was talking about. Before she could even guess his intentions, he wrapped his arm around her waist, pulled her forward, and smashed his lips against hers. Pain, mixed with the taste of blood and alcohol, penetrated her lips as she pushed against him. It was like pushing against a brick wall.

Her temper flared as she opened her mouth and chomped down, biting him. He pulled back, shouting as she stomped his foot. He lifted his injured foot and hopped up and down and howled. Clenching her fist, she swung. She felt the bones of his nose crunch along with a sharp pain in her hand. And down he went.

Arms came around her from behind, pulling her back. "Whoa, babe. He was only playing. We dared him to kiss the next freshman he saw."

"He's out cold," someone said.

"What's going on here?" a familiar voice asked.

Fae's heart sank when she looked up—Mr. Larsen, the dean of students approached. His eyes widened when he looked down at the unconscious form sprawled on the ground. Blood leaked from the corner of the kid's mouth and flowed from his nose.

"Who did this?" the dean asked.

All eyes turned on her.

"Fae Miller?"

A lump filled her throat as she nodded.

"You're coming with me," he said as he took her arm and dragged her toward the administration building. Almost as an afterthought, he yelled, "Someone call a doctor."

He barely gave her a chance to keep her footing. She lost a flip-flop in the process but didn't mention it. She had a feeling if she stumbled, he'd simply drag her across the ground. She looked up when they entered the building, and her heart sank. Why did he have to be there? Professor Chase stood in the reception area, his eyes wide.

The dean ignored all the onlookers and dragged her into his office. "This is completely unacceptable behavior," he snapped, shutting the door.

"I was just defending myself," Fae said, her angst rising.

"And how did Mike Pendleton end up unconscious on the ground while you have scarce an injury?"

Fae could feel her lip throbbing and touched it. Blood coated her finger.

"A split lip is nothing compared with the injuries you inflicted on your victim. From the looks of it, he has a broken nose and possibly a concussion. It's highly unlikely he'll be able to play in the next big game."

"He grabbed hold of me and kissed me," Fae argued. "I tried to push him away, but he wouldn't stop. Are you saying I don't have the right to defend myself against a sexual assault?"

"Sexual assault?" His jaw dropped. "He only kissed you!"

"Hard enough to split my lip!" Fae clenched her fists. "This is so unfair!"

Mr. Larsen frowned. "I knew admitting you would be a mistake. People like you don't change. We can pull you out of the bayou and give you a bath, but we can't change what's inside."

"You have no idea who I am and what I've been through!" Fae bellowed.

"Oh, I know your kind." The dean's eyes narrowed.

"Excuse me," a deep, familiar voice spoke from behind. "I couldn't help overhearing. Perhaps I can help."

Fae turned to see Professor Chase poke his head inside the door. She turned her eyes to the floor and swallowed.

"And who are you?" Mr. Larson asked.

"Special Agent Nick Chase of the FBI."

"This has nothing to do with the FBI. This is a private school matter."

Professor Chase stepped fully into the room.

"Actually," he said, frowning at the dean, "I also teach Introduction to Criminal Justice System. And either way, protecting the innocent and prosecuting criminals has everything to do with what I do."

"I'll need to ask Mr. Pendleton if he wants to press charges against Ms. Miller," the dean said. "But even if he does, I don't know why the FBI would concern itself with this affair."

"From what I understand, Ms. Miller is not the perpetrator of a crime; it's Mr. Pendleton who faces sexual assault charges."

"What?" The dean paled. "But he's the one who ended up bleeding on the ground."

"Mr. Pendleton was the instigator of the assault and Fae Miller was within her rights to defend herself."

The dean shook his head, obviously stunned. "Wait a minute. You know her?"

"Fae is in my class."

Fae glanced over at Professor Chase. He wasn't smiling, but a sparkle lit his eye. A warm trickle trailed down her lip onto her chin, and his amusement turned to a scowl. He reached into his pocket and pulled out what looked to be a handkerchief.

Who carries handkerchiefs these days?

Stepping toward her, he lifted it to her lip and pressed. "Hold that there until the bleeding stops."

She nodded.

"And you might want to have a doctor look at that. Human mouths are dirty things—especially the mouths of drunk football players."

She smiled. "Thank you."

"I don't think you understand the situation," the dean said. "Mr. Pendleton is an exceptional athlete and a good student. Ms. Miller was homeless, up until a short time ago—living in the backwoods, prostituting herself."

"That's a lie!" she said, stepping toward him.

Professor Chase moved in between them and frowned at the dean. "You do realize that unless you have evidence to support your claim, you are committing slander against Ms. Miller."

A loud thump and a commotion came from outside the office.

"I need to see her," a voice wailed. "Get away from me. I need her!"

Mike Pendleton exploded into the room and rushed like a freight train toward Fae. She barely had time to gasp when he plowed into her, knocking her to the floor. Nick Chase was on him in a moment, pulling Mike off her and slamming him face down on the floor.

"Get off me," Mike wailed. "I just want one more kiss. Just one more."

Professor Chase muscled Mike's arms behind his back and handcuffed him. "Mike Pendleton, I assume?" He looked over at the dean, who was too stunned to answer and then he turned to Fae. She nodded as she rubbed the back of her head. It throbbed from the impact.

"I just need one more kiss," Mike moaned. "Just one more."

"Mike Pendleton, you have the right to remain silent..." Professor Chase drove his knee into Mike's back as continued to read him his rights. When he finished, he pulled out his cell phone and called for a patrol car.

"What's wrong with him?" Fae asked.

"You probably gave him brain damage," the dean said through his teeth.

Professor Chase turned to him and snapped, "You. Shut up!"

"You can kiss your teaching job goodbye, Agent Chase."

"I'd be more worried about your job."

"But I...I didn't do anything wrong," the dean said.

"And that's how screwed up you are," Professor Chase said. "You don't even realize how wrong your behavior is."

Within the hour, Mike was off to jail and the dean faced an inquiry. Fae sat quietly on a bench outside the administration building, shivering. The sun had gone down, and the air chilled her, raising goosebumps on her skin. She would have wrapped her towel around her shoulder, but she'd lost it somewhere along the way. Hopefully, someone would turn it in to the lost and found. She only had one towel. Could this day get any worse?

At least the questions had ceased. Professor Chase spoke to an officer but kept glancing at her. He seemed concerned, though after hearing the dean accuse her of prostitution, it was highly unlikely that his concern meant anything. He couldn't possibly still be interested in her—if he had been in the first place.

She looked down at the handkerchief she wrung in her hand. The bleeding on her lip had stopped, but the cloth had a fair amount of blood on it. It seemed to be a nice handkerchief, with the initials NTC embroidered on it. Fae didn't even know people still carried these things around. Did he want it back? Probably. Why else embroider your initials on it? Though she should probably wash it before she returned it to him—it was covered in her blood.

Nick Chase finished talking to the officer and sauntered over to sit down beside her. "I'm really sorry all this happened to you, Fae."

He reached over as if to hold her hand. Her breath caught in her throat. "I'll take that back." He tugged the kerchief out of her hand. "Looks like the bleeding has stopped."

"Are you sure you don't want me to wash it for you?" she asked. Her voice sounded strained.

"Nah, don't worry about it." He shoved it in the pocket of a worn jacket. "Would you like me to walk you back to your dorm room?"

Fae looked up, her eyes widening in surprise. Then she looked toward her dorm hall. A good number students still hung around in small groups. Her chest clenched. There were probably some angry football players among the stragglers. "Um, yeah. I'd appreciate it."

"No problem," he said as he stood. He looked her up and down. "Are you cold?"

"A little."

He shrugged out of his jacket and draped it over her shoulders. She breathed in a scent of leather and spice.

Nick led the way, and she walked beside him. He seemed to know his way there. Of course, he was a professor, and the student housing was hard to miss.

"Listen," she said, "about what the dean said about me."

"You don't need to explain."

"I just don't want you thinking..."

"That you're a prostitute?" He glanced over to her.

"Yeah." She put her head down as heat rose in her cheeks.

"I already know you're not."

Her eyes snapped up. "How?"

"I've met a lot of prostitutes—in my line of work, or course." He cracked a smile.

She chuckled. "Of course."

"I've learned to read people pretty well. You're no prostitute."

Appreciation swelled in her chest. "Thanks for believing me."

Student housing came into view. She searched the area. Most of the party-goers had gone home and left a lot of garbage on the ground. A group of students with trashcans were spearing garbage with pokey sticks. Her heart skipped a beat when her eyes landed on a gray mound of fabric—her towel. "Oh, thank heavens." She ran forward and picked it off the ground.

"Yours?" he said, jogging to keep up with her.

She smiled. "Yeah. I'm glad I found it. Now if I can just find my flip flop." She scoured the ground.

"I noticed you were missing one."

"Yeah, I left here in a hurry."

"More like you were dragged from here."

"Yeah."

"For all the difficulty Mr. Larsen gave you, I think it shouldn't be too much to ask the school to reimburse you."

Fae shook her head. "I don't want to cause any trouble."

"Sometimes it's okay to cause trouble." He raised his eyebrow and smiled. "I do it all the time."

Fae grinned. "I'll bet you do."

Nick chuckled. "Now look who's reading who."

They reached the doorstep and stopped. Nick stepped toward her. Fae took off his jacket and handed it back.

"Listen," Nick said as he pulled out a piece of paper and a pen and jotted down some numbers. "If that idiot football player gives you any more trouble, or if you need anything at all, feel free to call me."

Fae nodded as she took the paper and clutched it in her hand. "Thanks."

Nick locked eyes with her, and her knees felt weak. Her heart fluttered in her chest when he lifted his hand and brushed an errant strand of hair from her face. His touch made her skin tingle. "I'll see you tomorrow," he said, and reached for the door handle. He hissed a curse and pulled his hand away.

"Is there something wrong?" Fae asked.

"No, no. I'm fine. I have a sensitivity to iron. Doorknobs are usually not a problem for me, but this is an old campus." He rubbed his hand. "It's no big deal."

Fae nodded and opened the door herself. "I'll see you tomorrow."

"I look forward to it." He smiled. Moments later, she watched him walk away.

Chapter 4

Emeric stepped forward, feeling the familiar ache in his joints. He turned to address his comrades. "My fellow guardians, it is time for me relinquish command to my next in line." He stepped out from under the worn, canvas canopy and approached Lafayette, who sat in the center of the guard. Emeric looked him over. Lafayette's head was lowered, his weathered hands in his lap. The creases around his eyes seemed to lengthen as if the thought of leading caused him to age a decade in moments.

"Lafayette." Emeric put his hand on his shoulder, and Lafayette lifted his head to look at him. "I have taught you all I know. I have the utmost confidence in your abilities to lead this group and protect the fountain. You, more than anyone else, know the appeal and the terrible danger the Fountain of Youth poses for all who touch or drink its waters." Emeric coughed—deep and hard. He could feel the beginning stages of cancer infiltrating his lungs, counting down to the end of his days.

"But it's not just the guardians of the fountain I entrust to you. Most of you know about my legacy...my son."

Several eyes widened at his announcement. "He will be coming to finish his training. I expect no special treatment for him. He will have to earn his place

48

among you like any other guardian. Do not go easy on him. It is in the hottest embers that the strongest blades are forged.

"Like each of you has already done, I expect him to forsake all personal desires. The duty of a guardian of the Fountain of Youth is immense. For seven generations, my family has protected the waters. Few have touched it, desiring its healing powers, and those who have met with the consequences of their act—our blade in their hearts. My three times great-grandfather revealed in great detail what becomes of those who partake of the fountain: a madness so acute that one would kill any and all who come between the thief and his cursed youth. It is our duty to keep the water's secret and protect the location even at the cost of lives—including your own." All were nodding with firmness in their eyes that told him they knew the gravity of their calling.

"I do not like long goodbyes, so I will offer none. I leave the protection of the fountain in your capable hands." He rose and flung his pack containing his meager belongings over his shoulder. "I do ask for a few moments of privacy, though—while I say farewell to my beloved fountain. I swear on my life that it will be safe until I am gone. I ask that I not be disturbed while I offer my goodbyes and go my way. You may send guards in ten minutes' time."

Nods all around let him know they trusted him completely. Not a hint of doubt clouded anyone's eyes at the sincerity of his words. A handshake and heartfelt goodbye from all, and he finally left. His excitement built as he drew closer to the fountain of youth. The power of the waters called to him.

Rafael came into view only yards away from the water's edge.

"Hello, my boy," Emeric said, cheerfully. At barely twenty years old, "Boy" was not really an exaggeration. But he made up for his youth with a stone hard commitment to his guardianship.

"Commander," the boy answered with a bow.

"I am no longer the commander. That title now belongs to Lafayette."

"It's done?"

"Yes, I just need some time alone with the fountain." He smiled.

Doubt flickered in the boy's eyes. "Will you come for me when you are done?"

Emeric shook his head. "Someone else will be coming to take over in a few minutes."

Rafael nodded. "I'll miss you."

Emeric nodded, with a hint of a smile. "As will I."

The boy stomped through the trees, and Emeric found himself alone. He stepped forward and knelt at the water's edge.

"Here we are again," he spoke to the waters. "You, my master, and me, your faithful servant. I have fought for you. I have spilled blood in your honor. I have led those who defend you. And you have given me so much more in return."

He reached his hand out, his fingers hovering over the surface of the fountain. He knew firsthand the power those waters held. They worked quickly. In just moments, his cancer would be gone, his youth restored. He would have years of life returned to him.

A sharp pain sliced through his chest. Suddenly dizzy, the world spun around him. His hand splashed down in the water. Horrified, he lifted it out quickly. Falling back, Lafayette's face spun into view.

He laughed and shook his head. "Oops, you broke your own rule. Never touch the waters of the Fountain of Youth. Stupid old man."

"Lafayette?" Confusion filled Emeric's heart. This was his friend, his ally, his most trusted soldier. "Why?" Emeric asked, his voice already weak.

"Why am I killing you?"

Emeric nodded, his head swimming with questions.

"You're not that stupid. You know why. I'm getting old. I have many days behind me and few days ahead of me. I would have asked you to join me, but we both know you wouldn't do it. Honor is too important to you."

Emeric's eyes searched the forest, desperate for someone to stop Lafayette.

51

"Oh," he said, smiling. "They're not coming. A vile of poison can come in handy when put into the celebratory wine. But I noticed you didn't have any. So, I had to change my plans a bit. I think this end is more fitting for you anyway. The great commander shouldn't die lying in his own vomit. Oh, and don't worry about your son. I will take care of him quickly and painlessly when he gets here. After all, what are best friends for?"

"But before you go to that great fountain in the sky, I have a toast of my own to make." Lafayette took out a tin cup, dipped it into the waters, and then lifted it up, brimming. "To a long and healthy life," he cracked a wicked smile, "for me." He drank, long and deep. His smile widened as he lowered the cup. He sat unmoving for several moments before doubt flickered in his eyes. His smiled faded. He looked down at the cup and then his eyes darted to the fountain. Confusion clouded his features.

"I don't understand. I don't feel any different. I know the fountain has power, you and I have both seen it. I should be feeling different—younger, more vigorous. Why isn't it working for me?"

Emeric fell back, his eyes on the sky framed by towering trees. Darkness filtered in from the edges and clouded his view. A mixture of thoughts and feelings tumbled through his mind as he died—relief that Lafayette would soon reach the end of his days and despair that he failed to protect what he held most dear. The Fountain's power was gone.

Chapter 5

Fae stepped into her room, and arms flew around her in a tight embrace.

"Fae!" Morgan shouted.

Fae's heart pounded as she stopped herself from pushing her roommate away. She wasn't used to getting surprise hugs.

"I heard what happened," Morgan said as she pulled away. "Are you okay?" She looked Fae over, and her eyes went to her lip. "Did he do that?"

Fae nodded. "Yeah."

"That idiot Mike Pendleton!" Morgan narrowed her eyes. "He's lucky my uncle's in prison. If he wasn't, I'd have him beat Pendleton bloody."

"I'm fine. Really. Agent Chase took care of things."

"The FBI teacher?" Morgan's eyes went wide.

Fae couldn't help but smile. "Yeah."

"Wow." Morgan flopped down on her bed. "That is so flippin' romantic."

"Romantic?" Fae said, confused.

"Being saved by a hot FBI agent? Absolutely!"

"It was pretty amazing."

"I'll say," Morgan said with a dreamy look in her eyes. "Are you going to see him again?"

"Of course," Fae said. "I'm in his class."

"That's not what I meant. Did he ask you out?"

Fae shook her head. "We're not allowed to date. Remember?"

"That wouldn't stop James Bond. He would've had you stripped down naked by now."

Fae could feel heat rising in her cheeks. "You have an overactive imagination, Morgan."

She shrugged with a hint of a smile. "Just sayin'."

"No one is stripping me down and getting me naked. Haven't you ever heard of abstinence?"

Morgan showed mock confusion. "Abstinence? Nope. Never heard of it."

"Well, you might want to look it up, because that's what I practice."

Morgan chuckled. "You're joking."

Fae raised an eyebrow as she held Morgan's gaze.

Morgan's eyes flew open wide as her jaw dropped. "You're not joking!"

"Do you know how many times I've been propositioned by scumbags?"

Morgan shook her head slowly.

"Well, neither do I. I've lost count. I don't know what it is, but I seem to attract crazies. Take what happened tonight, for instance. That is not unusual for me. And it seems these guys only ever want one thing..."

"Sex?"

Fae nodded. "I've made up my mind. If someone wants to have a relationship with me, they're going to have to prove to me they love me for who I am. They'll have to wine and dine me. The real me. The me inside here." She tapped her temple. "And there will be no sex until we get married. That should weed out the bad ones, don't you think?"

Morgan shrugged. "I don't know. I know a lot of women who married men that treated them badly."

Fae shrugged. "No plan is perfect. But I think this is my best shot at finding true love."

"You really believe in true love?"

Fae scrunched her eyebrows and pursed her lips. "Yes." She nodded. "I really do."

"Well, we agree on one thing. I just plan to find it a different way. By the way, there's someone I want you to meet."

"A boy?"

"Of course not."

Fae raised an eyebrow. If there was one thing she'd learned about her roommate this week, her mind was on boys twenty-four/seven.

"He's a man."

Fae chuckled. "Oh, sorry. My mistake."

"Mason Chevalier. He's an upperclassman majoring in Business. He thinks he can turn my art into a gold mine."

"Oh, really? And is this Mason cute?"

"Cute is for boys. Mason is downright sexy."

"Sexy, huh?"

"Yeah," Morgan sighed. "He's a weightlifter. He can bench press like three of me."

"Wow. That is impressive."

"He wants to go out."

"How long have you known him?"

"That's the problem." Morgan frowned. "I just met him once. I don't know about going out alone with someone I just met."

Fae's estimation of Morgan's wisdom raised about ten notches. "Yeah. I'd feel uncomfortable with that too."

"So," Morgan said. "What do you think about a double date?"

Fae shook her head. "I haven't gotten to know any guys yet."

Morgan's face fell.

"But," Fae said, feeling sorry for Morgan. "How about you give me a chance to look around for someone I might want to ask out?"

Morgan's eyes lit up. "Sure! You've got 'til next Saturday."

"A week?"

"That shouldn't be a problem. You're so beautiful, you could probably get any guy you wanted to go out with you."

"I highly doubt that," Fae said, "but still, I don't know anyone here." Nick's face flashed in her mind.

No. He was off limits. She'd have to find someone else. "I'll see who I can scrounge up."

Morgan's smile widened. "I knew I could count on you."

Fae's heart pounded as she stood in front of the arts building. She'd exhausted every other job on her list. This was it. Glancing down at her watch, she closed her eyes and took a deep breath. She could do this.

She held her head high as she pushed the door open and stepped inside. Cool, floral-scented air greeted her. A wide room with art displayed along a curving wall surrounded her. In the center of the room stood sculptures—several mounted on display columns. One held the bust of a woman. The whole thing looked odd. Fae tried not to look at the breasts, though they seemed the strangest of all—as if they were melting down the side of the stand.

There was no way she could pose for someone who might portray her like that. She turned to leave when a woman put her hand on her shoulder.

"Hello, darling." The woman smiled brightly. "Are you Fae Miller?"

Fae nodded. "Um, yes."

"Oh, thank heavens." The woman sighed dramatically. "I'm Ms. Kline, and you, my dear, are a breath of fresh air. I've interviewed seven applicants today, and none of them would even remotely work for what we need." She stepped away and inspected Fae from head to toe. "But you...you look absolutely perfect!"

"Um, I..." Fae said, and then paused. "I don't know if I can do the job."

"Oh now, don't underestimate yourself. It's easy. All you have to do is stand in the same position for about a half an hour, forty-five minutes, tops."

"No, that's not it." Fae shook her head. "I don't think I can stand in front of a class full of people with my clothes off."

"Very few of your poses will be nude."

"I'd rather none of them were."

Ms. Kline once again put her hand on Fae's shoulder. "Everyone feels like that." She gave Fae an understanding look. "The first time's the hardest. After that, it only gets easier." She continued to study Fae, a frown settling on her face. "You still don't think you can do it?"

"No, I don't."

"Listen," the woman said, her voice lower. "The key is to not look anyone in the eye. You are a prop—an image for the artist to base their work on. They are not allowed to touch you, talk to you, or contact you at all. Any violation of that will result in academic probation. There is no tolerance for sexual harassment."

"I still don't—"

"Wait," she said gently. "Let me put it this way. Have you ever had a doctor's appointment?"

"Um," Fae answered. "No."

"Never?"

Fae shook her head. She'd never been sick a day in her life.

"Okay, well, let's say you get very sick and you get a new doctor to see you. How would you feel if your doctor had only seen pictures of human bodies and never actually examined a nude woman before? Do you think that could be a problem?"

"I see your point."

"Artists, to really capture the human figure, need to see a real human body. Art is an artist's life, it's part of who they are. We cannot deny them the knowledge they can gain from working from real life. Don't you agree?"

"I guess so."

A smile broke across the woman's face. "Good! I'm so glad you can appreciate the important work you will be doing for our students. Now I'll need you to start tomorrow at four o'clock, room one-seventy right here in this building."

Fae opened her mouth to speak.

"And," the woman interrupted. "I'll be increasing your pay. You have an interesting and unique look that is worth more than the average model."

Yeah, right. This woman was just plain desperate. Still, more money would be good.

Fae nodded and managed to say, "Thank you."

No," Ms. Kline said. "Thank you for your contribution to the arts and to the future of our students."

Fae left a half an hour later with a sinking feeling in her chest. At least now she had a source of income.

Chapter 6

Something wasn't adding up. The woman who haunted Nick's dreams and his waking hours presented a mystery. Should he put his investigative skills to use and find out everything he could about Fae? Or would that be considered an invasion of privacy? After all, she wasn't a suspect in a case. She was a student and a woman he would like to get to know better. She had also obviously had a rough life. He should let her reveal things naturally as he gained her trust.

Yes. That's exactly what he would do. He'd just have to ignore the itch to know everything immediately.

"Nick!" Don stood above him.

"What?" Nick asked, perturbed.

"Are we a little distracted?"

Nick ignored the question. "What's the big emergency?

"The bodies of sixteen people were discovered in a compound twenty miles off the Dixie highway. Fourteen were victims of an obvious poisoning, the fifteenth was stabbed through the heart, and the sixteenth was beheaded."

Nick swore. "Do they have any leads?"

"Yeah, they think these are the elusive protectors of the Fountain of Youth."

"You're kidding me."

"Nope."

"I thought that was a myth."

"The Fountain of Youth is a myth; this group of radical worshipers obviously is not. We leave now."

"I can't."

Don stopped and looked back, stunned.

"Did I hear you correctly, Agent Chase?" a familiar voice came from behind.

Nick turned around. "Hello, ASAC Young."

She looked up at Nick and sneered. "You will help in this investigation."

With dark brown hair, steel-blue eyes, and a body with curves in just the right places, Nick had at one time found Cheryl Young attractive. That time was long gone. Her sour personality overpowered everything appealing about her.

"Absolutely," he answered, "but I'm busy this morning."

"Doing what?" she blurted.

"I'm teaching a college course. Thank you so much for recommending me."

She swore under her breath. "This is a big case."

"And teaching college is a big responsibility. I'm guessing that if I don't show up, that would be *bad* for public relations, am I right?"

She scowled at him. "Come in your own car as soon as your class is done. I'll send you the coordinates."

"Yes, ma'am," he said, resisting the urge to mock her with a salute.

Two hours later, Nick approached a line of news vans a mile long parked along the side of the highway. He double-parked beside an ABC news van. Orange cones and police in yellow jackets directed the cars away from the scene—giving the FBI room to work.

Stepping from his car, he reporters bombarded him with questions. He simply said, "Just arrived. Don't know a thing."

"Do you know if this really is the Fountain of Youth?"

That question caught his attention. Nick looked over to see the person who'd asked it. There were too many reporters to ascertain the individual.

Still, Nick didn't bother answering him. He doubted he didn't need to—his expression showed it all. That reporter was an idiot.

A local deputy glanced at Nick's raised badge. The deputy lifted the yellow crime-scene tape to let him through. "It's straight through—"

"Yeah," Nick interrupted. "I'll just follow the trampled path." He gave the deputy a friendly smile.

The officer chuckled. "I guess it is pretty obvious now."

The camp was crawling with law enforcement and FBI agents. Nick spotted his partner next to a pond fed by a small spring. Several backhoes dug in the ground around the water, and a victim lay face up at the water's edge. It looked to be a male in his late seventies with what appeared to be a stab wound to the chest—the likely cause of death.

Nick looked at the backhoes. "Are the other bodies buried?"

Don shook his head. "The sixteen we found— including this guy—weren't, but Richards said that the depressions in the ground and discrepancy in the growth of vegetation around this pond has him thinking these are graves sites. We're here to see if there may be more victims."

"I'm guessing we've already scoured the place for evidence."

"Oh, yeah," Don said. "This investigation is by the book. I'm sure we'll all be under a magnifying glass in this case."

"Whoa!" someone shouted.

Nick looked over to see the claw of the backhoe raise and the machine turn off. He and Don ran over to the site and stepped to the edge of the hole. About five feet down, amid rocks and dirt, he could see something pale, almost white—bone.

"I'd say we found another victim," Don said.

"Looks that way," Nick said. "How may graves does Richard suspect?"

"At least five. And he says they all look to be dug decades apart. The earliest one seems to be from twenty years ago, and the others—who knows? Decades before. He even swears that there's one grave from over a hundred years ago. How in the world he could possibly know that, I have no idea."

"Yeah," Nick said, frowning, "but Richards is rarely wrong." Nick raised his eyes to the crew and shouted. "Clear the area around this. You will remove every speck of dirt until we have each and every bone. Understand?"

Everyone nodded.

Another shout from the backhoe on the other side had Nick and Don running again. Nick frowned when he looked down at the partial remains of a skull. This one looked to be much older than the first victim.

Don scowled. "These crazies have been killing for a long time. Why are we only finding out about it now?"

"That's not the biggest question," Nick said.

Don looked at him, startled. "What?"

"Look at these holes, and then look at the pond." Nick followed Don's eyes as they went from the open grave to the water, uphill only a few yards away.

Don's eyes widened. "That's impossible. These graves should be flooded with water."

Nick raised his head and turned to the excavation crew. "Someone get a pump in here. We need to drain this pond."

"That's not going to happen." Two men in dark suits stepped out from behind the trees.

"Who do you think are you?" Nick asked.

"I'm Special Agent Smith and this is Special Agent Jones," the older and slighter of the two said without a hint of humor. "Our division title is classified."

"Sounds like your names are classified, too," Nick said. "Or are you really Smith and Jones?"

Jones smiled and turned to Smith. "I like this guy."

Smith looked at Jones with surprise in his eyes. "You sure?"

"Absolutely," Jones said. "We should keep him around."

Smith turned to Nick. "What's your name, smart-aleck?"

Nick grinned at the old-fashioned nickname. "Special Agent Nick Chase."

"Okay, Agent Chase," Smith said. "You can stay. But everyone else needs to leave. Our division is taking over the investigation."

"What?" Don's voice rose. "Under whose authority?"

Agent Smith pulled out a folded piece of paper and handed it to Don. Don blurted out an uncharacteristic slew of profanity.

"What is it?" Nick grabbed the paper. He looked down and his eyes grew wide. "The Director? Seriously?"

"Yes."

Don shook his head. "I don't believe it. Why can my partner stay, but I have to leave?"

"We're not at liberty to say," Smith answered.

"Well, this just bites," Don said.

Smiling, Jones turned to Smith and mumbled something. They both chuckled.

Don took an intimidating step toward them. "You see something funny in this situation?" His eyes shot daggers at the two agents.

Smith's humor disappeared as he stepped nose to nose with Don—obviously not intimidated.

Jones stepped forward and put his hand on Smith's chest and nudged him back. "Murder is never funny," he said, looking at Don. "Now, if you could join the rest of your team, we can get this investigation underway."

Don narrowed his eyes. "You haven't seen the end of me. I'll be following up to make sure you do your job. One false move, and even the director won't be able to save your sorry self." He turned his back and stomped into the woods.

Nick approached the two strange men. "So, the president of the United States knows about what's going on here?"

"Probably," Jones said.

"Let's stick to the details of the case," Smith said. "And let me inform you, Agent Chase, that what you see and hear will remain with this team. Any sharing of information about this case or anyone working on this case will be considered an act of treason punishable by execution. That includes sharing information with anyone in your local field office, am I clear?"

Is this guy for real? "Yes, sir." Nick swallowed the lump in his throat. He looked up to see his friends and colleagues filing out from the crime scene with stunned looks on their faces. Even ASAC Cheryl Young was being escorted out. She locked eyes with him and shouted, "Why does Agent Chase get to stay? He's only been in the field for three years."

The man next to her shook his head and spoke to her as he kept his hand on her elbow. The fierce glare she shot him gave him a smug satisfaction. Still, this turnabout in events was the strangest thing he'd ever witnessed.

"Now that I'm part of the team," Nick said, "can you tell me what your division is called?"

"You're not part of the team," Smith said. "For now, we'll consider you an outside consultant."

"Right," Nick said, doubtful. "And what are you consulting me about?"

"That's classified," Smith said.

Nick shook his head. "If I'm to understand it right, you can't reveal to me my own expertise?"

"Exactly," Smith said. "Now, I think you'll be of more use with the recent murders." He gestured north.

Nick raised his eyebrows. "Yes, sir."

The scene was not quite as gruesome as he imagined it would be. That was, until the stench hit him—vomit mixed with feces and rotten flesh. Oh yeah. This was a murder scene.

"Hey," a tall, lean man raised his hand and stepped toward Nick. "You aren't supposed to be here."

Nick motioned toward the waterfall. "Mr. Smith told me I could stay."

"He did, huh?" He pulled out his cell phone. "Smith, did you give the okay on an outsider?... Jones cleared him?... Let's hope he knows what he's doing."

He replaced his phone in his coat and put out his hand. "Agent Chase?"

Nick shook his hand. "That's me."

"I'm Agent Thomas." He nodded. "What's your first impression?" He looked around, his eyes lingering on the oozing corpses of fourteen people lying haphazardly around a campsite.

Nick narrowed his eyes. "I'd have to agree; it looks like a poisoning. You can see the uneaten food and vomit on and around each of the victims."

"A ten-year-old could have told me that. What do your instincts say?"

Nick looked again. There were remnants of uneaten pastries, breads, lamb, desserts... "Looks like they were celebrating something." He saw benches set up in a semi-circle. "And either someone gave a speech, or there was some kind of performance. No. It was a speech. These people don't look like the performing type."

He stepped over to the one body that was different—this one was missing his head. He knelt to examine the wound. "The blade that caused this was very sharp. This wasn't done by anything you'd find in a sporting goods store. Has anyone found the head?"

Agent Thomas gestured several feet away at the base of a tree. The face looked up toward the sky and held a distinct expression—despair.

"I think this one was the last to die," Nick said. "Most likely stumbled onto the scene and was killed from behind."

"How do you figure?" Agent Thomas asked.

"He doesn't look afraid, he looks devastated. And why he would feel that way? Because friends and possibly family members are lying dead at his feet. And the fact he wasn't poisoned like the rest suggests a late arrival."

"Not bad, Agent Chase." Agent Thomas walked over to a black bag and retrieved a camera. "I want you

71

to document everything you think is important, and everything you don't think is important. I want every inch of this crime scene photographed from ten different angles. Understand?"

"Sure thing, Agent Thomas. What about the scene around the waterfall?"

"No. Definitely not. They have a different crew working that area."

Nick shrugged, his suspicion raised. This division ran with a lot of secrecy. "No problem."

When Agent Thomas's turned his back, Nick slipped a transmission chip into the camera that would send the images to his phone. There was something seriously off with this team, and he didn't trust them at all. What they didn't know wouldn't hurt them, right? And Nick was determined to cover his butt.

He snapped about a thousand shots and made it to the woods between the camp scene and the scene by the waterfall. Looking around, everyone seemed absorbed in what they were doing. Nick turned his camera to the area around the falls. He zoomed in to see if he could get a better look.

The area seemed void of investigators—which was odd. It should be swimming in them. They did, however, have strange lighting set up. He couldn't see where the light originated from, but the whole area was cast in some sort of green illumination. Suddenly there was activity... Movement came from several agents and one woman being carried from the scene. Unconscious? Looked like she'd taken a plunge in the water. She was completely drenched, the water dripping from her flowing dress. Who wore a dress to a crime scene?

Nick had the impression that someone was approaching. He turned and aimed the camera toward the camp and continued to snap pictures.

Agent Thomas came into view.

"I think I got shots at every possible angle," Nick said.

"You're out kind of far from the camp."

"Didn't want to miss the forest because of the trees—if you know what I mean."

Agent Thomas nodded. He took a quick glance behind Nick and said, "Yeah, I know what you mean." He reached his hand toward the camera. Nick pulled the strap over his head, his heart pounding in his chest. How in the world would he pull out the chip—

"Hey, Thomas," a shout came from behind. "You gotta see this!"

Nick didn't waste the chance while the agent's attention was diverted. He slipped his chip out of the camera and then handed the camera back. Agent Thomas looked back at him and mumbled, "Thanks," as he took the camera and stomped over toward the voice. Nick followed, his curiosity peeked.

A bulky man with a bald head came out of a tent carrying a worn, heavy book. He took a step back as soon as his eyes met Nick. "Who's the new guy?"

"Agent Chase," Agent Thomas answered. "Meet Agent Williams. Jones cleared him."

"That's cool." He shrugged. He stepped forward and pulled out an ancient book. "Take a look at this. This is the only book left from a whole library of journals. Looks like the rest were taken somewhere. This one would probably have been taken too, but I found it in a tent on the far side of the camp. It seems to be detailed documentation about The Fountain of Youth. Maybe Jones can use it to help the lady—"

"Yes, thank you," Thomas interrupted. He took the book and tucked it under his arm.

"Does the journal mention the members of the society?" Nick asked.

Agent Williams nodded. "Oh, yeah, and detailed accounts about the fountain. It looks like it restores youth, but causes insanity. Maybe the murderer is named in there. I'll bet he's an old guy—or at least he used to be old."

"So, you think we're on the lookout for a newly young, crazy guy?" Nick smiled.

"Young, yes," Thomas said without a hint of humor. "Crazy? Maybe."

Nick continued to chuckle. "Right." His laughter died when he realized they were completely serious.

"You don't really believe in the power of the Fountain of Youth, do you?"

Thomas raised an eyebrow. "If I told you the things I've seen, you'd think I needed a padded cell."

"We've seen," Williams added.

"Yeah," Thomas said.

The men in this division were certifiably insane.

Chapter 7

Fae sat with her eyes glued to the crime scene before her. A woman lay on a bed, her clothes and her bedding scattered on the floor. She appeared to be sleeping off a wild night with a lover. But she wasn't sleeping. She was dead.

"Okay," Nick said, stepping up beside the image on the screen before him to address his class full of students—in fact, it looked like there were more students here today than the first day. "I want you to take in every detail you can and let's see how much you can remember." He waited a few moments and turned off the screen. The class groaned.

"Now," he said, "write down as many details as you can remember. And I'll give you ten bonus points if you can tell me how the victim died."

Fae jotted down everything she could recollect. The victim lay sprawled on her back in white, lacy underwear. The bed was a high-end four-poster with light blue bedding. The victim didn't have a mark on her, that Fae could see. The clothes strewn across the floor consisted of a red t-shirt, blue jean shorts, white socks, and a pair of pink and yellow tennis shoes. The window was closed; the bathroom door open. She wasn't lying on a pillow. It sat on the floor and had a tiny smear of something red. Lipstick? The same color as the—

Fae's hand shot up.

"Ms. Miller?" Nick said.

"I know how she died," Fae said with pride in her voice.

"You do, do you?" He raised his eyebrows. She'd obviously surprised him. He looked around the class. "Does anyone else have a clue?"

The students were silent. "No one?" Nick asked.

When no one made a move, Nick turned back to her. "Okay, how was she killed?"

"She was smothered to death. The smear of red on the pillow is the same color as her lipstick."

Nick broke into a wide smile. "Very good."

He gave them a few more minutes to finish up their lists before speaking. "Okay, class. I want you to practice your observation skills." He turned on the projector and clicked. A web address popped up. "Here's the link for some activities. I want you to do the first one in class and the others as homework, which you'll need to turn in on Tuesday."

Fae continued to write down more of what she remembered as the rest of the class began to file out. When the last student left, she finally decided she had written enough.

"That's a lot of items. You're very good," Nick said. She looked up at his smiling face.

"I've always been pretty observant."

"I can see that." He raised an eyebrow.

Her heart sped up as he continued to watch her.

"Um," she said, "your class is really good. I've learned a lot."

"I'm glad you think so. Look, I was wondering..."

When he hesitated, she said, "Yes?"

He sighed, and his countenance soured. Fae felt like she'd been washed in cool water. "Don't forget the rest of your assignment is due Tuesday."

"Oh, um. Yes. I'll remember." She gathered her things. "I'll see you next class."

"Absolutely," he answered with regret in his eyes.

As she walked away, she heard him mutter something.

She turned back. "Did you say something?"

He shook his head. "No. It's nothing."

Fae left the building with a mixture of thoughts floating in her head. She felt a strong attraction to her professor. Every time she caught his eye, she could barely breathe. Aside from that, she took pride in the fact that she seemed gifted in her chosen major. She ached to put her investigative skills to use in her own life. She had to find out who she was and where she came from. Only one person held the key to those answers. Fae dreaded having to face her. She dreaded it down to her bones. But first, she had to do something else she dreaded nearly as much.

She had to go to work.

The linoleum tile was cold under Fae's bare feet. She pulled the cotton sheet tight to her chest. *What am I doing? I seriously can't do this!*

"Ms. Miller?" a light, feminine voice called. "The class is ready for you."

Fae looked up and met the eyes of a gray-haired woman with understanding written on her face. Looked like she could see Fae's fear. Fae swallowed back the lump in her throat. "I don't think I can do this." The woman stepped forward and took her hand. "The first time's always the hardest. And this one's a good way to start. Have you ever worn a bikini before?"

Fae nodded.

"Well, this costume covers more than a bikini."

"But everyone will be looking at me."

"Have you never done any acting?"

Fae shook her head.

The woman pressed her lips together—her eyes sympathetic. "You'll do fine."

"Okay." Fae took a deep breath. "I can do this," she said, mostly to herself.

"Good girl." The teacher led her through the door.

For a split second, Fae caught the curious looks of the class members, and she dropped her eyes.

The teacher tugged the sheet away, leaving Fae dressed only in a silky, toga-like thing that barely covered her. As bad as this seemed, it could be worse. Thankfully, the class was learning how to draw fabric along with the human body. She seriously needed to look for another job.

Stepping up to the stool, Fae sat down, leaving one leg extended and the other resting on the crossbar. She leaned back ever so slightly and looked up.

"Perfect," the professor said. "Don't move. All right, students..."

Fae didn't pay attention to the rest of the introduction. She tried to focus on her happy place—a wooded area with a small stream trickling through some rocks. The light penetrated the forest in green-tinted beams that dropped to the moss-covered ground, lighting the whole area in a soft glow.

She let her imagination go, dreaming of a fantastic adventure—complete with woodland animals, fairies, and a small cottage. She herself was not what she appeared. She had magic flowing through her veins, and everything she touched came to life.

A cottage lay before her, beckoning her. The woodland creatures flocked her, blocking her way. It seemed that they didn't want her to reach the quaint house. But she knew exactly who lived there and she simply had to see him. Stepping up to the door, she gave a little knock.

The door opened just a crack—enough to see the eyes of a man that made her heart pound and her knees tremble. At first, he seemed irritated. And then he recognized her.

Nick opened the door and put out his hand. She tentatively took his grip and a moment later found herself pressed against his chest. He looked down at her, his eyes penetrating hers, his gaze filled with heat. When he looked at her mouth, her heart flip-flopped in her chest. Slowly he lowered his mouth so that it hovered just above hers.

"Miss Miller?"

Reality thrust its way back into Fae's mind at hearing the professor's voice. *Just when my daydream was getting good!*

"Thank you so much," the professor said, helping her off the stood.

Looking around, Fae saw the classroom was nearly empty. She'd really zoned out! She swayed a bit, finding her left foot asleep. Thank heavens she could right herself before she fell over.

The professor chuckled. "You'll have to walk it off. Sitting in one position for forty-five minutes is bound to put something to sleep."

"Yeah," Fae breathed, still trying to shake off the daydream. What was she doing daydreaming about Professor Chase, anyway? It wasn't like it could ever come true.

"I'll see you Thursday, same time."

Fae nodded.

Right. Her job. Maybe it wouldn't be so bad after all.

She looked up at the clock and her heart sank. Mr. Wright would be here to pick her up in about twenty minutes.

Fae stepped out of the car and took a deep breath. Glancing up, the jail loomed ahead. It almost looked like an elementary school—except for the sparse windows with bars. Fae had always wanted to attend school, but seeing this building, she wondered what in the world she had been thinking.

"You don't have to do this, Fae," Mr. Wright said. He watched her with pity in his crinkled, brown eyes. He wore a light gray suit and brown loafers. With those clothes and crazy white hair and mustache, he looked more like Colonel Sanders than an attorney. He didn't even need to be here. She had no money to pay him, but that didn't seem to matter to him.

"I really do." Fae's voice quivered. "As much as I'd like to leave my past behind me, I need to know who my real parents are, and she's the only one who has the answers I need."

Mr. Wright nodded. "Just let me know if you'd had enough. And Fae?"

She turned when he hesitated.

"Don't let her get to you. She's a deeply disturbed woman."

Fae nodded.

She easily passed through security. She didn't carry a bag, just a small wallet, which they inspected and passed back to her. Her low heels clicked against the floor as a chill broke out over her skin. Places like this always ran the AC on high. And her stomach turned at the smell...a mixture of industrial cleaners, sweat, and urine. Fae pushed back the guilt that threatened to rise. Brigitte was responsible for her own actions and the consequences of those actions.

The corrections officer manning the security station looked at her with his eyebrows raised and gave a friendly smile with just a hint of pity. He didn't bother saying hello. This was not a place one went to chat or socialize—unless you were visiting with a loved one.

She walked down the hall with Mr. Wright's hand on her back. He seemed to know she needed assurance that she wasn't alone.

There were several other visiting family members hovering around a closed door. Fae stood at the edge of the group. The steel door opened, and an officer stepped into the hall.

"Those visiting inmates Heather Connor, Patricia Staudman, and Brigitte LeCrue may enter through here." He stepped aside. Fae's heart pounded in her chest as she paused.

Gathering courage, she stepped into the room and found several booths with thick glass separating the inmates from visitors. Identical tan phones hung on the wall inside the enclosures. The guard directed Fae to the booth at the far end.

She stifled her surprise when she saw Brigitte. The dark circles under her eyes and the wrinkles that had sprouted on her face gave Fae a twinge of regret. Brigitte looked like she'd aged a decade in the last few months.

Fae sat on a plastic-lined metal chair and lifted the phone.

"Fontaine," Brigitte said, her southern Florida accent coming through. "I knew you'd come to see me eventually. You're too sweet a girl to turn your back on the woman who raised you."

"Raised is a very loose term," Fae said. "A person who raises you doesn't usually lock you away and keep you prisoner."

"You talk as if I kept you prisoner all your life," Brigitte said. "I didn't have to lock you up until you tried to run away."

"I was twenty-one years old, and you kept me padlocked in a shed for over a month. You threatened to kill me if I escaped. What kind of mother is that?"

"You don't understand," Brigitte said. "I never said *I* would be the one to kill you. Everything I did, I did to protect you. I had to teach you a lesson."

"The lesson I learned was how cruel you could be." This was the exact conversation she'd been determined to avoid. She needed information, and she'd better get it now before she lost it completely. "Listen, I didn't come to argue. I need to know about my parents...my real parents."

Pain flashed across Brigitte's face. "I can't talk about it."

"Because it would incriminate you?" Fae said.

"No!" Brigitte said adamantly. "You know that's not the reason. If I told you, you would be in danger."

Fae wanted to shout that she wasn't in any danger. Brigitte was delusional. But Fae kept her mouth shut. She'd have to be clever if she wanted to get any answers from Brigitte.

She'd have to lie.

"Mom, please," she said, nearly choking on the word "mom." The day she found out Brigitte wasn't her real mother and that Brigitte had kidnapped her, she'd sworn she'd never call her mom again. But desperate times called for desperate measures—which was why she'd also decided to forget her vow to never lie again— just for today. She'd need to find out the truth from Brigitte. Today was a day for broken resolutions.

"I promise," Fae said. "I won't tell a soul. I just need to know."

"If I tell you here," Brigitte looked over to the guard, "they'll know."

Fae shook her head. "No, they won't. Mr. Wright knew you wouldn't say anything if they were listening. He was able to get a court order to have our conversation remain private—you know, like client/attorney privilege."

Brigitte looked doubtful. "Are you sure he wasn't lying to you, honey baby?"

"I'm sure," Fae said. "I heard the approval from the judge himself." Guilt gnawed at her. There was a time she never would have lied to her mother—no, Brigitte wasn't her mother. *I have nothing to feel guilty about! Brigitte was the one who kidnapped a baby and hid her away deep in the bayou.*

Brigitte's eyes shifted from Fae to the guards and back. "Your birth mother got too close," she whispered. "Much too close."

"Too close to what? Who is my mother?"

"Your mother is dead, honey baby. I don't know her name. I don't know where she came from. I only know that she was murdered."

"Murdered? How? Why? What did she get too close to?"

Brigitte chewed on her bottom lip—something she always did when she was extremely nervous.

"Please, Mom. Answer me."

86

"The Fountain of Youth," she said. "You were born in the waters of the Fountain of Youth. You are special, baby."

Fae only half listened to the rest of the conversation. It was too crazy to be believed. She spoke of guardians, sacred oaths, and murder. Nothing made sense.

Several excruciating minutes later, the guard approached. "It's time, Ms. Miller."

Brigitte snapped her mouth shut as Fae turned to the guard. "Thanks."

Fae didn't offer Brigitte a goodbye. She gave her a regret-filled glance as she hung up the extension. Fae got all she was going to get—the delusions of a crazy woman. She left with her heart heavy in her chest. She had no clue as to who her parents were. Perhaps she would never find her family.

Fae held back tears as she got in Mr. Wright's car.

"I'm really sorry, Fae." She nodded. He'd heard the whole thing. He knew exactly how crazy Brigitte was. How had Fae not truly seen it before? The woman actually believed the Fountain of Youth was real. She thought Fae was some kind of... What? Supernatural being?

Fae closed her eyes and clenched her fists. She was far from special. She was far from extraordinary. Unlike most people who grew up with a normal family and had a life with school, friends, dance lessons, girl scouts, Fae grew up with a crazy woman who thought magic existed and danger lurked behind every corner.

Maybe she was special. But it was definitely not in a good way.

Your mother is dead. The words replayed in her mind as Fae choked back tears. Was her mother truly dead? Or could this be just another delusion? Brigitte had said she was buried near the Fountain of Youth—somewhere west of Dixie highway. From what Brigitte described, it was a simple pond with a trickling waterfall fed by a spring.

It probably didn't exist.

But Fae didn't have anything else to go on. If only she had access to a car.

"Here we are," Mr. Wright said, pulling Fae from her thoughts.

"Thank you...for everything."

"Sure thing, sweetie."

Chapter 8

Several days later, Fae still hadn't gotten over her visit with Brigitte. It would take her a long time to process all her emotions: anger, guilt, despair, regret...

Maybe someday she could find it in herself to forgive Brigitte. But that day wasn't today.

Fae walked into her empty dorm room, eager to feel the cooling comfort of slipping between her bed sheets. Morgan was probably working late on a class project somewhere. Stripping down to her underwear, she slid her white, lacy nightgown over her head.

Just as she stepped up the first rung on her ladder, her phone vibrated. Her bare feet padded over the cold, linoleum floor as she stepped over to her dresser. Morgan's name lit up the screen.

"Hello," Fae answered.

"Fae," Morgan said, her voice ringing with anxiety. "Are you in our room?"

"Yeah," Fae said. "I'm just headed to bed."

"Oh, no, you can't go to bed yet. I've got a big problem. Mrs. Albrecht said someone is moving into our old room, and I just remembered. I left a box with some of my jewelry in it on the top shelf of my old closet, pushed clear to the back. I was going to grab it when we moved, but I totally spaced it. Can you go get it for me? I don't want the new girl moving in and laying claim on it. I have my grandmother's ring in there. I should have listened to my mom and left it home."

"No, no," Fae said. "Don't worry about it. I'll get it."

"Thank you so much," Morgan said. "You are the best roomie ever! Listen, I've got to go. Can you text me when you find it?"

"Sure," Fae said as she stepped from her room into the hall.

Fae approached the door and hesitated. What if the girl was already there? Raising her fist, she knocked. She waited a minute and knocked again. Still no answer.

Should she just go in? Or should she get Mrs. Albrecht? No. The girl obviously wasn't in, and Morgan really needed her jewelry back.

She tried the knob, and it turned easily in her hand. Stepping into the dark room, she turned on the light, and her heart skipped a beat. Someone had moved in.

"Oh, shoot," she whispered. She needed to get out fast. Rushing to Morgan's old closet, Fae threw open the door and slapped her hand over her mouth.

Beside the hanging sweaters and blouses, just above the rows of designer shoes, a young woman dangled from the curtain rod. Her milky eyes were open and her mouth hung askew. Her skin was white—not just pale, but freakin' white! And her hands and feet.... Fae fought the sudden nausea that threatened to cause her to lose the contents of her stomach then and there.

Fae backed away and shut the door. She swallowed bile as her mind raced. Here she was, breaking into a room, and she finds a dead body. Knowing her luck, she would end up cell mates with Brigitte. But still, she had to call the police. She—

Wait a minute. She had Nick's number. He did say to call him if she needed him for anything. And he was an FBI agent—one who knew her and seemed to actually like her.

Pulling out her phone, she dialed his number.

"Fae?"

"Listen, you said I could call you if I needed help." The words rushed from her mouth.

"Is something wrong?"

Her breath came out in gasps as the reality of the situation seemed to crash down on her. Tears flooded her eyes. "You could say that."

"What's wrong?"

"There's a..." she swallowed, "dead body in my roommate's old closet." The image flashed in front of her eyes, and she began to shake.

Nick paused on the other end of the line. "Is this a joke?"

"No. I swear, there's a...there's a..." Fae was trembling so hard her teeth began to chatter. Her

91

stomach twisted in a knot. "I think I'm going to be sick."

Nick swore. "Fae! Fae, listen to me. Are you still in the room with the body?"

"No. I closed the closet door."

"Good, good. I want you to go out into the hallway. You need to be around other people."

"I don't feel so good," she said when her stomach lurched and darkness seeped into the edge of her vision.

"Close your eyes and breathe."

"Are you...coming?" she asked as she stumbled into the hall. There wasn't anyone around. She slumped to the floor and put her head between her knees.

"I'm on my way. I'll call it into the campus police."

"There..." Fae closed her eyes. "...wasn't any blood." She focused on breathing and calming down. What kind of investigator would she be if she fell apart at a murder scene?

"What?"

"She was as white as a sheet and her hands and feet...were gone. But there was no blood on the floor beneath her. Not a drop. There wasn't a drop of blood anywhere. Isn't that strange?"

"Yes, it is," he answered calmly.

She could hear him mumbling in the background—probably calling the police. She sat and tried her best to focus on her breathing.

"Fae?"

"Yes," she answered.

"The police are almost there."

Moments later, the door from the outside burst open and two campus cops rushed in. They locked eyes on her. "Are you Fae Miller?"

"Is that them?" Nick asked.

"Yes," she said, answering them both.

"Who are you on the phone with?" one of the officers asked.

"Special Agent Nick Chase," she answered.

"Fae," Nick said. "I'm going to hang up now so you can talk to them, but I'll be there in just a few minutes."

"Okay," she said. "Thanks, Nick." She hung up and looked at the cops.

"Are you okay?" the younger of the two asked. He was a hefty, short man who looked to be no more than twenty. His name badge said Officer Holden. The other officer—Layman—looked older, but not much. He was in better shape and much taller.

Fae nodded weakly. She remained on the floor. She didn't trust her legs to hold her up.

"Where it is?" Layman asked.

It? Fae's stomach sickened at the thought that that girl, the one who had great taste in shoes, the girl who couldn't have been more than eighteen years old, had been reduced to an "it." She looked at the door to her old dorm room. "She's in there. In the closet."

They both nodded. Officer Layman reached for the doorknob.

"Stop!" Fae shouted.

The officer jerked his hand back and put his hand on his gun.

"No, no...I'm sorry. I just think you should dust for fingerprints first. The murderer was probably the last one to enter that room—well, before me. You don't want to miss the chance to pull his prints off the doorknob."

Officer Layman frowned at her. "This isn't our first investigation."

"How many murders have you had on campus?" she asked, genuinely interested.

Layman must not have taken her question in the spirit she'd asked it because he simply answered with a scowl.

Officer Holden whispered to Layman, "Maybe we should wait for the investigators."

"Fine," Layman snapped. "I really don't want to see a dead student anyway. Let the meat wagon handle her."

At the mention of meat wagon, the image of the girl surfaced in her mind—her body hanging from the curtain rod, her hands and feet missing. She had to put her head between her knees again.

Chapter 9

Nick ran across campus. He could hear the fear and panic in Fae's voice. If anyone so much as put a hand on her, he'd rip them to shreds.

Bursting through the doors, he spotted Fae immediately through a group of campus police officers. She looked ghostly white. With her white-blonde hair and light blue eyes, the paleness of her skin made her look washed out—like a ghost. Adrenaline pumped through his veins, seeing her in this state.

He ignored the campus 'girl scouts' and went straight to Fae. Kneeling, he brushed her hair away from her face. "You okay?"

She blinked back tears and nodded.

He looked up at the crowd and then to the campus officers. He lifted his badge. "I'm Special Agent Nick Chase. I need you to seal off the exits and take the students and staff to the common area. When the other investigators get here, the students will all need to be questioned and the building will have to be searched. I appreciate that you didn't enter the room. You don't know how many idiots have ruined perfectly good evidence by blundering through a crime scene."

They nodded and mumbled their agreements.

Minutes later, the place was crawling with investigators. And seconds after that, the news reporters descended like vultures looking for scraps.

Nick decided he would be the best one to question Fae. He knew how investigators could be— hounding her with questions while she was still in such a fragile state. He would not allow her to be put through that.

He reached out his hand. "You think you can stand?"

She started to nod, but then shook her head. "I don't think so."

Scooping her up off the ground, he felt her trembling in his arms. She was in shock.

Nick spotted Don coming through the door. "Don," he shouted. "Can you get her a blanket?"

Don looked over and frowned. "Sure."

"I guess you're rethinking whether I'd make a good investigator now," Fae said. "I see one dead body and I fall apart."

"Fae," Nick said disapprovingly. "Even a seasoned investigator would have a hard time stumbling onto something this grisly—especially off the job. The agents coming on the scene now have had time to mentally prepare."

Carrying Fae behind the entrance desk, he lay her down on a couch. He shrugged off his jacket and rolled it to place under her head. The place was empty—the dorm mother had been taken to another location to be questioned.

"How are you feeling?" he asked.

"Better," she said with her eyes closed.

"Is it okay if I ask you a few questions?"

"Yeah," she breathed.

Don handed Nick a blanket, and he draped it over her.

"Are you sure you're ready to talk about it?"

She nodded.

Pulling out his electronic recorder, he switched it on. "Tell me what happened."

"My roommate called tonight and told me she forgot her jewelry box in her old closet."

"Her old closet?"

Fae nodded. "That used to be our dorm room. They moved us out when a pipe broke and it flooded. I went in the room, opened the closet door, and there she was."

Nick's heart skipped a beat when he thought about how close Fae might have come to being murdered herself. "Was it your roommate hanging there?"

Fae shook her head adamantly. "Oh no. Heavens, no. I don't know that girl...at least, I don't think I do."

"You've never seen her before?"

"No. Morgan just called and told me Mrs. Albrecht said a new girl was moving in and she was worried about her jewelry box. She said she'd forgotten she'd hidden it in the closet. She wanted me to get it before the new girl moved in."

"How long was it between the call and when you opened the closet door?"

"Not long. About a minute."

"I see. Did you see anyone coming or going in the hall?"

"No. It was completely empty."

"You didn't hear anything?"

"No."

"Can you think of anything usual? A new face? Anything out of place?"

Fae's brows creased as she seemed to be thinking hard. Finally, she shook her head. "No. But then, I'm pretty new here. Everyone's a stranger."

"Agent Chase?" Don muttered, and Nick looked up. "When you have a minute, I have some information you might be interested in."

Nick nodded. He looked back at Fae. Her coloring was better and she'd stopped shaking. "I'm going to talk to my partner for a minute. Are you going to be okay if I leave you?"

Fae gave a weak smile and nodded.

Nick breathed a little easier. She was going to be fine.

"What'd you want to tell me?" he said in a low voice.

"The room mother gave me some disturbing information," Don said.

"What isn't disturbing about this case?" Nick asked.

"I think Fae Miller was the intended target."

Nick felt a quick shot of adrenaline shoot through his veins. He stopped himself before raising his voice. Fae was just beginning to calm down; she did not need to hear him shouting. "What makes you think so?"

"Mrs. Albrecht said she found her file cabinet broken into and a file missing. It was Fae's. Apparently, her room number was still listed as the room where the victim was found."

Nick swore. "This was not a random murder. Didn't the room mother report the theft?"

"She said she told security, and they checked on the whereabouts of some guy named Mike Pendleton. He had assaulted Fae earlier and is now being held at the hospital, in the psychiatric wing. His alibi is air tight."

"What makes you think its Fae and not her roommate in danger?"

"Morgan's documentation was still in the cabinet and it had already been updated. The room mother said she hadn't had a chance to change Fae's yet. And as of yet, the victim hadn't been added to the file at all. According to the file, Fae was the only occupant of that room."

Nick looked over at Fae. She had her eyes closed and her head back. She looked exhausted. "She'll need protection."

"The school administrators have already arranged for twenty-four-hour security here at the dorm, and they're adding security cameras at all exits."

"She'll be safe here, but not anywhere else."

Don shrugged.

"I'm going to ask her to come home with me."

Nick waited for Don's reaction. He didn't have to wait long.

"Are you crazy?" Don hissed. "You shouldn't be getting personally involved."

Nick frowned and looked at Fae. Yes, she was beautiful, and in any other situation, he would welcome a relationship with her. But that wasn't the main reason for his desire to protect her. It was something else. She had a mixture of strength and vulnerability the likes of which he'd never seen before. She drew him to her like no other woman, and not just physically, but emotionally. "I'm already personally involved."

Don put his hand on his shoulder and leaned in. "You didn't sleep with her, did you?"

"I haven't even kissed her yet."

"Well, you better not. Young is still ticked at what happened at the Fountain of Youth murder investigation."

"You think? So, that's why she put me on two weeks' paid leave," Nick said in mock surprise.

"You're pathetic, you know that?"

"Looks like my leave will work to my advantage. Now I've got the time to keep a close eye on Fae."

"Fae's not just a person of interest in a murder investigation, she's your student. Getting involved with her would be bad for your teaching career."

"I don't have a teaching career; I teach one class. And if keeping Fae alive messes that up, I'd say it's worth it." Nick stepped away.

Sitting down next to Fae, he put his hand on her leg. She opened her eyes and said, "What did you find out?"

Nick frowned as he considered how he would break the news to her.

"It was me he was after, wasn't it?" she asked bluntly, stunning him.

"How did you know?" he asked.

Fae didn't answer.

"Is there something you haven't told me?"

She shook her head and sighed. "I have the worst luck in the world. Seriously!"

"You're not safe here," Nick said. "I'd like you to come home with me."

Fae's eyes widened in shock. She scrunched her eyebrows. "I don't think that's a good idea. You know. School policy."

"I could care less about school policy." He touched Fae's chin, and she raised her eyes. "Someone wants you dead, Fae. That girl hanging in the closet was supposed to be you."

She sucked in a breath, and what little color she had gained fled. He could kick himself for striking her when she's down. But the thought of her staying here without protection... Absolutely not.

"Do you have friends or family you could stay with?" he asked.

Fae shook her head.

"Then you're coming with me."

Fae looked at him, her eyes wide and haunted. Finally, she nodded.

Nick kept his arm around Fae as they stepped out the door. He held her small duffel bag in his hand. Investigators had taped off the area, and a crowd formed, lining the perimeter and pressing against the tape.

A female student waved and shouted, "Fae!"

Nick recognized the girl from the first time he met Fae. Fae didn't seem to hear her. She avoided making eye contact with those around her and flinched every time a flash went off.

Fae's friend ducked under the tape and ran toward them. Before she could reach them, an officer intercepted her. The girl raised her finger and pointed. "She's my roommate," Nick could barely hear her over the sounds of the crowd.

Nick led Fae toward the girl and caught the girl's attention. "Morgan?" he said. The officer turned, and Nick showed him his badge. He took a quick glance at the officer's name tag. Lieutenant Hunter. Ah, a detective.

Morgan nodded vigorously.

"She needs to be questioned," Nick said to Hunter. "Take her to talk to Special Agent Don Fuchini."

"Wait," the girl shouted. "I need to talk to Fae."

Fae slipped out of Nick's grasp and made her way to Morgan. The girl threw her arms around Fae. Tears flooded her eyes.

"I heard what happened," Morgan wailed and looked her friend over. "That was you? You found the body?"

Fae nodded.

"Are you okay?"

"I'm alright," Fae answered. "Really, I am."

"You don't look all right," Morgan said. "Where are they taking you?"

"She's not allowed to say," Nick said.

Morgan's eyes turned to him and widened. "Professor Chase?"

He nodded.

"Is someone after Fae?"

"I can't say."

"Listen," Morgan raised her voice. "I'm her roommate. I have a right to know."

"It's okay, Morgan," Fae said. "He'll make sure I'm safe."

Morgan stepped up to him and jabbed her finger into his chest. "You'd better not let anything happen to her. If she gets so much as a paper cut, I'm coming after you."

Her bravado impressed Nick.

"Are you threatening a federal agent?" the police officer growled as he stepped toward her.

Nick put his hand out to hold him back. "It's okay." He turned to look at Morgan. "I promise; I'll personally see to Fae's safety."

Morgan nodded and turned to Fae. "Call me as soon as you can."

"I will," Fae answered. "And I'll be in school tomorrow."

"I'll meet you outside your first class."

Fae nodded and turned away.

"Wait!" Morgan shouted. "Are we still on for Saturday night's date? Did you find someone to take? Are you even going to be up for it?"

"I'll try," Fae said.

"I'll bring her," Nick said. He had no idea if she already had a date, but if she did, she'd just have to cancel. Her safety was more important than hurting the feelings of a post-high school kid. And the fact Nick didn't want to see her on the arm of another man had nothing to do with it.

A sparkle lit Morgan's eyes. "Okay. Good."

Nick kept his focus on the crowd as he led Fae away. Students lined the walkway. He wondered if the perpetrator was there. Could he know that he'd gotten the wrong girl? Could the murderer be another student? There were too many unanswered questions.

Nick guided Fae to his car. Her eyes widened when she saw his car parked on the sidewalk just outside the entrance gate. He didn't comment on his parking job. She was smart enough to know he had been in a hurry to get to her, and with the FBI markings on the tags, no one would dare tow or move it.

After getting Fae in the passenger side, he put her bag in the trunk and then got in behind the wheel.

"Um," Fae said. "Are you sure you're okay with having me stay with you? I mean, you don't have to go out of your way. I know how to stay under the radar."

"And where did you learn that skill?" he asked as he bumped over the curb and pulled out into traffic.

Fae paused before she spoke. "From the woman who raised me."

"Your mom?"

Fae shook her head.

"A relative?"

She shook her head again.

"Ah, you were in the foster system."

Fae once again shook her head—surprising him. A couple things clicked into place. Fae was raised by someone who had no legal right to have her in their custody. And she'd been asking how to find the parents of child with no identity. "You were kidnapped."

Fae's head snapped up. She sighed as she shrugged. "I should have known you'd figure it out. Most people don't."

"I *am* pretty smart."

She gave a weak laugh.

"So where is your kidnapper?" he asked.

"She's in jail awaiting trial."

"And you have no idea who your real parents are," he said matter-of-factly.

"Not really. Brigitte is crazy, and I mean certifiably insane. She said my mother is dead and buried near the Fountain of Youth."

Nick took a quick intake of air and clutched the wheel tightly in his grip. This was an insane coincidence. "The Fountain of Youth? Like the park?"

"No. The real Fountain of Youth. At least, that's what she said," Fae said, doubt saturating her voice. "I have no idea how to figure out the real story. I've spent my whole life hiding away from a figment of Brigitte's imagination. She was so paranoid that she never even put me in school."

"From what happened today, I'd say you have a reason to be cautious."

Fae's eyes darted to him and widened. "I guess so. But that has to be a coincidence."

"Probably," Nick said to placate her. He was even more confident in his decision to take Fae and keep her under his protection. From the sounds of it, Fae may be indirectly involved in the Fountain of Youth murder case. Perhaps her mother's remains were there at the scene.

"Listen," she said. "I know you're worried, but I can take care of myself."

"Right," he said, half to himself.

"No," she said, straightening up. "I have black belts in Kenpo and Aikido, I'm an expert with both the rifle and handgun, and—"

"Whoa, whoa. Wait a minute," Nick interrupted. "Brigitte taught you all this?"

"Some of it," Fae said. "But I also learned from the experts in those areas."

"So, she didn't sign you up for school, but she got you into martial arts?"

"Yeah."

"Is Fae Miller your real name?"

Fae shrugged. "I guess it is now. The court made it official—until I find out who I really am."

"How did you find out Brigitte wasn't your real mother?"

"I always suspected she wasn't. But I tried not to think about it. It was easier to buy into the conspiracy thing than to admit she was mentally ill. I finally came to the point where I couldn't deny it anymore. I really wasn't out to get her arrested. I just wanted her to get help."

Nick sighed. "I'm really sorry."

She shrugged. "There's nothing to be sorry for. I'm sure things will be sorted out and Brigitte will get the help she needs."

Nick frowned. He doubted it would work out as nice and neatly as she thought.

They neared the Applewood Assisted Living Community, and he slowed down to turn into the gate.

"I know you're older than me." She smiled weakly. "But I didn't know you were *that* much older."

"Oh yeah, I'm ancient." Nick smiled back. He paused, obviously enjoying her confusion. "This community isn't just for the elderly; it's for disabled residents, too."

She looked at him, doubtful. "Disabled?"

"Becca—my little sister—has Muscular Dystrophy."

All humor vanished from her expression. "Oh, I'm sorry." From what Fae could remember, Muscular Dystrophy was one of the really bad diseases. It took away your ability to function. There was no cure and it was eventually fatal.

Nick shrugged. "It sucks big time. MD is rare enough, but for a woman it's really rare—especially as severe as Becca's condition. But there's not much we can do about it. Brace yourself. What she lacks in ability to move, she makes up for in sass."

A spark lit Fae's eyes, and she smiled once again.

Chapter 10

Fae watched the increasingly large houses pass by. This was a high-end community. Agents made pretty good money, but this neighborhood seemed a bit posh even for FBI agents.

"Professor Chase?" she asked.

"We're not in class, Fae." He looked at her, smirking. "Call me Nick."

"Okay, Nick?"

"Yes." He smiled.

"If you don't mind me asking," she said. "Where are your parents?"

"They died three years ago. Car accident."

"Oh." Fae's heart clenched. "I'm sorry."

"Yeah," he said. "It was not a happy time. Becca took it especially hard."

"How's she doing now?"

"She puts up a good front, but I know she's still mourning—both my parents and her old life. She's always known she has Muscular Dystrophy, but her type is usually mild, so she didn't expect problems until she was much older. My parents knew even before they adopted her."

"She was adopted?"

"Yep, we both were. They got me first. And then when I was five, they brought me home a little sister— a two-year-old hellion."

He slowed and pulled into the driveway of a large home. Next door, a woman with white hair and a thick middle held a water hose and showered her flowers. She raised her head and waved. Nick smiled and waved back.

Stepping out of the car, he yelled, "Hello, Mrs. Tunston. Your flowers sure are looking vibrant this year."

"It's all in the fertilizer," she answered with a smile.

Fae opened her own door as Nick retrieved her bag from the trunk. She stood and took in the sights. Nick's home was a mixture of brick and wooden slats— very expensive looking, and very different from the backwoods shacks Fae had grown up in.

There were no steps to the front porch. It was all ground level, and the front door was a double entryway that appeared to be made of some kind of solid, dark wood.

Nick opened the door, and cool, pine scented air greeted Fae. A wide entryway opened up before her. Dark wood floors shone, and a crystal chandelier hung from a vaulted ceiling.

A whirring sound came from the right, and Fae turned to see a beautiful woman in a motorized wheelchair. Her hands were gnarled, and her head was tipped to the side. She smirked at Fae.

"Well, well. He brought you home, huh?"

Fae turned to Nick.

"Becca," he said in a reprimanding tone.

"This is Fae, right?" She blinked innocently.

"Yes, this is Fae." He glared at his little sister.

"Fae, this is Becca." He turned to Fae. "Don't listen to anything she says."

"If you don't want it repeated," Becca said, "don't say it." She smirked again. "My brother is your professor, huh?"

"Yes," Fae answered.

"You know," Becca said, looking at Nick. "In my brief time at college, I never remember any of my professors bringing their students home, or going out with them. Of course, most of them were ancient and it would have been really disgusting."

"We're not going out, Becca," Nick said. "Fae is a witness in a murder on campus."

Becca held back a smile. "A murder?" She laughed. "I'd come up with something more believable than that if I were you." Turning her wheelchair around and rolling away, she called out, "Mrs. Anchovy is almost done making dinner."

"Mrs. Anchovy?" Fae asked as she turned to Nick.

"Mrs. Anchinly," Nick corrected. "Becca calls her Anchovy because she knows Mrs. Anchinly hates it."

Fae chuckled.

Nick smiled. "I told you she had sass."

Fae's mood had lightened considerably in the last hour.

"Are you feeling up to eating?"

"I could probably eat something."

Nick gestured to an adjacent room. "The dining room is that way. I'll be there in a minute. I need to call my partner."

Fae nodded, her chest tightening.

Minutes later, Fae sat down at the table across from Nick. There were only two place settings. "Isn't Becca joining us?"

"She prefers not to eat in front of other people. She can't work her arms very well, so Mrs. Anchinly has to feed her."

"Oh," Fae said, not sure whether she should offer an "I'm sorry."

They ate in silence for a few moments. "How are you coming on your Assessing the Crime Scene assignment?" Nick asked.

"Oh crap." Fae frowned and dropped her fork. "I left it in my dorm room. I'm only halfway done."

Nick shrugged. "I'll give you extra time. I think what happened today is a good excuse to get an extension."

"Thanks," she said as she picked up her fork and took a bite of salad.

"No problem," he answered.

"Speaking of crime scenes," Fae said. "What did you find out about the murder? Do they have a suspect?"

Nick shook his head. "It looks like no one saw the murderer come or go."

Fae wondered briefly if there might have been anything to Brigitte's paranoia.

"You look like you've had a thought."

"I was just wondering if Brigitte was right. Maybe there is a secret society out to get me."

Nick dropped his fork, and Fae's eyes shot up. He swore under his breath.

"What's wrong?" Fae asked, her stomach twisting into knots.

He sat silent for several minutes. "There's someone you need to talk to."

"You do think there's something to it," she accused.

"Possibly."

"Nick," she said, grabbing his hand. "What do you know?"

"I can't tell you." He looked her in the eye. "Really, I can't."

She pressed her bottom lip between her teeth as worry crept in. She'd lived in fear of hidden dangers and whispered secrets. She'd thought that was over the day she spoke to the authorities about Brigitte, but she just couldn't get away. "What are you keeping from me?"

"I wish I could tell you."

Fae stood, with every intention of storming out the front door. She was sick of all the veiled danger and mysterious threats she'd experienced throughout her life.

"Fae, where are you going?"

"I'm leaving. I'm sick of lies. I'm sick of deception. I don't want any part of this." She stomped toward the front door. A hand locked around her arm, and Nick pulled her back against him. Out of reaction, she grabbed his hand and threw an elbow toward his chin, preparing to throw him over her hip. He grunted as he blocked her strike. The next thing she knew, she lay flat on her back and he was sitting on her, straddling her hips.

His face swam into her vision. "Are you okay?"

She fought to catch her breath, and trembled from the adrenaline in her system. "Where did you learn to do that?" she gasped.

"I'm an FBI agent," he said as if that explained everything. He brushed her hair away from her eyes. She could feel his skin burn across her cheek.

"I didn't hurt you, did I?" he asked.

She took in a few deep breaths but couldn't shake the quivering in her chest. "Just my confidence."

"I'm really sorry," he said. "I couldn't let you leave. You don't understand the danger you're in."

"And you do?" she asked.

A looked passed over his face. His eyes looked haunted, burdened by tragedy and dread. He nodded. The fear and vulnerability she glimpsed in his face pierced her heart. He was honestly worried about her. The adrenaline in her system that had fed the flight or fight part of her brain changed into something else. Fae had the insane urge to pull him down for a kiss. Nick seemed to read her mind. His gaze intensified. He looked at her lips and lowered his head.

He's going to kiss me.

His lips were warm, and he tasted like heaven. Fae hesitantly reached up and wrapped her arms around his neck. He growled at her touch, and the kiss grew more fervent, overwhelming her senses. Everything about him drew her in—his taste, his touch, his smell. He put his arm around her waist and pulled her against him. His corded muscles moved and flexed against her and she held on as if he were a lifeline. His lips tore away from hers and he trailed hot kisses down her neck into the crook of her shoulder as her breath came out in gasps. She could feel the flutter of his fingertips against her sternum. Her body wanted more, but she was mindless to exactly what that meant. Still, instinct took over as she moved in sync with him.

"Hey, Nick?" Becca's voice filtered in from the doorway like a splash of ice water.

Nick pulled away and rocked back, breaking free of Fae's arms. Fae turned to see Becca's disapproving gaze settling on them as she came through the door. "Nick, you do realize you have a bedroom in this house, right?"

Heat rose in Fae's cheeks. Her chest heaved.

"This isn't what it looks like," Nick said, breathless himself. He stood and helped Fae to her feet. She swayed, and he caught her around the waist. "I was just showing Fae some ju-jitsu."

Becca raised an eyebrow as her glance flickered down to Fae's chest. Fae followed her gaze. She stifled a gasp as she clasped her blouse together. It looked like she'd had a couple buttons come undone.

"Right," Becca said, drawing out the word. "Listen, I'm going to watch a movie. If you two don't have anything better to do, you can join me."

"Sure, I'll watch it with you," Fae said, a little too quickly. "It sounds like fun." She could feel Nick's gaze on her.

"Yeah," Becca said, smiling, "much more fun than rolling around on the floor with my brother."

Fae seriously doubted it would be that fun. She slipped a quick glance at Nick. He watched her with an unreadable expression on his face. Looking back to his sister, he said, "I'll come too."

"Great." Becca smirked, her head wobbling as she nodded. "I'll find something with action." She turned and left, leaving them alone.

"Come on." Nick led her to the table, his arm still around her waist. "Your dinner is getting cold, and Becca doesn't like to be kept waiting."

They ate their dinner in silence. Fae realized in those quiet moments that she had a major problem.

She'd not only kissed her professor, she desperately wanted to kiss him again. No. Desperate was not a strong enough word. It took supreme effort not to jump out of her seat and throw her arms around him.

"Um," she said, and cleared her throat, "that probably shouldn't have happened."

Nick didn't say anything. A scowl settled on his face.

"I mean," Fae continued, "this could complicate things. I don't want you to feel you need to give me a good grade, just because you might..."

"Might what?" he asked when she didn't continue.

"I don't want to put words in your mouth," she said.

"Right," he said.

Was he angry? Heat rose in her cheeks. Why did she have to act like such an idiot around him? She was nothing better than a school girl with a crush. She stood, gathered her dishes, and mumbled, "I don't want to keep Becca waiting."

"Fae?" Nick put his hand on her arm. She turned to face him.

"Leave the dishes."

She could feel her hands shaking as she set them carefully down.

"How about I tell you how I feel?" he asked. "That way you won't be putting words into my mouth."

"Okay."

"Sit down," he ordered with a quick glance at her seat. When she hesitated, he said, "Please."

Fae sank into the chair.

He looked her direct in the eyes. "I think you're the most beautiful woman I've ever laid eyes on. And I think that kiss was enough to let you know, I'm attracted to you."

Fae swallowed and gave a shaky nod.

"But the truth is, I am your professor. That means, this relationship cannot move further than what it is now. That is, until the end of the term. And no, I won't be giving you any grade you don't deserve. But, once the term ends, all bets are off. I intend to pursue you. I expect keeping my hands off you will be difficult in the meantime. I think we are both reasonable adults and have enough self-control to keep things at a professional level. Right?"

Fae nodded, feeling a bit relieved. "I do have one question," she said.

"Yes?"

"You said our relationship couldn't go further than it is."

"Right," he said.

"And we've already kissed."

A frown settled on his face. It looked like he could guess where she was going. Warmth flooded her cheeks. She asked in a small voice, "So, can I kiss you again?"

He closed his eyes and shook his head, chuckling weakly. "You're going to make things difficult, aren't you?" When he opened his eyes, he stood up, pulled her out of her seat, and wrapped his arms around her. Her eyes widened and her heart pounded as her body melded against his. He looked down and gave her a smoldering look as the scent of his cologne teased her senses.

"I can't think of any alternate reality where I would ever say no when you ask me that question." With that said, he leaned forward and kissed her so thoroughly, she could scarcely remember her own name.

Chapter 11

Lafayette peered through the blinds of Room 13. The lingering scent of cigarette smoke wafted to him from the dirty, worn curtains. He hated staying in motels, especially ones as rundown as this one. But he couldn't take a chance of being followed.

Everything had gone wrong! Fae had fought him like a wildcat high on drugs. She'd kicked, she'd scratched, she bit him.... In the end, he'd had to break her neck.

Lafayette snarled as he punched the wall. The wall gave way under his pounding fist. He wasn't supposed to kill her! Killing her was the last thing he wanted to do. But if he didn't, someone would have heard her, and he would have lost his chance.

Stepping toward the grocery bag sitting on the bed, he removed the case of mason jars. At the most, he had five quarts of blood. Five! He was supposed to live forever!

No. He wouldn't take this gift for granted. He'd been given more life than anyone else ever had. Fae's blood was the elixir to grant him many more years— worth a million times its weight in gold. He wouldn't spend time regretting the fact he had to kill the source of his blood.

He'd been beyond careful not to lose a drop. Gravity had been his friend when he cut off her hands and feet. He simply had to wait for each limb to drain completely into the trash can.

He didn't relish the idea of drinking out of the garbage. He'd fill the jars first and then measure the blood carefully.

If the journal writings were correct, it would take a cup to restore his youth—taking him back to his early twenties. Then if he waited and drank every fifty years, he would have enough blood to last a thousand years.

Would her blood really remain fresh for so long? According to the writings, it would. But could he trust it? No one else had tried to keep it as long as he planned. Should he freeze it? What if freezing it changed it? Made it so it didn't work?

He'd have to trust the writings—have faith that they were true. He was never very good at faith.

Lafayette carried the can into the bathroom. Placing the plug in the sink, he sat a jar in the middle of it. Then he went to retrieve the blood. Gingerly, he lifted the trash bag from the wastebasket. He had tied it off tightly. If it tore, he could lose precious years.

Placing it on the counter, he cut a small hole in the bag and poured the crimson fluid into the jars, filling nearly five. Then he took out the measuring cup and filled it. He added some herbs to the life blood and stirred, then prepared to drink.

"Well, this is it," he said with hope in his voice. "A moment of truth."

He lifted the blood to his lips and drank deeply. It was thick, warm, and had a deep, coppery taste to it. He suppressed the urge to gag.

Finally, the he drained the cup completely.

Raising his eyes to the bathroom mirror, he searched his face for the first signs of change. It should come quickly. His heart pounded as he looked carefully at every wrinkle, every age spot, and at the gray hair on his head.

The minutes ticked by.

Nothing.

No change.

When five minutes elapsed, his excitement burned away into anger.

It wasn't working!

Why wasn't it working? It was supposed to work immediately.

Six minutes passed.

He continued to pace. When a full twenty minutes passed, he picked up a jar and hurled it against the wall behind the bathtub. It shattered; blood and glass shards splattered across the tile. He yelled and cursed as the other jars followed. His rage burned so hot he couldn't contain it. A slew of profanity spewed from his mouth.

That idiot college student wasn't Fae. She couldn't be. He'd made a mistake. When the last jar joined the others, he looked around for something else to throw. Or even better, something to hit.

Or someone.

Stomping into the next room, he pulled out a number he'd been saving for "after." Dialing the phone, he waited for the familiar voice.

"Hello, this is Angel," a sweet voice said.

"Hello, Angel," Lafayette answered, careful not to let any of the anger he felt come through in his voice. "I need you for an hour. It's still a hundred dollars, right?"

"You betcha, sweetheart."

He provided her his location and hung up.

Pacing the room, he felt like a caged tiger. His mind raced over the events of the night. He'd made the mistake by rushing in. He was so eager to reclaim his youth, he hadn't even found out what Fae looked like. He'd made assumptions as he watched the girl from his hiding place in the closet. The room obviously belonged to her, and that was Fae's room. Where had he gone wrong? Could he have overlooked something? His mind had dulled over the years. He was making too many mistakes! It had to be his age. He needed to talk to Brigitte. She had the answers. He looked up at the clock and frowned. What was taking the prostitute so—

A faint knock at the door interrupted his thoughts and lightened his mood.

Holly Kelly

She was here.

He opened the door and saw her initial reaction—disgust. Her expression changed quickly to a pleasant smile, but he'd seen how she really felt. Yeah, he was an old man. But old men had needs too.

He motioned for her to come inside.

"I'll need the money first," she said as he closed the door.

"Of course," he answered, and opened the end table drawer. "Cash, right?"

"Yeah, sweetheart. I don't take check or charge. Oh, and there's a few rules..." Her voice dropped off and her eyes widened when she got a look at the duct tape in his hand.

Chapter 12

Fae had never felt so conspicuous. Nick walked to her right, a half a pace behind. Nearly every female they passed had her eyes on him. Did he have to deal with that kind of attention all the time? Fae's mind flashed back to the first time she saw him.

Oh yeah, he'd had her full attention.

She really wished she could link her arm in his. She wanted to claim him so the other women would back off. But he wasn't hers. They weren't even allowed to date—at least not yet.

"Be sure you sit close to me," he muttered at her back.

She nodded, suddenly reminded that any one in the sea of faces passing her could be a murderer. "Are you able to carry your gun here?" she asked.

"Of course," he said. "I always carry when I'm out in public."

This was one instance when knowing there was an armed man on campus made her feel safer. She'd feel even safer if she could carry her own 9 millimeter Ruger with her. Right now, it was doing her no good, locked in a storage shed. "Do you think I could get special permission to carry too?"

"Definitely not," he snapped.

She frowned at his quick dismissal. "You sound as if you think I'll shoot myself in the foot. I'll have you know, I learned to shoot before I learned to ride a bike."

"I'm not questioning your ability, Fae. There are strict gun laws for college campuses that cannot be waived for any reason."

"Oh," she said, stunned. "And you—"

"I'm FBI."

"Every time you teach class, you're carrying?"

"Yes."

"That's good to know. Do you think I'd make a good agent?" The question popped out of her mouth before she had a chance to think it through. What if he said no?

"I think you'd make an excellent agent."

"Really?"

"Absolutely. You *are* my star pupil."

"Don't you think you're biased?" she asked.

"I am biased," he answered without hesitation. "Regardless of that, there's no denying that you are brilliant."

A grin spread across her face before turning to a smirk. "More brilliant that you?"

Nick narrowed his eyes and fought back a smile. "Sweetheart, no one is as brilliant as me." The sparkle in his eyes told her he was joking. Or was he?

Without thinking, Fae stepped up to the vending machine.

Nick chuckled. "You and your Coke."

"It keeps me alert."

"Most people use coffee for that," he said.

"Coffee makes me jittery. I can't handle too much caffeine."

Minutes later, they stepped through the door of the classroom. "I'm giving you a heads up," Nick said. "I have someone coming to visit the class. He wants to talk to you."

"Really?" Fae's heart lit up. Maybe this was an expert in the field Nick wanted her to meet. Fae had set her sights on being a police detective, but perhaps the FBI would be a better fit. Seeing as she had just started college, she had a long time to think about her career. But it was something to consider.

Nick kept Fae in his peripheral vision as he started class. Ten minutes into his lecture, Special Agent Thomas strolled in. Thomas's eyes flickered over to Fae, and then he took a seat at the back.

Fae had been taking notes, but stopped and raised her head and glanced over her shoulder. As she turned back, Nick could see the confusion on her face.

Without missing a beat, Nick continued. "The rate of incarceration has tripled in the last thirty years. And of those incarcerated, only forty percent are violent offenders. Couple that with the fact that our prisons are overflowing with inmates, and we can't build prisons fast enough, we are faced with a major problem. For those of you looking to go into law enforcement, how does this information affect how you would do your job?"

The answers were the kinds he expected: it would be disheartening, we should focus on violent offenders, drugs should be legalized...

When Agent Thomas's hand went up, Nick was surprised. He called on him. "Yes, Mr. Thomas?"

"If I were to choose what to do with criminals, I'd say arm all the dangerous ones, drop them on an island, and let them fight to the death. And then all the non-violent offenders should be put into camps and forced to do hard labor fourteen hours a day."

Nick had to force back a smile when the class erupted in a hum of angry voices. Nick gave the seasoned agent a thanks-a-lot glare and shook his head. Nick spent the rest of class reeling in the chaos and getting the discussion back on track.

When Nick dismissed class, the students filed out, most of them glaring at Agent Thomas while a couple others smiled appreciatively.

When the last of the students trickled out, Nick approached the agent. "Thanks a lot for livening up my lecture."

"I knew that would get them going," Thomas snickered. "So, who did you need me to talk to? I must say, I didn't expect to hear from you again."

Nick turned back to invite Fae to join them. What he saw unnerved him. She was glued to her seat, obviously terrified.

"Fae?" he asked gently. "Is something wrong?"

Her eyes were locked on Agent Thomas. She nodded her head.

"Do you know Agent Thomas?"

She shook her head slowly.

"Fae, what's wrong?" he asked. Her eyes turned to him and then snapped back to Thomas.

Nick looked at the agent and found his expression a strange mixture of shock and apprehension. Thomas carefully rose from his seat and raised his hands. "I'm not going to hurt you, Fae. I promise."

"What are you?" she asked, her voice quaking.

What are you? Not, who are you?

Thomas's eyes darted back and forth from Fae to Nick, finally landing on Fae. "What do you see?"

She swallowed. "You look like a man..." she hesitated, "but you're not."

Nick's heart sank. Fae was having some kind of a psychotic episode.

131

Nick could hear Thomas's sigh. He looked back at the man and saw resignation in his eyes. "I'm what you'd call a shape-shifter."

"I don't understand," Fae said.

"What are you talking about?" Nick snapped at the man.

Thomas looked back at Nick. "My kind originates from the wilds of Alaska."

Nick locked his arm around Fae's waist and stepped back, pulling her with him. "Fae, we're leaving."

Turning toward the door, he prepared to storm out and nearly ran Thomas over. *That man can move insanely fast!*

"I know this is hard to believe," Thomas said. "But it's true. Fae is not crazy. She has a sight. She can see things as they truly are."

"I've never seen anything or anyone like you."

"There aren't many of us around—especially not here." Thomas looked back to Nick. "You wanted Fae to talk to me. What did you need her to tell me?"

"You're insane," Nick breathed. "You stay away from her."

Thomas frowned. He closed his eyes and blew out a slow breath. When his eyes opened, Nick stumbled back. Fae grabbed his arm to keep him from falling.

Thomas's eyes were a golden yellow! "This can't be real," Nick muttered as he closed his eyes. He opened them again. The man's eyes were still yellow. "It's a trick."

Thomas reached out his hand and held Nick in a vise grip, sharp fingernails digging into Nick's skin. "It's not a trick, and my time is very valuable. You said that Fae had something to do with the investigation."

"Threatening me will get you nowhere," Nick growled.

"What investigation?" Fae asked.

Thomas turned to her. "Twenty-five bodies have been found near the Fountain of Youth—sixteen recent murders and nine others from decades before."

Fae blanched white and sank into a nearby chair. "No," she breathed.

Thomas let go and approached Fae. "What's wrong?"

"Brigitte..."

"Brigitte?" Thomas asked.

"She said my mother was buried there."

"How long ago?" Thomas asked.

"Twenty-two years."

"I think I know which one she is." He frowned. "We'll need a DNA sample from you. We'll see if we can match it."

Fae sighed. "I'd always hoped I'd find my mother alive. I thought she might be looking for me."

"I'm sorry," Thomas said. Hesitantly, he reached out to her hand. "May I? I just need a small sample of blood for the test."

Fae nodded.

Taking her hand in his, he lifted his index finger—an inch-long claw extended from it. He nicked her finger, sopped up the blood on a handkerchief, and placed it in a zip-lock bag.

"This is insane. You really are a..."

"Kushtaka," Thomas supplied.

"And the division...they know?"

Thomas nodded.

"Is Thomas really your name?" Nick asked.

Thomas smiled and shook his head. "My name is Kaare, but my friends in the division call me Thomas."

Fae lifted her finger and sucked on the blood.

"Is that still bleeding?" Nick asked her.

Fae nodded.

Nick pulled out a handkerchief from his jacket only to find it covered in blood. "Oh, right. I guess I never got this washed." He replaced it in his pocket, and a flash of red caught his attention. Wet blood coated his hand.

"That doesn't make sense. The blood should have dried by now."

Thomas was there in a moment, grabbing Nick's bloody hand and lifting it to his nose. He inhaled deeply, his eyes narrowed. "There's something unnatural in her blood."

"I have hemophilia. My blood never clots. I do heal quickly, though. So it's not usually a problem."

Nick's brows pressed together. "But it should dry."

"You were in the Fountain of Youth, weren't you?" Thomas asked.

Fae's eyes snapped up. "Brigitte said I was born in it. But, how did you know?"

"That's not important." He looked at Nick. "Fae needs protection."

"She's already got it."

Thomas's eyes narrowed. "Why?"

"Someone tried to kill her. A case of mistaken identity cost another girl her life."

"That makes no sense," Thomas said. "Fae's more valuable alive."

"What are you talking about?" Nick asked.

Thomas ignored his question. "Was the girl drained of blood?"

The hairs on the back of Nick's neck stood on end. "Yes."

Thomas narrowed his eyes and looked Nick up and down—apparently sizing him up. "Don't let her out of your sight. Whoever the perpetrator is, he's dangerous."

"Are you going to tell me what's going on?" Nick asked.

"I need to talk to Jones first," Thomas said.

"I want in on that conversation," Nick said.

"That's not going to happen."

"I need to know what's going on," Nick growled.

"You will," Thomas said. "I'll tell you everything. I promise."

"You'd better," Nick threatened.

Chapter 13

"You look beautiful."

Fae looked up to see Becca sitting in her wheelchair in the doorway of Fae's temporary room—the largest and most beautiful room she'd ever slept in.

"Thanks," Fae said and gave a weak smile. "You're welcome to come in."

Becca smiled and rolled inside.

"I really appreciate your brother taking me on this date tonight," Fae said as she wrapped her blonde hair around a curling iron. "My roommate was really counting on me."

"Oh, yeah," Becca smirked. "It's a real sacrifice for Nick." She coughed, her head lolling with the movement.

"You okay?" Fae asked, concerned.

"I'm fine." She cleared her throat. "I know my brother. He's head over heels for you. I just want to know how you feel about him. Are you going to break his heart?"

Fae shook her head. "I...I don't know how I feel. I was rarely allowed to make friends. A boyfriend was out of the question. And Nick...? Well, seriously, who wouldn't want to be with him? He's kind, he's smart, he's funny... Not to mention, he's the sexiest man alive."

"I'll have to take your word on that one." Becca winked, and then coughed softly.

Fae chuckled, her laughter dying off into a sigh. "I guess I'm not ready to think beyond the fact that I like being with him. He makes me feel safe, and I do like to kiss him."

Becca cracked a smile. "I guess that's good enough for now."

Fae finished curling her hair and clipped it back. Then she took a look at the overall effect.

"You look stunning," Becca said with a smile on her face, but there was a trace of sadness in her eyes.

Fae's heart sat heavy in her chest. Becca was not quite halfway into her twenties and had a classic beauty of her own. If only...

Fae turned to her. "Why don't you let me do your makeup?"

A spark lit Becca's eyes. "You don't know what you're getting into. Do you have any idea how terrible Mrs. Anchovy is at putting on makeup? And Nick's even worse. If you do a good job, you'll just have to take over."

Fae smiled brightly. "I'd be happy to." She stepped over to Becca and pulled her hair back, securing it with a band, and then she got to work.

Minutes later, Nick stepped into the doorway. "Wow, Becca. Who knew that Fae could work miracles? You actually look pretty."

Becca narrowed her eyes and stuck out her tongue. "Very funny." She raised her eyebrows. "Hey, did you get a haircut?"

"Nope."

"Hmm." She looked him over. "You look different."

He shrugged. "It's just the same old me."

He turned to Fae, his expression warm. "You look beautiful."

Fae's cheeks burned when she said, "Thanks."

"You ready to go?" he asked.

"Yes," Fae said, and then she looked over to Becca. "Why don't you come with us?"

"Oh, no, no!" She looked horrified. "This is your night. I'd just be a fifth wheel." A cough rose in her throat, leading into a serious coughing jag.

"You okay?" Nick stepped up to her and brushed the hair from Becca's face.

"I'm fine," Becca said, recovering. "I just need a drink of water. Mrs. Anchovy can get it for me. You two need to get going."

Nick looked conflicted. His eyes darted from Becca to Fae, and then back to his sister. "Okay, but if you need me, you'd better call."

"I will."

"Becca." he said, his eyes fixed on hers.

"I said I will. Now hurry up, you've got people waiting for you."

Fae had her arm through Nick's as she walked down a dark path along a stone wall of the Castillo de San Markos—a fortress that resembled a stone castle. Morgan's high heels knocked against the pavement just behind them. Fae made a quick glance back. Morgan had her date in a death grip. If Morgan didn't want to be scared out of her mind, she shouldn't have suggested they take the St. Augustine Ghost Tour.

Actually, Morgan probably knew exactly what she was doing. This tour provided the perfect excuse to get cozy with Mason. Morgan's date was a polar opposite of her. He hadn't spoken two words, and from the looks of it, a smiled hadn't cracked his face in a very long time. What did Morgan see in this guy? Probably his muscle-build. It was pretty darn impressive—and that was seeing it through a t-shirt. He was even more muscular than Nick—though he didn't have Nick's height.

"And over here on the other side of this wall is a secret room." The tour guide stopped and pointed to a wall that looked identical to the others they'd walked by. "It was discovered nearly two hundred years ago. A man named Lieutenant Tuttle had been studying the architecture of the building when he discovered an area had been closed off. He removed a brick from a wall adjacent to that spot and the unlikely scent of perfume hit him. Peering through the hole, he found a space with no entrances and no exits. He removed more bricks to gain access and found a hidden room. Inside that room hung two skeletons chained to the wall—a man and a woman. Come to find out, these skeletons may have been the key to solving a mystery. Fifty years before, a Spanish general, General Marti, moved here with his young wife, Dolores. She was a beauty who always looked and smelled her best—wearing tasteful clothes and generous amounts of expensive perfume.

"General Marti had a man under his command named Captain Abela—a young and handsome soldier. General Marti was a busy man and didn't spend much time with his outgoing bride, and she must have felt neglected. Dolores spent time socializing with the soldiers and their wives and seemed to take a liking to Captain Abela.

"On one occasion, the general called a meeting in which Captain Abela attended. The general couldn't help but notice a distinct aroma coming from the Captain—his wife's perfume. Soon after this, both Captain Abela and Dolores abruptly left the country, never to return. The general claimed his wife had taken ill and went to be nursed back to health by a distant relative and Captain Abela had been sent on a special mission to Cuba. Fifty years later, the evidence pointed to a different fate for the supposed lovers—the two skeletons chained to the walls as retribution for their adulterous acts."

Fae turned to Nick and whispered, "Didn't they have divorce back then?"

Nick nodded his head. "Yes, but it was uncommon. And what's worse, the general couldn't have built out a hidden room on his own. He probably had help from his soldiers who were in on the crime."

Morgan whispered, "I'm really glad things like that don't happen today."

Nick looked at her, his eyes wide in surprise. "No. We just have girls murdered and left in dorm room closets."

Morgan's expression soured. "Yeah, I guess things haven't changed that much after all."

"One interesting note," the guide continued, "this entire structure is made of limestone. Does anyone know the significance of that?"

An eager young woman raised her hand. "Limestone magnifies paranormal energy."

"Very good." The guide smiled. "So, if you watch carefully, you just might catch a glimpse of the ghostly couple."

Chills broke out across Fae's skin when she noticed one of the other members of the tour—an older man with gray hair—watching her. He had a hefty, black backpack slung over his shoulder. He didn't appear to be with anyone.

Fae tried to ignore the strange man as the tour continued. A half an hour later, Fae began to get spooked. She felt as if something more than just the stranger watched her. If she'd believed in ghosts, she would have sworn it was a spirit.

This tour was going to her head.

Shouts caught Fae's attention. She turned to see a cloud of mist billowing toward her. Nick's arms came around her as he guided her away. "Hold your breath," he snapped.

She's only just gasped in a deep breath when someone shoved her hard from the side. Nick went down first and she soon followed, landing on top of his chest. With a grunt, she took another breath and inhaled an unusually sweet scent that turned her stomach. Someone was shouting, but it sounded far away—and it grew fainter by the second.

Chapter 14

Drip, drip, drip...

Fae smacked her lips.

They were so very dry.

Drip, drip, drip...

Taking a deep breath, she coughed. Pain shot through her wrists. She couldn't feel her fingers. Flexing her hands, she tried to get the circulation moving. She scooted back to relieve the pressure on her wrists and shivered at the cold washing over her legs and backside. Was she sitting in a puddle of water?

Where was she?

Peeling her eyes open, she shrieked. A face hovered just inches from her own.

"Are you really awake this time?" the stranger said. "Or am I still General Martin?" He chuckled. No, he wasn't a stranger; he was the man from the tour group, the one who had been watching her. His eyes narrowed, wrinkles sprouting from the creases in his leathery face.

"Who are you?" she asked. Fae blinked as her awareness increased. Cold stones pressed against her back, her wrists were shackled above her head, and she was sitting in about an inch of water with darkness enveloping the air around her.

"Where's Nick?" her voice rasped.

"That's the FBI agent you were with, right?" A smile cracked his face. This man was tall and bony, with white hair cut military style.

She pressed her lips together and glared.

"He's probably waking up in a hospital right about now."

Fae's eyes widened.

"Oh, don't worry about your precious bodyguard. He's fine. Just shaking off the effects of halothane—along with all the others from our tour group. I, on the other hand, happened to be lucky enough to bring along a gas mask."

"Who are you? Why did you bring me here?"

"My name is Lafayette, and this, my dear, is your new home. Get used to it. You'll be here a long, long time."

"Why? What did I ever do to you? I've never even met you before tonight."

"Ah, now that's where you're wrong. We met once before. Many years ago." He rose and paced in front of her, his feet sloshing in the water as he spoke. "The day you were born, actually."

Fae's eyes flew open wide. "My mother was murdered the day I was born."

Lafayette stopped and raised his hands. "Hey, that wasn't me."

Fae frowned and then glanced around the room—trying to see through the oppressive darkness.

The only light came from the Lafayette's cell phone, clipped to his pocket.

"I'll admit your mother had it coming," he continued. "I mean, she was actually in the Fountain of Youth. Talk about desecrating a sacred place! There was a time we would have hung her by her own intestines for such an act. She's lucky she didn't have to suffer. But then you were born," he stopped pacing and faced her, "right there in the waters of the Fountain."

"So, what?" Fae asked, doubt heavy in her tone. "Did it turn me younger? How much younger could I get, I was a newborn."

"It didn't make you younger—though you won't age past twenty-two. No, what it did to you was something much more significant. You are the Fountain of Youth."

"You're crazy. That doesn't make...sense..." Fae's voice trailed off as a thought came to her. "That girl in the closet. You were the one who killed her and drained her blood." She blew out a nervous breath as fear clenched her chest. "You really believe what you say."

"I acted rashly," he said. "She made me angry, and I was desperate. I'm not proud of what I did."

Fae breathed, slightly relieved. Perhaps he had a trace of a conscience. After all, he did regret murdering that girl.

"I mean, if that had been you," he continued, "I would have had a thousand years at the most. Luckily, it wasn't. Though when I drank her blood and didn't regain my youth, I must say I was disappointed. But I soon realized I had a second chance."

"You don't regret that you killed an innocent girl?"

He scrunched his eyebrows. "Why should I? She means nothing to me."

"She means something to someone. Her mother, father—"

"Not my problem," he interrupted as he continued to pace. "What I would have regretted was killing you. But, I calmed down, and this time I stuck to my plan. Now I'll have you for...well, forever. With your blood, I'll never have to die." He stepped forward and knelt down beside her. "And now it's time for me to get what I came for." He pulled out a knife, the steel glinting from the cell phone light. With the knife clutched in his trembling hand, Lafayette lifted it.

"Look." He cracked a smile. "I'm so nervous, I'm shaking."

Fae quickly pulled her leg back and kicked out as hard as she could. Lafayette went flying and landed with a thud against the stone floor.

He gasped as he struggled to his feet. When he finally caught his breath, he cursed. "You think you can stop me?" The anger in his voice reverberated off the walls. "I've killed two other women just this week. If I have to, I'll kill you too. Do you want that?"

Fae glared back at him. He moved in. She kicked again, and pain exploded in her foot. Her scream echoed off the walls of the dungeon. Looking down, she could see the point of his knife coming out of the top of her foot.

"It's no use fighting me, Fae," he said calmly.

Fae huffed as she tried to get on top of the pain—it was excruciating! Still, she couldn't let it stop her.

"Brigitte taught you to fight, didn't she?" he asked, gaining her attention. "I need to let you in on a secret. I taught Brigitte, and she was a complete disappointment. Definitely not a natural-born fighter."

"You were a guard?" Fae's heart pounded.

He nodded as he stepped forward and jerked the knife from her foot. She screamed. The pain ten times worse coming out as it did going in.

"I still am a guard. Which is why I'm here with you. I'm the last."

Fae breathed, her body shaking. "Brigitte is a guard," she said.

"Not anymore."

Fae blinked, and then her eyes widened. "What do you mean?"

"You can't be a guard if you're dead."

Her chest tightened. "That's impossible. She's in jail."

"You wouldn't believe how little it took to bribe the cook—just a case of cigarettes. Wolf's bane works fast and looks like natural causes."

She shook her head in denial. He had to be lying! But even as she thought it, she knew he was telling the truth. Despair overwhelmed her. Darkness seeped into her vision as she sobbed. She was about to lose consciousness.

No! She couldn't afford to. Focusing on her breathing, she tried to will the pain and anguish to go away. Brigitte may be gone, but that didn't mean Fae was ready to die too.

Lafayette moved in closer, the bloody knife raised.

Fae wanted to fight back, but she knew it was futile. She needed to stay alive long enough for Nick to find her. He had to find her. It's what he did. It's what he excelled at.

"Please don't—" Fae said when she could feel the steel against the side of her neck. She gasped as she felt a slash of pain and then whimpered, terrified at the warmth dripping down her neck.

Lafayette cringed for a moment. "Sorry, that's a bit deep." He leaned forward, and she could smell his sour breath and body odor.

"No." She tried to move away from him.

He grabbed her shoulders firmly. "This'll only take a minute." His cold, dry lips pressed against her neck, and he began to suck on the wound. When he swallowed, her stomach took a turn.

This crusty old man was drinking her blood! She tried to buck him off her, but he held her shoulders tightly, digging his fingers painfully into her. He pulled her closer, slurping the blood. She could feel it flowing from deep inside, and she could feel her energy leave her. The more she struggled, the tighter his grip became. She felt her strength wane even as his hold on her increased.

"Please, stop," she begged. He didn't hesitate or even acknowledge he'd heard her.

"Please," she said, her voice barely above a whisper. Feeling so weak, a whisper was all she could muster. "You're killing me."

He didn't stop drinking from her; in fact, he drank more vigorously. He sucked hard on her neck, drawing the blood out faster and faster as his grip grew tighter and tighter. Spots of light swam in her vision. She was losing too much blood.

Out of the darkness, notes chimed out. It had to be from his cell phone. Lafayette froze. He was shaking hard when he finally pushed her away, his wide eyes fixed on her throat. Her blood was dripping from his mouth and staining his teeth red, but that was not even close to the most shocking thing Fae saw.

This man was young—every bit as young as she was!

His face was handsome, too, but his eyes were wild with thirst. Fae didn't believe in vampires, but this guy looked like he was experiencing blood lust as strong as any fictional vampire she'd read about.

"I've got to..." his eyes looked away and landed on the phone on his belt. He swore under his breath. He pulled the phone out and must have swiped it off because he replaced it on his belt without answering the call.

The veins stood out on his neck as he seemed to be having an internal struggle. He muttered a curse. "I almost forgot. The herbs." He pulled a small muslin bag from a pack by the wall and dumped what appeared to be dried leaves into his mouth. His expression soured as he sucked on the powdery substance. He visibly relaxed, and then grabbed a water bottle from the pack and drank half of it.

He lowered the water and said, "Red clover and burdock root—the only sure way to completely neutralize the blood lust." Lafayette coughed and drank the rest of the water down, and then wiped away the water mixed with blood and herbs off his mouth. "You know, I'd read about how insanely strong the compulsion is. But imagining it doesn't even come close. I swear I've never tasted anything better or gotten a bigger rush. I wonder if this is where the legend of vampires comes from. Drinking blood, living forever...I guess I am a bloody vampire." He chuckled.

151

He raised his hands to inspect them. They were definitely not the hands of an old man.

"It worked," he shouted with a smile on his face. He pulled out a pocket mirror and studied his reflection. Shaking his head, he said, "I forgot how devilishly handsome I was."

He raised his eyebrows as he looked at her and corrected himself. "Am. Well, my dear," he said, "this is where we say goodbye—until I need to drink again. Now that I don't have to conserve the blood, I'll give it ten years."

"You don't..." Fae said in a weak voice. She felt like a half-drowned kitten. She could still feel the blood flowing down her neck. "You don't really plan on keeping me here, do you? Even you aren't that cruel."

"You don't have any idea how cruel I can be, Fontaine." The cold look in his eyes terrified her more than anything else that had happened this evening. He looked away and shrugged. "Besides, this is the perfect spot. A constant flow of water to keep you from drying out, and this dungeon hasn't been opened in two hundred years, so I have no fear of you being rescued any time soon. I'll keep an eye on the place, just in case someone decides to do some archeological exploring, or the underwater spring decides to take a different course. Who knows, I may have to move you a hundred years from now. But we'll worry about that when the time comes."

"I'll bleed to death...or starve," Fae said. Her chest tightened so severely, she was having a hard time taking a breath.

"Not so, my dear. Your blood may not clot, but your wounds will heal. From what I understand, you heal very fast. You'll be fine. As for starving...sure, you'll be hungry, but give it a week, and you'll be asleep."

"Asleep?"

"Yeah." He nodded. "A sort of hibernation. Sleeping and ageless."

He knelt beside Fae, his coppery breath brushing over her face. His teeth were now white as he smiled. His youthful, boyish appearance was at odds with what he planned to do with her. She would end up another skeleton in this dungeon.

"Nick will find me." She said the words as much for herself as Lafayette. "You won't get away with this."

Lafayette laughed as he stood and stepped away. "Whatever keeps you going, my dear."

"Wait!" Fae shouted. "Why not take me with you? I promise I won't run away. And now that you're young, you're actually pretty good looking. Maybe you can benefit from more than just my blood." She licked her lips and gave him her most smoldering look. She wondered if she was even close to pulling it off.

He raised an eyebrow and looked her up and down, undressing her with his eyes as he approached, smiling. She suddenly felt exposed, but she carefully kept her composure. If she could get him to release her, she just might be able to figure out how to get away from him.

He came in close and squatted down beside her. His eyes lowered as his finger brushed over her skin where the swells of her breasts met the top of her blouse. She trembled and swallowed her revulsion.

"It's too much of a risk to release you, though I can't say I'm not tempted." Fae's heart took off in a sprint as she tensed. "But you and I are going to be around a long, long time." He raised his eyes from her breasts to meet her gaze. "I hope someday you'll come to me willingly."

Over my dead body. He seriously thought she would warm up to a man who kidnapped, murdered, and tortured women? This guy was crazier than she thought.

Leaning forward, he pressed his lips to hers and then traced his tongue over her mouth. She stopped herself before she bit him. She might need his cooperation to release her. He couldn't possibly be serious about leaving her here for years. He was bluffing. He'd be back.

"Mmm." He licked his lips. "The taste of you still gives me a buzz."

He got up and stepped toward the wall. The light from his phone revealed an opening in the stones. "Goodbye, sleeping beauty. I'll wake you in a decade."

The shadows swallowed him up as he disappeared through the gap.

Seconds later, Fae could hear some scraping sounds. A mason trowel appeared along with Lafayette's ghostly face. He dumped mortar on the lower part of the opening. Using the trowel, he then spread the mortar and lowered a stone block into the hole. He was bricking her in!

Fae's screams echoed off the walls as he laid the last brick.

Chapter 15

"He's been in and out," a female voice said. "Agent Chase? Can you hear me?"

The smell of antiseptic and the beeping of a monitor let Nick know he was in a hospital. But how did he get there? He tried to think, but his mind was fuzzy and his head pounded.

He struggled to open his eyes, but they were weighed down. Finally, he raised his eyebrows and lifted his eyelids. A hazy face framed in black hair came into view. "Agent Chase. Can you tell me your first name?"

He licked his dry lips. "It's on my badge," he rasped.

"I need to know that you know your name."

"Nick."

"Good, Nick. Now, do you recognize where you are?"

He tried to swallow. Why was his throat so dry? He looked around. "Looks like a hospital."

"And what day is it?" she asked.

"September twenty-third, I think."

"You think?"

"Unless it's after midnight. Then it's September twenty-fourth."

"And the year?"

"We don't have time for this." Don's frustrated voice surfaced, as did his concerned face, coming in from behind Nurse Twenty-Questions.

"Nick," Don said, and uttered a curse. "What happened?"

"How did you know I was here?" Nick asked.

"I'm your emergency contact, you idiot. Now you tell me why anyone would want to knock out a group of tourists? And what were you doing in the middle of it? I thought you were supposed to be keeping an eye on your girlfriend."

"A tour group?" Nick said, trying to sit up. His head pounded at the movement. He covered the side of his pounding head with his hand and closed his eyes. "My head's killing me."

"You may have a concussion," the nurse interjected. "You hit it pretty hard when you fell."

Nick's mind wandered back to what Don said. Something about a tour group. The date! "Where's Fae?" he asked as his eyes flew open and he shot up. The room began to spin. He closed his eyes and held tight to the mattress.

"Whoa, slow down," Don said, putting his hand on his shoulder.

"Sir," the nurse said. "You really shouldn't be upsetting him. He needs to rest."

Nick opened his eyes, grateful the room decided to stay put. He grabbed Don's arm. "Is Fae here?"

"You were with Fae?" Don's eyebrows rose.

That question chilled Nick to the bone. "Is she here?" he asked again.

Don shook his head.

Nick punched the mattress and swore. "I need to make a phone call."

"Don't worry about it," Don said. "I'll call in the team."

"Not our team."

"What...?" Don narrowed his eyes. "You don't mean Division X."

"They told you what they're called?"

"It's what I call them. Why bring them in?"

Nick debated what to tell Don. He'd known Don for years; he was the closest thing he had to a best friend. Normally he didn't keep any secrets from him. This whole Division X stuff was wreaking havoc with their friendship.

"Don," Nick frowned. "I wish I could tell you. If I did, I could be charged with treason."

"You're joking?" Don jerked back.

Nick shook his head slowly.

"You're not joking."

"Nope."

Don swore under his breath.

"Where is she?" a deep, angry voice shouted from somewhere down the hall. "Where's Fontaine Miller?"

It took a moment for Nick to realize the significance of what he overheard, but when he did, he ripped off monitors and stumbled out the door.

"Agent Chase," the nurse shouted behind him. "You need to return to your room."

"You need to tell me where she is," the angry voice shouted again, letting Nick know exactly what room the man was in.

Nick stormed through the door and found Mason struggling with the doctor.

"I need some help," the doctor shouted.

"I'll help," Nick snarled as he pushed the doctor aside, took Mason by the throat, and slammed him back against the mattress.

"Who are you?" the doctor shouted.

"Special Agent Chase of the FBI," he said, glaring down at Mason. "What do you know about Fae? You just met her. You never said three words to her. So why all the concern?"

Mason sneered as he struggled to breathe. "I don't have to answer you," he rasped through his clenched throat and then tried to buck Nick off. Nick held firm.

"Agent," the doctor said. "I really must insist you let the patient go."

"Is he injured? Did the knockout gas harm him?"

"Well, no. He seems to be okay, but I won't know until I do a full examination."

"And I need to know what happened to the innocent college student under my protection," Nick said to the doctor. "She already survived one attempt on her life. And now someone went to a lot of trouble to abduct her. This man shouldn't know her from Eve. I'd like to know why he's so concerned over a stranger."

Mason snarled, "Go to—"

Nick increased the pressure on his neck.

"Don," Nick said, as he continued to glare at Mason. "Call Agent Thomas." He listed off the numbers, and Don dialed his cell phone.

"How do you know Fae?" Nick asked, loosening his stranglehold. "What is she to you?"

"I'm not telling you a thing," Mason rasped.

"So what, you want your lawyer?" Nick snarled.

"I want you off me." Mason pushed against Nick again, but Nick held fast.

Nick turned to the doctor. "Do you have restraints?"

The doctor sighed. "Yes, we do." He turned to the nurse, standing stupefied in the doorway. "Sierra, can you get out the straps?"

She nodded and moved forward. Mason growled and struggled in Nick's grasp. Don moved in and held down his shoulders. Nick increased the pressure on his throat, only easing up when Mason's eyes rolled back in his head.

"Is he okay?" the nursed asked.

"He's fine, just unconscious."

As soon as Mason was strapped down to the bed, Nick stepped into the hall with Don.

"Where did you meet this guy?" Don asked him.

"Fae's roommate asked her to go on a double date with her, and since I was protecting Fae, it made sense for me to go with her as her date. Mason is Fae's roommate's date."

"Right," Don said, and then raised an eyebrow. "So, going out with her was all in the line of duty."

Nick couldn't bring himself to smile. Not with Fae missing. Maybe even dead. No! He couldn't go there.

"I'm falling for her," Nick said and sighed. His heart felt like lead in his chest. The image of her face flashed across his mind. He slammed his fist against the metal doorframe and swore. "Why did I take her out in the open? I should have kept her inside. I knew someone was after her."

"Don't even go there," Don said. "This isn't your fault. What lunatic uses knockout gas to take out an entire tour group? This is not your run-of-the-mill criminal."

Nick looked back to the room. Mason was his biggest lead, and he wasn't talking.

Twenty minutes later, Nick paced outside the door while Thomas spoke to Mason.

"Please tell me that when this is all over," Don said, "you'll be leaving Division X behind for good?"

Nick turned to him. "What? I could care less about Division X! I don't even care what happens with the bureau. The only thing I'm concerned with, the only thing that matters is getting Fae out of the hands of a cold-blooded killer."

"You really are head over heels for this girl," Don said.

Nick pressed his lips together. He couldn't bring himself to analyze his feelings. There was no room in his head for that. All he could think about was finding her.

Twenty minutes later, the door to Mason's room opened, and Thomas stepped out. Nick rushed over. "What did he say?"

Thomas looked over to Don and then back to Nick. "I'll tell you in the car."

Nick raced to keep up with Thomas.

"See you around, partner," Don shouted at his back.

Nick could feel the tension in those words.

He turned around and nodded, somberly.

As soon as Nick shut the car door, Thomas said, "Mason Chevalier comes from a long line of guardians. He was due to train after his father retired as the leader. When Mason got to the fountain, he found everyone dead, including his father."

"He told you all this?" Nick asked.

"I can be very persuasive when I want to be. Besides, his organization and my organization have what you might call a working relationship."

"How did he find Fae?" Nick asked.

"Blind luck."

"What, he just stumbled onto her?" Nick frowned at Thomas.

"No, he saw a woman he recognized on TV. A woman he'd seen at the camp when he visited his father. Her name was Brigitte Rose."

"The woman who raised Fae," Nick said, recognizing the name.

"Yes. Mason watched the jail closely and when Fae came to visit Brigitte, he followed her in, pretending to visit another inmate."

"So, what did he learn?"

"He learned that the Fountain of Youth has no power, and he thinks he knows why." Thomas paused.

"Why doesn't it have power?"

"The power was transferred."

"To whom?"

Thomas turned to look at Nick. "I think you know."

"That's crazy."

"Do I need to remind you? You've seen crazy things before."

Nick swallowed. "Right." A thought struck Nick—why the first victim was drained of blood, and why Thomas had mentioned that Fae was worth more dead than alive. "The power's in her blood, isn't it?"

Thomas sighed and then nodded.

Nick's phone rang out the newest Danielle Voltaire song—Becca's favorite.

"Do you need to take that?"

"Yeah, it's my sister." Nick swiped the screen and put the phone to his ear.

"Mr. Chase," Mrs. Anchinly's voice was frantic. "Thank heavens you finally answered. You need to meet us at the hospital. Becca is being put on a ventilator."

Chapter 16

Fae's eyes fluttered open, though it seemed they were still closed. She'd never been in such complete darkness. It was extremely disconcerting—as if being chained to the wall of a dank dungeon wasn't bad enough.

The shaking of her body caused the iron chains to cut into wrists. Her lips were dry and cracked, and her stomach clenched in hunger…thirst? It was hard to tell which.

She had no way of knowing how long she'd been here. Lafayette told her she'd go into hibernation in about a week. She had until then to figure out how to get out of this place.

"Hello?" she shouted—not truly because she thought someone would hear her, but because she couldn't bear another moment of silence. "Please, help me." Her voice rasped like dry sand over her parched throat. She tried to swallow, but there was no moisture. Too bad she couldn't drink the water she sat in. The chain was too short. *Water, water everywhere, and not a drop to drink.*

"Please," she pleaded.

Dangling in silence, jagged stones pressed into her back. Her foot throbbed. Her mind moved in and out of consciousness with no clear boundaries between asleep and awake. She remained this way for hours...days? She had no idea.

"Hello?"

Fae's eyes flew open. *Was that a voice?*

"Hello? Is anyone there?" she responded.

Silence.

Her breathing calmed down, as did her heart. She must have imagined it. No one could possibly—

"Hello?"

That was a voice! It sounded like a woman. "Hello! I'm here. Please help me!" Fae tried to shout, but her voice came out dry and raspy.

From out of the darkness, a pattern began to emerge—slashes of horizontal and vertical black stripes. As the image became clearer, she could make out blocks, stacked one on top of another—extending from the floor and arching over her head. Was she imagining this? The image was very hard to see in the oppressing darkness, but what little she could make out was familiar. This was her surroundings. Why was she only now seeing it?

The light increased, and she could make out more detail. There had to be a light source somewhere. Was it seeping through cracks in the wall? Perhaps she hadn't been here for days. Maybe it'd only been one night. Could this be sunrise? It seemed impossible. The cell had appeared impenetrable. But then, maybe it wasn't. She had heard a voice.

She opened her mouth to call for help one more time, but only a croak came out. Her throat was just too dry.

"Please don't leave me here!"

Fae jumped when she heard the voice crying out, echoing in her thoughts and chilling her. Dolores? No. That was insane. There was no such thing as ghosts. But then...a short time ago she hadn't believed in the Fountain of Youth, either. And then Agent Thomas... he definitely wasn't human.

"I don't want to die."

The ghostly voice wailed, causing panic to rise in Fae. Was this what she had to look forward to? Dying in here and becoming a ghost herself?

The light continued to increase—taking on a blue tint. At any moment now, Fae expected to see the apparition of the woman. She squeezed her eyes shut, afraid of what she might see.

"No one is coming."

This time it was a man's voice. That had to be Dolores's lover...what was his name?

Captain Abela. The name popped into her head as if someone placed it in there. She was probably going mad. People in solitary confinement did—or so she'd heard. And hearing disembodied voices was crazy.

But still...she'd seen a lot of insane things lately. Was it really so far-fetched to believe ghosts existed?

And if they did exist, could they be trying to communicate with her?

"I don't know what to do," Fae said.

Minutes later she heard him again. *"The shackles are weak."*

The shackles are weak? Maybe she was reading too much into this. He could be replaying the tragedy that occurred two hundred years ago, but then again, he might be trying to tell Fae something.

"Are you talking to me?" she asked hopefully.

Silence stretched on for several long minutes. And then a faint, melancholy voice answered, *"Yes."*

The shackles are weak. Of course! With all the moisture in here, iron shackles would be rusted. If she could break them, perhaps she could figure out how to chisel a hole in this ancient wall.

Turning around, she pressed her foot against the wall, got a grip on the chains, and pulled until she felt she might pull her own arms out of their sockets. The chains didn't budge. Perhaps she needed to yank on them.

She jerked hard—once again to no avail. What did she expect? That this would be easy? She prepared to go again, this time determined to pull as hard as she possibly could. Giving the chains some slack, she pushed with her good foot and pulled back as she grunted. The air burned her raw throat as it breezed out. A loud snap rang in her ear, and she flew back, her head cracking against the stone floor.

Fae awoke with a pounding in her skull and water lapping at the nape of her neck.

Turning on her side, she pushed herself off the floor. She was free!

First things first; if she didn't get a drink, she would literally die. Leaning forward, she put her mouth to the water and began to slurp. It was filthy, it was gritty, and she couldn't get enough.

Minutes later, she was water-logged and fighting off nausea. Yeah, it probably wasn't smart drinking so much of the foul stuff. Who knew what kind of parasites or diseases she would get? Still, she was beyond grateful to have the raging thirst gone.

Staggering to her feet, she steadied herself against the wall, trying her best to keep her weight off her injured foot. It felt as if it weren't healing. Perhaps she'd lost too much blood. Her leg felt like wet spaghetti underneath her. Limping around, she studied the wall, looking for loose or cracked stones.

She found one!

At chest level, there sat a stone that was cracked and partially broken. Jamming her fingers into the cracks, she pulled at the loose chunks. They splashed to the floor near her feet. When she'd gotten all she could out, she felt a breeze. Her heart leaped in her chest. It wouldn't be long.

Minutes later, her fingers were raw, and the rest of the block seemed unbreakable. She looked down at the shackles still on her wrists. A long metal spike protruded from the cuff. Taking it in her hand, she began to chip at the rock. It was slow going, but the rock began to flake off under her pounding. She found the mortar was the key; it crumbled away much more easily than the hard stone. She concentrated her efforts there.

Hours later, the stone began to shift. She pushed at the block and it grated, moving under her pressure. Finally, she could push it through. It landed on the other side of the wall with a deep thud.

The hole she'd created wasn't huge, but she should be able to squeeze through. At least, she hoped she could. As weak as she felt and as much time as it took her to loosen the first stone, she didn't think she could do another. Sinking to the floor, she sat down and tried to gather the strength she'd need.

Ten minutes later, she felt even more exhausted than she had before. What was wrong with her?

She needed to get out of here before her weakness made it impossible to even move.

Getting to her feet proved to be a difficult feat, but she finally did it. Reaching forward, she decided her shackled arms should go through the hole first. When her head came through, she met her fist obstacle—her chest. Most thought being well endowed was a good thing. But, it may very well kill her. If she got stuck in here, she'd die.

Taking a deep breath, she pushed forward. The jagged remnants of the mortar grated against her— tearing her clothes and scraping her skin while her breasts were flattened painfully against her body. She inched through slowly, biting back cries. She blew out all the air in her lungs and wiggled her body whenever it got stuck. Finally, she experienced some relief when her chest came out the other end. The relief soon turned to horror when she tried to get her hips through. Blowing out air, would not make her hips any smaller.

Bracing herself for the pain, she pushed hard with her hands, and her body began to scrape through. She felt like she was leaving chunks of grated flesh behind with every push. Her jeans refused to make the journey with her and slid down as she continued to squeeze through the hole. Finally, blessed relief came when she got through.

The relief was short-lived when she realized that there was nothing to stop her descent to the floor.

Reaching out, her hands took the brunt of the fall, followed quickly by her head, and then rest of her.

"Ouch," she moaned, lying on the ground. Pulling her raw, aching body off the floor, she sat up and looked around. It looked like a continuation of the room she'd been in—except she couldn't see the other side. Crawling forward, she tried not to think about the possibility that there wasn't an exit in this room either. There simply had to be one!

When dark slashes came into view, her heart sank. A few more feet forward and her hopes were completely deflated. There was no exit. She'd escaped one dungeon only to find herself locked in another.

And this one had no water.

Chapter 17

Nick pressed a kiss into his sister's forehead. The hissing of the ventilator reminded him that if not for that machine, she would be dead. He closed his eyes to hold back tears. Both of the women he loved were in danger. Becca would eventually succumb to her illness. The ventilators couldn't save her indefinitely. She found peace with her fate. Nick still struggled to accept it.

But Fae? She was healthy. No, she was more than healthy. She was immortal. But she was not immune to death. She could be dead, even now. Nick held tight to the hope that Thomas had given him. If her abductor knew what Fae really was, he would know she was worth more to him alive than dead.

Nick looked his sister over. She looked pale, and the spark that always lit up her face had dimmed. She lay unconscious before him, but maybe she could still hear him. He had so much to say. So much on his mind.

"You know I love you." He choked back the lump that formed in his throat. "You may have been a royal pain, and drove me absolutely insane at times, but I love you, Sis. You know that. You could always read me like a book. I bet you knew exactly how I felt about Fae even before I did, didn't you?"

173

He sighed. "And now she's in trouble. She's in the hands of an evil man—a man who has killed people. He already tried to kill Fae once." He took her hand and gave it a squeeze. He sucked in a breath when her eyes opened.

"You're awake." Nick breathed a sigh of relief.

Her eyes darted around to the machine at her side and down to the plastic tube coming from her mouth. She looked confused for a moment before recognition saddened her face. She knew the end was coming. And then her eyes went to the door. Her gaze held for a moment before she looked at him and back to the door.

"What is it?"

Once again, she looked at him and then back to the door.

"You want to see the doctor?"

Her head moved. It looked like she might be attempting to shake it.

"You don't want to see the doctor?"

She rolled her eyes—typical Becca.

"All right, so you don't want to see the doctor. Wait. How about you blink once for yes, and twice for no?"

She blinked hard once.

"Okay, so you want me to...leave?"

One blink.

"Why? Why wouldn't you want me to stay?" Her eyes went back to that stupid door. Nick blew out a breath of frustration. "I can't leave you. You really think I'd leave when you're scared and lying in a hospital bed?"

One blink.

Nick scowled and then a thought hit him. "You heard me?"

One blink.

His heart felt like it was being torn in two. "You want me to save Fae?"

A tear leaked from her eye and trailed down her cheek when she blinked—once.

He leaned down and kissed Becca on the forehead. "You know I love you too, right?"

One blink and another tear.

He breathed out a curse. "I hate leaving you."

Again, her eyes went to the door.

"I'll leave when you're asleep again." Two blinks.

Nick blew out a quick breath. "You want me to leave now."

One blink.

"Why do you have to be so self-sacrificing?" he asked, and then paced the floor. He stopped and sighed. "I'll do it, but you have to make me a deal. You cannot leave while I'm gone." He couldn't bring himself to say die. Becca rolled her eyes and then turned to the door once again.

"All right, I'm going, but I'll be back, and I'll bring Fae with me. Okay?"

One blink.

Nick stood unmoving, his heart pounding in his chest. He was literally tearing apart. How could he leave his baby sister while she may be dying? But then, how could he not go and do all he could to save the woman he loved?

Becca gave another hard look at the door and then glared at him.

"I'm going," he said, and then kissed her forehead. "Love you, squirt," he mumbled as his lip brushed against her skin.

A moment later, Nick stepped through the door and took one last glance at his dying sister.

Thomas met him in the hallway and looked at Becca's door. "I'll understand if you can't help in the investigation. We can cover this."

"She understands. Let's get to work."

Thomas nodded. "Okay." He took a deep breath. "The name of the man we're looking for is Demarquis Lafayette. People call him Lafayette. He was second in command to the leader of the Guardians of the Fountain of Youth. The leader was a man named Emeric, and Lafayette was due to take his place. Mason is Emeric's son. He got to the fountain shortly before we did and found everyone dead. He made the call that brought in investigators."

"Mason's a Guardian?" Nick asked.

"Was. The Fountain of Youth lost its power. It no longer needs Guardians. But Fae does. That's why Mason came. Now he feels it's his duty to protect *her*."

"You do realize how crazy this all sounds, right?"

"You haven't begun to see crazy yet. I think it's logical to say that Lafayette is a person of interest in not only Fae's abduction, but also the murder of the college student, the victims at the Fountain of Youth, and then another murder in a motel room not far from here."

"Another one?"

He nodded. "It looks like he wasn't too happy when he realized he'd gotten the wrong girl. He took it out on a prostitute. Broke nearly every bone in her body before he drowned her. A maid found her in a tub filled with not only water, but the college student's missing blood."

Nick swore under his breath. And Fae was in the hands of that lunatic!

"How do we find him?" he asked.

"I don't know," Thomas said. "We've come up against a brick wall."

"What about Brigitte?" Nick asked.

Thomas shook his head as they headed out to the parking lot. "That's a dead end. And I mean literally."

"He got to her?" Nick asked as they approached the exit leading into the garage.

"Yeah and besides Mason, she was our biggest lead."

"How'd she die?"

"She was poisoned," Thomas said.

Nick swore.

"Lafayette is proving formidable," Thomas said.

Frowning, Nick narrowed his eyes. "What do we have to go on?"

"We have a cell phone bought under the name Marcus DeCruise."

"I need all the information you have on that phone," Nick said.

Thomas clicked his keys, and a new model Mercedes chirped.

Nick raised an eyebrow. "Looks like your division pays better than mine."

"Like you, I have a few things on the side."

"Huh," Nick said. "I'll need my personal computer."

"Are you a hacker?"

Nick shrugged. "I know my way around."

An hour later, Nick poured over Lafayette's activities from the last week. He was only mildly interested in who he had called. He was more interested in where Lafayette had been. With two screens open, he was able to get the coordinates and see the satellite images of his exact location just before Fae was abducted.

Six forty-seven P.M., he'd parked in a handicapped parking spot near the location where the Ghost Tour began. He entered the trolley for the tour at seven o'clock—just behind Nick, Fae, Mason, and Morgan.

Nick looked at the photo they had of Lafayette. He remembered the man vividly. He was in his mid- to late-seventies, with a yellow tinge to his eyes that let Nick know his liver was in bad shape.

After the knockout gas was released, Lafayette's phone stayed in the same general area. He'd stayed there from that time until long after the ambulances had come and gone. Could he have hidden her somewhere at the scene and waited until it was quiet to remove Fae?

Probably.

Eventually, he made his way to the airport and got on a flight to Denver Colorado.

How would he get Fae on a plane? Unless he could coerce her.

Nick got into the airport surveillance and studied the images of the flight he took. After twenty minutes, he slammed his fist into the desk. He wasn't there.

"He's smarter than you think." Thomas's voice came from behind.

"I don't understand," Nick growled. "I looked at baggage check-in, the gate, and even studied every person getting on that flight. He wasn't there. But his phone was. That doesn't make sense!"

Thomas raised an eyebrow. "You're looking for a young man, right?"

Nick turned his head slowly toward Thomas, his eyes wide. And then he turned back to the computer screen and cursed. A blur of faces came and went, but then...

"That's him," he snapped. "At the luggage check-in desk." He blew out a breath. "He has the same bone structure, same height. That man can't be more than twenty-five!"

Neither of them spoke for several long moments.

"So, it's true." Nick's voice sounded hoarse.

"Yes," Thomas said, resigned.

"I don't believe it."

"Believe what you will. It's true."

"Why isn't Fae with him?" He said, his stomach sickened. *Please let her be alive.* Nick continued to follow the man at 10x speed.

"He could be keeping her somewhere around the St. Augustine area," Thomas said.

Nick's eyes widened. "What is he doing?"

Thomas turned to look at the screen and leaned in. "It looks like he's leaving the airport."

"He never got on the flight."

"Just his bag." Thomas narrowed his eyes.

"He knew we'd be able to track him by his phone. So, he put it on a plane to throw us off track."

"Makes sense," Thomas said. "He probably didn't think investigators would recognize him."

"But where is Fae? He didn't go anywhere! He went straight from the Ghost Tour to the airport."

Nick's eyes widened as he and Thomas turned to look at each other. Not a second later, they were rushing back to the Mercedes.

Nick and Thomas stepped up to the Castillo de San Marco. It looked less eerie but more imposing in the daylight. The gray-stoned structure rose from a wide lawn and simple, trimmed grass. There was only one way in and one way out.

"She has to be here," Nick said. "How far can an old man carry a full-grown woman?"

"Fae doesn't weigh much," Thomas said, "so I'm guessing as far as he needs to. Too bad the place is closed at night, and they have no one on duty after dark, so it's unlikely someone saw something here."

Nick looked down at his phone. "I wish this was more precise. According to this, he didn't move from this spot. But the range is a hundred yards. She could be anywhere."

"Let's go inside and see if we can find any clue as to where she was taken," Thomas said.

Nick walked into the Castillo de San Marcos and felt as if he'd stepped into another age. The place smelled ancient and the temperature dropped, raising goosebumps on his skin. His senses heightened, and he felt...

Well, there was no way to describe the feeling. Something was off about this place. He'd never felt anything like it. Nick didn't believe in ghosts, but if he did, he'd say this place really was haunted.

They wandered for nearly an hour when Nick came to a sickening realization. They had explored every inch of the place, and found no sign of any secret, unexplored room or place to hide someone.

"That's disappointing," Thomas said.

"We need to go again," Nick said somberly.

"Okay," Thomas said without hesitation.

Three hours later they had combed the entire building—inside and out.

"Perhaps he had an accomplice," Thomas said.

"If he did, we're screwed." Deep in his gut, he felt she was here—somewhere nearby. But short of taking apart this historic fort brick by brick, he was at a loss to figure out where.

Chapter 18

Fae awoke shivering. Cold seeped through her damp clothes and permeated into her bones. She couldn't complain too strenuously. Not only did it help her to realize she was still alive, it also dulled the pain. She hurt in so many different places, she felt like one large open wound. Usually, she healed quickly, but this time, she wasn't recovering. Maybe her loss of blood had something to do with that.

Her eyes blinked open, and she could see that faint light she'd seen before. After fruitless searching, she had to admit there was no logical place it could be coming from.

"You're awake."

Fae jerked—her eyes wide. She was hearing voices again. She struggled to push herself off the floor. Weakness overwhelmed her.

Looking around the room, she sucked in a startled breath. In the corner of the room, a faint flicker of an image materialized out of her imagination. It was a young woman. Fae couldn't see her clearly. She could only make out her general shape, but then the figure raised her eyes—eyes that Fae could see clear as day.

"Who are you?" Fae whispered, afraid she would disturb the spirit.

"My name is Dolores." The woman's answer blew across Fae's skin, bringing with it the faint smell of perfume.

Fae swallowed and squeezed her eyes shut. She'd never believed in ghosts. But here she was, talking to one. Opening her eyes, she frowned, disappointed to see the woman remained.

"Why are you here?" Fae asked.

"There's no way out."

"You're a ghost," Fae muttered. "You can move through walls."

Confusion passed over the ghostly countenance. Then she blinked—her eyes taking on a far-off look. *"They didn't find you."*

"Who?" Fae's heart sped up. "Who didn't find me?"

"They came for you."

"Who? Who are you talking about?"

Dolores's image began to fade as sadness darkened her countenance.

"No!" Fae shouted. "Don't leave. I need to know who came."

Seconds later, Fae sat in complete darkness. The sound of dripping water tormented her through the opening in the wall. Soon, her thirst would drive her to squeeze back through—if she even had the strength to. She blinked back tears. Gently pressing on the open abrasions on her hips, her fingers came away dripping wet. Those scrapes should have healed by now—yet they hadn't. She oozed blood from more places than she could count.

"Nick," she said, wishing desperately that he could hear her. "Please don't give up on me. You've got to find me." Her voice broke and tears began to fall.

"Please."

Chapter 19

Nick tried his best not to gawk, but he found it impossible. The woman standing before him was stunning, with an ethereal beauty that seemed otherworldly.

"This is Agent Adams," Thomas said.

Nick nodded and shook her hand. Her fingers were like ice, but that wasn't what bothered him. There was something off about her, something he couldn't quite put his finger on.

"I think Adams is our best bet at finding Fae," Thomas said.

The woman looked at Nick briefly with disinterest as he studied her, and then her eyes locked with his. A look of surprised confusion passed over her features, and then a slow smile spread across her face. "Do I unnerve you?" she asked, her voice low and seductive.

"Nope."

Her smile widened. "You're lying." She turned to Thomas. "Jones is right. He's not your ordinary human."

Human?

"So," Nick said, "what are you?"

Her smile faded as she turned back to him, but the amusement remained in her eyes. "That's a rude question."

"You're not offended," Nick said, shaking his head.

Her smile returned, and then she chuckled. "No, I'm not." She didn't say more. Obviously, she didn't want him to know exactly what she was. Nick had the feeling he stood before another supernatural creature.

"Avira will be accompanying us to the fort," Thomas said.

Avira was her first name? It was strange how Thomas used such an informal way to address an agent of his. Was there something going on between him and Avira?

Minutes later, Nick once again approached the fort with Thomas and Avira at his side. The structure towered above them—a dark silhouette against the night sky. The eerie feeling Nick had felt before compounded.

"You okay?" Thomas said. At first Nick thought Thomas was talking to him, having witnessed Nick's distress. But his eyes were on Avira Adams, and it was easy to see why. She looked stricken, haunted. In fact, her whole countenance took on an unearthly glow. Thomas's figure cast a shadow as he stood in her radiance.

"I'm so hungry," she said. She bowed her head and closed her eyes. "So many lost souls."

"Avira, I need you to focus." Thomas lifted her chin. "Look at me. Come on, baby. Look in my eyes."

Well, that answered the question of them being an item.

Her eyes flew open and immediately searched out his. "I've never felt so many."

"I know. I'm sorry. And I'm sorry you must do more. But I need you to talk to them. We are looking for Fae Miller, remember? If she's alive, we need her to stay that way."

If she's alive? Nick's chest tightened as he pushed back the possibility that she might be—

No. He wouldn't even consider it. She was alive.

Avira swallowed and then nodded. "Yes." Her eyes were pleading when she asked, "But after?"

Thomas brushed his hand across her face, lingering at the corners of her eyes and mouth. "Just one."

She smiled with intense relief in her face. "Thank you."

Thomas had a hint of a smile when he leaned forward and kissed her. Oh, yeah, Thomas definitely had personal involvement with this agent. Their kiss intensified within moments, making the situation awkward for Nick. And then Avira tore her mouth from Thomas's as she pushed him back.

She dropped her face into her hands and whispered, "I can't. The hunger is too strong. I don't want to hurt you."

Thomas hesitated a moment before he pulled her into his chest. "I understand. I'm sorry. I shouldn't have kissed you." His chest heaved as he tried to simultaneously talk and catch his breath.

And that's when a strange observation struck Nick.

Avira wasn't breathing hard. Either that kiss wasn't nearly as intense for her or...

He watched closely, waiting for the gentle rise and fall of her chest.

Nothing. Not a hint of movement.

She wasn't breathing at all! That's what had unnerved him from the start. This woman didn't breathe.

Nick wanted to question her. Wanted to know what kind of creature she was. But now was not the time. He had to find Fae and this woman—whatever she was—may be his only hope of finding her.

Pulling away from Thomas's embrace, she said, "Okay. I'm ready."

Nick moved to follow.

Avira raised her hand to block him. "I need to go alone."

Nick opened his mouth to protest.

"No," Avira interrupted before he could get the words out. "I...I just need to talk to them. I promise I'll bring you in as soon as I learn anything useful."

"How long's this going to take?" Nick asked.

"I don't know, but it shouldn't take long." She stepped through the doorway, and darkness swallowed her up.

Within minutes, Nick had trampled a path in the grass as he paced back and forth.

"Relax, Chase," Thomas said. "Adams is very good at what she does."

"I sure hope so," Nick said as he dragged his fingers through his hair. He felt restless. With his sister dying and Fae in trouble, he wasn't handling waiting very well. He wanted—no, he *needed* to act. Instead, he waited for a stranger to talk to ghosts. Nick stopped and turned to Thomas. "How long have you known her?"

Thomas blew out a breath. "A very long time. We used to be on opposite sides. I was hired to hunt her down and destroy her."

"Obviously, that didn't happen," Nick said.

Thomas shrugged. "I came close."

"So, what is she, a vampire?"

Thomas chuckled. "Nope. You'd have to have a deep knowledge of the mythical world to even be able to guess what Avira is."

"What other creatures don't need to breathe?"

"You noticed that, huh?"

Nick nodded.

"I'll bet you a hundred bucks you won't figure it out."

"Won't she be mad—us betting on her?"

Thomas shook his head, smiling. "Nah. She'll probably want in on the bet."

"How much time do I have?"

"I'll give you a week."

"Okay," Nick said, almost smiling. "You've got yourself a bet."

Avira came out a few minutes later. She didn't look happy.

"You weren't able to find anything?" Nick asked, his heart sinking.

"Oh," Avira said. "I found something. We're going to need some tools to get through stone blocks. And—"

"You know where she is?" Nick interrupted.

"I think so, but we're also going to need a doctor." Avira sighed. "The ghosts told me she's injured, but I already knew she was. I could smell her blood."

Nick swallowed back the lump that formed in his throat.

"I'll get the tools and call for help," Thomas said.

"I need you to take me to her," Nick said.

Avira nodded. "Follow me."

Nick raised the lamp as they entered the building. The place—though darkened by shadows—was familiar. Their shoes echoed off the stone walls as they walked down the narrow hallways. The smell of dust and mold permeated the air. The same eerie feeling he'd felt before washed over him. Avira stopped.

"Here we are," she said.

Nick looked up and down the passage. There was nothing but bare stone, dirt, and cobwebs. "Where?"

Avira looked at the wall. "See, here?" She laid her hand against the stone bricks. "Look closer."

Nick studied the wall. There was a slight difference in the area under her hand—more mortar between the bricks. "This is new," Nick said, astonished. "The stones are old, but the mortar is new."

Avira nodded. "Yes. Someone did not want her to leave."

"Or someone else to find her," Nick added, his chest constricting. His worst fears were coming true. "Does this mean she's..."

"She's alive."

Nick struggled to believe her.

Thomas came minutes later with a crowbar in hand.

"We need to get through this wall," Avira said.

Thomas nodded and they got to work—chipping at the mortar between the stones.

"Lafayette would have had an easier time of it," Thomas grunted as he chipped away a big chunk of the sealant. "The old binder would have been weaker."

Brick by brick, the wall came down. When it was finally big enough for them to get through, Nick lifted the lamp to see inside. "There're some stairs going down."

He entered first. "Is there a doctor coming?"

"She's on her way," Thomas said.

At the bottom of the stone steps stretched another passage. They walked along, the lamp barely penetrating the darkness.

Chills broke out over Nick's skin.

"This is it," Avira said.

"You say that every time I get the creeps."

She turned to him, surprised. "Really?"

Nick nodded his head.

"You kissed her, didn't you?" Her question held a tinge of accusation.

"How did you know?"

Avira shrugged. "Just a guess."

They started to work on the wall, chipping away fervently. When the first stone was removed, Nick moved in and lifted his lantern. "Fae. Are you in there?" He searched the darkness. "Fae," he bellowed.

Silence.

"She has to be in there," Nick said, wanting to scream at the doubt in his voice.

"Let's keep at it," Thomas said.

Another stone fell with a deep *thud* to the ground. They kept at it as stone after stone dropped to the floor.

"I think it's wide enough," Nick said as he pulled Thomas back.

"I don't think so," Thomas said.

Nick didn't listen. He stepped in with his right foot. It hit the floor with a splash. He attempted to wedge his body through as he searched the darkness. The room seemed empty, and it was flooded with water.

"Avira," he growled as he strained to squeeze through. "Are you sure this is the right place?"

"I'm sure," she answered. "Come on." She pulled him back. "You aren't going to fit. The hole needs to be wider."

Mumbled voices echoed off the walls as he slipped out of the hole.

"Fae," Nick shouted. "Is that you?"

"I don't think that's Fae. It's coming from behind. Rose!" he shouted. "We're down here."

Nick could hear steps as he shoved the crowbar into the wall. The block cracked in two and tumbled down, nearly landing on his foot. He could care less who was coming. He needed to get inside that room. Frustrated at the slow progress, he swung the crowbar. When it hit the wall, it reverberated into his bones. Undeterred, he swung again and again. Chunks of stone broke away with each blow.

"Thomas." Avira's voice sounded concerned. "Stop him before he hurts himself."

"I'm not going near him swinging that thing," Thomas said.

"There goes covering up any evidence we've been here," Avira said.

When Nick was sure he could get through, he dropped the crowbar and rushed in. Voices mingled at his back while he searched every corner of the room. "Fae? Fae!" He slammed his fist against the back wall as he snarled.

She wasn't there.

"Hello?" A ghostly voice had his heart thundering in his chest.

"Fae?" he asked, his voice pleading.

"She's here."

He followed the sound of the voice, confused at where it could be coming from. And then he saw it. One of the stones was missing from the far wall.

Heavy footsteps came from behind. "I can't believe you found her in here." Nick turned to see Mason and a tall woman with long, red hair step alongside Thomas and Avira.

"What are you doing here?" Nick asked, scowling.

"I came to help. That is, unless you decide to strangle me again."

Nick narrowed his eyes. "If you're here to help, then do it. Just don't expect me to trust you. And if you so much as touch Fae, I'll do more than strangle you."

He turned back to the opening. Avira touched the stone, and her fingers came away covered in red. "Blood," she said simply. "She must have scraped herself getting through that hole." She moved to taste it when Thomas snatched her hand back.

"I wouldn't do that," he said.

"Fae," Nick said loudly. "I need you to move away from the wall."

They waited several moments for her to answer. When she didn't, Nick shouted, "Fae, do you hear me? Can you get away from the wall?"

Still, she didn't answer.

"We'll have to remove the stones carefully," Avira said.

The job of removing the stones went much faster with the old crumbling mortar, but it still felt like an eternity to Nick. Finally, the way was clear.

He entered the room and nearly stepped on her. His heart stopped when he looked down. She lay on her back, her lifeless eyes open and her deathly-white face haloed in a pool of red blood.

"Fae," Nick breathed as he dropped to his knees.

"Let me through," Rose said. "I'm a doctor."

She came up beside him and knelt. Reaching forward, she pressed her fingers to Fae's throat, looking for a pulse.

"It's faint, but it's there." She looked up to Thomas. "Call 911. We need an ambulance; she won't last much longer."

Chapter 20

A white leather ball came barreling toward Lafayette. He clasped his hands together and got in position. It slapped against his skin and flew up. The blond woman on his right got it next and set it perfectly. He didn't waste any time as he rushed forward, jumped, and spiked the ball over the volleyball net between the other two players. The ball hit the sand hard as the blonde in the pink bikini cheered.

"Game point," she shouted and then jumped into his arms. Her face beaming when she looked at him. "We make a great team."

He beamed back at her. "Yes, we do."

The couple on the other side of the net frowned. The young man lifted his head and shouted, "Good game."

"For us," Lafayette shouted back with a sneer. The woman in his arms chuckled—he couldn't remember if her name was Jenny or Julie.

"Whatever," the man grumbled back.

Lafayette traced his finger over her lips. "My dear, what do you say we go back to my place and celebrate our victory?"

Her smile widened. "Sure."

She turned back and shouted, "Hey Olivia! I won't need a ride back; I'm going with Marcus."

"You sure?" a voice called back.

"Yeah," she answered.

Lafayette looked to see who she spoke to. It was another woman—a bit older than what's-her-name. This woman frowned as she looked at him, almost as if she could guess he wasn't a safe person to be leaving with. Well, he had no intention of harming her friend.

"All right, but call me if you need a ride," Olivia said.

"Sounds like a good friend," he mentioned casually.

"She's my big sister. Ever since our mom died, she's been a bit overprotective. I'm surprised she's not having me call her when I get to your apartment."

"I own a house," he said.

"Even better." She smiled.

Lafayette narrowed his eyes as he looked back at her sister. Oh, yeah, she was suspicious of him. He wondered if she could guess what he planned to do with her baby sister.

Probably.

What a day and age this was! She still let her leave with him.

Hours later, Lafayette stepped over to the table at his new house. Well, it was new to him. It was actually an older clapboard farmhouse with peeling paint and uneven floors. The style was like other homes built around the time he was born. It had a lot of wear and tear on it. Still, it was the only place he could find that fit his needs. The best part—it had an owner with no close family ties to raise suspicions when the man signed the deed over to Lafayette and took an extended vacation—six feet under in the backyard.

Stretching his arms and back, he tried to work out the kinks. This day had been both exhilarating and exhausting.

He opened his laptop to check on Fae. The night vision security cameras were easy enough to install at the fort. He just tapped into the electrical lighting system, drilled a narrow hole through the wall, and mounted them. He took out the red lights so that they wouldn't flash. Fae would go into hibernation faster with less stimulus.

Looking over at Jenny lying sprawled across the bed, he thought perhaps he should have taken Fae up on her offer to come with him. He'd had fun with the blonde with the beach body, but he could only imagine what it would be like with Fae. He'd have to be more gentle than he'd been with this girl. He needed to protect Fae like he protected his own life. She *was* his life.

He clicked open the camera images and his heart stopped.

She was gone!

The chains were broken, dangling from the wall. And the wall he so recently bricked up gaped open.

"No," he snarled as he stood, knocking his chair over. He bellowed a string of profanity as he paced the floor and clawed at his hair. Why had he waited so long to check on her? How did she get out? How did they find her? He knew exactly who had her. He'd caught a glimpse of a familiar face on campus. And Lafayette wasn't equipped to retrieve her from the Order. But—

He stopped pacing as a thought struck him. *The enemy of my enemy is my friend.* Perhaps he did know who could help.

He gathered his clothes that were strewn across the floor, put them back on, and snatched his keys from the end table. He was about to walk out the door when he remembered Jenny. He couldn't just leave her there. She'd start stinking up the house soon.

Walking over to the mudroom, he looked at the old deep freeze. Hopefully, it worked. He didn't have time to dig a grave right now. Opening it, he smiled, relieved to find it empty. A stale musty odor wafted over him. He plugged it in and was pleased to hear the whir of the machine. Lifting his hand over the chest, he felt the air turn cold.

It worked!

Minutes later, Jenny was stuffed into the freezer and beginning to chill.

Lafayette wondered briefly why he couldn't seem to stop killing. Brigitte and guards were necessary, maybe even the girl at the dorm, but these last two weren't. Okay, so he'd planned on killing the prostitute from the start, but Jenny? He had no intention of killing her, he simply got carried away. And now her sister was probably frantically searching for her. He may yet have to take care of that loose end.

He shook off his thoughts. All of that didn't matter nearly as much as finding Fontaine Miller. And he had someone infinitely more wicked than himself to meet.

Chapter 21

"She's lost a lot of blood," an unfamiliar female voice said. "We've replaced most of it."

"So, is it hemophilia?" another unfamiliar voice asked.

"No, it's something I've never seen before." The first woman spoke again. "But the transfused blood is doing its job. It's now clotting."

Who are these people? Where's Nick? Fae thought.

A warm, rough hand brushed her hair away from her face as a familiar scent of cologne breezed over her. Nick.

"When is she going to wake up?" Nick asked. Relief washed over her at the sound of his voice.

"Should be any time now," the first woman said.

I'm already awake. Fae tried to open her eyes, but it proved much more difficult than usual.

"Nick," she rasped, her voice barely audible.

"I'm here," he said. "Fae, can you hear me?"

"Yeah," she breathed.

"Fae," he said softly. "You've lost a lot of blood, but you're going to be fine."

Fae tried to nod, but she wasn't sure she succeeded. Darkness pulled at her. "He drank it," she said, her words slurring. "My blood."

"I know."

"It changed him," she said, not sure he even understood her. Why was she so exhausted?

"I know, sweetheart."

Sweetheart? Her heart, though weak, beat a little faster at the endearment. But then her brain finally processed what he said.

How could he know? Even as she asked herself this question, she didn't have the strength to speak as sleep overtook her once more.

The steady beeping of a monitor was the first thing Fae was aware of, but that was soon followed by the extreme discomfort she felt in her chest and hips. Desperate to find a more comfortable position to sleep in, she attempted to turn on her side and groaned as her body screamed in protest.

"Fae?" a familiar voice said.

"Yeah," she whispered and groaned again.

"Oh, you're finally waking up. You've been asleep like forever, and they won't tell me anything!"

Fae peeled her eyes open and attempted to swallow, but her mouth was so dry. Morgan's concerned face came into view.

"I'm not even supposed to be here. I had to wait for Agent Chase to leave before I could sneak in. That took a lot longer than I thought it would and I doubt he would have ever left—except for the fact his sister is here. I think she's dying."

"What?" Fae croaked.

"Yeah. I wasn't supposed to know that either, but you know, when you're hiding, you hear things."

Fae attempted to process this new information, but moving through her thoughts was like trying to sprint through knee-deep mud. And Morgan continued to speak a mile a minute—as usual. Fae only caught about half of what she said—something about school and then something else about Mason.

"How long has Becca been here?" Fae interrupted.

"She was admitted the night of our disaster date. Do you know Mason won't even talk to me now? I don't know what his problem is. It's not like I was responsible for what happened!"

"Morgan," an unfamiliar, disapproving voice spoke. "Visiting hours are over."

Morgan leaned forward and discretely mumbled, "Visiting hours my butt." Then she looked up and smiled innocently. "I was just leaving." She patted Fae's head. "Don't want to wear my best friend out."

Looked like Fae had been promoted from roomie to best friend.

Morgan grabbed her purse. "I'll see you again soon, Fae. Oh, and I've talked with your professors and arranged to get your homework and copies of notes for the classes you are missing."

That was the one and only thing Morgan said that actually made Fae feel better. Fae couldn't afford for her grades to drop. Keeping her scholarship was dependent upon getting and keeping a good GPA. "Thanks," Fae said sincerely. Maybe Morgan really was best friend material.

"Hello, Fae, I'm Gertrude." An old woman smiled as she lumbered through the door. "I'll be your nurse today. How are you feeling?" She reached out and pressed her weathered fingers to Fae's wrist.

"I'm really thirsty."

"You can't drink anything until the doctor okays it. But I think I can get you some ice chips."

"Thank you."

The woman nodded.

"Can you tell me how Becca Chase is? I hear she's in this hospital."

"I'm sorry," Gertrude said as she pushed a button on the monitor and the cuff around Fae's arm began to fill with air, squeezing her. "I can't discuss another patient's condition without her approval."

Fae frowned. Her heart ached thinking that sweet, sassy Becca might be taking her last breaths. But wait! Her blood turned an old man into a healthy young one. Could it help Becca? Maybe turn back the clock to before she was sick and in a wheelchair?

She searched for her cell phone. No, it wouldn't be here. She hadn't seen it since Lafayette. Her heart constricted in her chest as she thought about him. Where was he now? Would he find out she escaped? Would he come after her?

Fae shook off those thoughts. Right now, Becca lay dying somewhere in this hospital. Fae had no room for any other worries.

"Gertrude?"

"Yes, dearie."

"Do you know Nick Chase?"

"The young FBI agent?"

"Yes, that's him. Do you know how to get in touch with him?"

"Of course." She smiled. "He's actually on his way. He wanted to know the minute you woke up."

"Oh, good. Thank you."

"Hello, beautiful." A warm, familiar voice filtered in through the door—Nick.

Fae turned to see him smiling as he walked toward her. Her heart caught in her throat when she noticed the dark circles under his eyes. It looked like he hadn't slept in days.

"I'll be back to finish taking your vitals," Gertrude said as she stepped out the door.

"You look tired," Fae said.

He chuckled, smiling weakly. "You look more tired."

"How's Becca?"

His countenance darkened. "It won't be long."

"Nick." She took his hand in a tight grip. "Give her my blood."

He shook his head even as the words left her lips. "Fae, you almost died. If they hadn't given you transfusions, you would have."

"Just give her some."

"Fae—"

"You haven't seen what I have," she said. "You haven't seen the power my blood has. It can turn an eighty-year-old man into a twenty-year-old in less than a minute. I know it can help her. Please, we have to try."

Fae was dumbfounded when he shook his head again. "You're wrong, Fae. I have seen it. And do you know what else I've seen?" He looked down and sighed.

"I've seen you on the brink of death. And then I saw you saved by the frantic effort of doctors and a team of nurses. And even then, it's been touch and go the last few days. Your body doesn't seem to want to accept new blood. Your heart stopped twice, and the doctors had to bring you back. You wouldn't stop bleeding and have been given three transfusions."

"Three?"

He nodded. "Eight units. There's probably not much, if *any,* of your own blood left in your system."

"But there may be some."

Nick blinked back a tear. "Maybe. I just...I don't want to get your hopes up, and I really don't want to give Becca false hope. She's at peace right now."

"You have to try. Just don't tell her. Give it to her through her IV."

Nick sighed. Weariness shadowed his features. "I'll talk to the doctor and see what she says."

"How are you going to explain something like this to a doctor?"

"Dr. Rose is no ordinary doctor."

Minutes later, Fae gaped a strange sight. A woman in doctor's gear, her strikingly beautiful face framed by curly red hair and pointed ears. She looked down on Fae with concern.

"Is it rude to ask...?" Fae began, and then she paused.

"What am I?" Dr. Rose supplied with a smile. She turned to Nick. "Thomas's right, she can see right through glamour." She turned back to Fae. "I'm elven."

"I thought elves were smaller."

The woman frowned. "Today's portrayal of elves is not very accurate dear. Except for Tolkien, he came pretty close."

"Do you think I can help Becca?" Fae asked.

"Probably not. Nick's right, you don't have much of your own blood left in your system. And you can't afford to give her much without risking your own life."

"But you're willing to try?" Fae asked hopefully.

Dr. Rose pressed her lips together in a fine line as she nodded. "Now mind you, at the most, this will only turn back the clock for a couple years, and if I'm not mistaken, she started showing signs three years ago. She'll probably still have some problems. And this solution is not permanent. She'll begin to age again immediately after the change."

"So, she'll need my blood over and over again?"

"Yes, but once your blood is fully yours again, it won't take much. And, there's another option."

"What?"

"We wouldn't be able to do it until you are fully healed. But..." She paused. A moment later, she shook her head. "No. I shouldn't have said anything. We arcn't supposed to interfere in humans' lives."

"What?" Fae felt desperate. If there was any way to save Becca, she simply had to do it.

"Oh, now look what I've done," Dr. Rose said. "Your pulse is still weak, but now it's racing."

"Please." Tears built in her eyes as she pleaded.

"Fae," Nick said. "You need to calm down."

"No," Fae said vehemently, even as darkness began to eat away the edge of her vision.

"A bone marrow transplant." Dr. Rose pressed her lips together in a fine line. She sighed and said, "That would make the change permanent."

"So, Becca would be...?" Nick said.

"Immortal," Dr. Rose said. "She'd be just like Fae."

Immortal? I'm immortal? She'd never thought about her own life and what it meant to have the power she had. She would live forever while everyone else aged and died—even Nick. Would she watch him die, too?

"What about Nick?"

Nick turned to her in surprise. "What about me?"

"Can I donate bone marrow to Nick, too?"

"A bone marrow transplant is excruciatingly painful, with a long recovery." Dr. Rose said. "You don't want to do it unnecessarily."

"Unnecessarily? I don't want to live forever if it means watching him die." Fae avoided looking Nick in the eye. Her experience in the dungeon solidified her feelings for him. She wanted nothing more than to spend the rest of her life with him.

"As long as you two are together," Rose said, "you won't have to."

"What's that supposed to mean?" Nick asked.

"It's not only her blood that has the power to restore youth. It's in all her bodily fluids, including her saliva. One kiss can shave months off you. A lifetime of them will make you immortal too."

Nick stared in disbelief. Then his eyes lit up. "So, that's why."

"Why what?" Fae asked, trying her best not to succumb to weariness.

"Everyone keeps asking me if I got a haircut, hired a personal trainer, or got my teeth whitened. I guess I look different, but no one can figure out exactly why." He shook his head. "I wondered myself what had happened to my gray hairs."

Dr. Rose sighed and raised an eyebrow. "What I don't understand is why you seem immune to the lust."

"Oh, I don't know about that. I've felt plenty of lust." Nick gave Fae a quick glance and then turned back to the doctor and cleared his throat.

"That's not the kind of lust I'm talking about." Dr. Rose smiled.

Fae was surprised she wasn't blushing. This conversation totally embarrassed her. She probably didn't have enough blood in her to properly blush.

Right. Blood.

Becca needed hers to survive.

Fae locked eyes with Dr. Rose. "You'll do it, right? You'll do it all for Becca? Including the transplant?"

Dr. Rose frowned as her brows pressed together. Finally, she nodded. "As soon as you're strong enough. But I have to warn you, giving Becca your blood now probably won't work—not with it so diluted. And she's not going to last much longer."

Fae nodded. "But it's worth a chance."

"Yes," Dr. Rose said. "It is."

Chapter 22

Standing over Becca's bed, Nick's heart pounded in his chest. This was the moment of truth. Becca slept fitfully as Dr. Rose injected her IV with Fae's blood. Despite the ventilator, Becca's oxygen levels didn't look good.

"I've got the blood infused with a mixture that should eliminate the blood lust."

"I didn't even think about that," Nick said, surprised at his own oversight.

"It's okay," Rose said. "I did. And we're lucky she has the same blood type as Fae, or Becca would have to ingest it."

Nick cringed at the thought. He watched as the red liquid swirled, filling the tube leading to the vein in Becca's arm.

Dr. Rose kept her eyes glued to the monitor as the blood disappeared, entering his sister's body. What was she looking for? An increase in the blood oxygen level? Heart rate?

Minutes ticked by, and nothing changed. A frown settled on the doctor's face along with a heavy dose of disappointment. She stepped out of the room. Nick followed.

"It's not enough," she whispered in the hallway.

Nick's heart sank. "Did you see any change?"

She shook her head. "She won't last long enough for Fae to recover. It'll be two months before the blood in Fae's body is replaced by her own."

Nick swallowed. "Becca doesn't have two months."

Dr. Rose looked up and met his eyes. "Becca doesn't even have a day."

Nick pressed his eyes closed against the burning tears that threatened to fall. Blinking them back, he took a deep breath.

He knew this day had been coming. Becca was at peace. He needed to find the strength to be strong for her. He didn't want her leaving this world worrying about him. She needed to think he would be fine without her.

He was definitely not going to be fine. But for her, he would give a good show.

"The longer we wait," Dr. Rose said, "the longer she suffers. She's already in a tremendous amount of pain. The sooner you let her go, the sooner she can be free of her suffering."

Nick nodded. "I need to talk to her first."

"Of course," Dr. Rose said, and Nick stepped back into the room.

Pulling a chair to Becca's bedside, he sat down. Weariness and misery engulfed him. Leaning forward, he lay down beside her and stroked her hair, like he'd done countless times before. When she was five, this was how he'd kept the monsters hiding under her bed away. In her young mind, his presence alone was enough to scare them off.

He couldn't keep the monsters away anymore.

Becca's eyes blinked open.

"Hey, squirt," he said softly.

A weak smile pulled at the corners of her mouth.

He looked down at his baby sister, and tears burned his eyes. One spilled down over his cheek.

Becca squeezed her eyes shut and then opened them, only to shut them again. When her eyes opened again, she looked agitated. She blinked twice once more, ending with an intense look on her face.

"What?" Nick said, his voice strained. "You don't want me to cry?"

She blinked once. *Yes.*

"You know what time it is, right?"

Yes.

"Sorry, baby sister," Nick said, another tear breaking free and trailing down his cheek. "You're dying. Your big brother is going to cry."

Tears welled up in Becca's eyes, spilling as she blinked again, twice. *No.*

"I love you," Nick said. "You know that, right?"

Yes. She closed her eyes, her face contorting as she began to shake.

"Are you in pain?"

Yes.

"Nick?" a small voice said from the doorway.
"Becca?"

He looked over and saw Fae standing, leaning heavily on crutches with Dr. Rose at her side.

"I thought you shouldn't be alone for this," Dr. Rose said.

Nick scowled at Fae's apparent struggle to stay upright. He rushed over to grab a chair for her. "You shouldn't be out of bed."

"Actually," Dr. Rose said as she helped Fae into the chair, "it's good for her to move around a bit."

Nick turned back to Becca. Her face, though still pained, had a look of peace. She seemed relieved.

He stepped closer to Dr. Rose and whispered, "What do I do?"

"It's simple," she said, somberly. "When you're ready, pull the plug to the ventilator."

"Will it hurt her?"

"It's not going to be pleasant. I offered to sedate her when the time came, but Becca was adamant that she be awake before she passes."

Nick nodded as he swallowed.

Turning back to Becca, he approached her. His tears were falling freely when he leaned down and kissed her cold forehead. "I love you, baby sister," he whispered so only she could hear.

Yes.

He choked back a sob and asked, "You ready?"

Yes.

Nick hesitated, taking one last look at Becca—
the girl with so much spunk that for a while he
believed she could beat muscular dystrophy by grit
alone.

But she couldn't.

He stepped over to the wall, grabbed the thick,
black cord planted firmly into the outlet, took a deep
breath, and pulled. The whirring of the machine
slowed, coming to a stop.

Nick turned around, leaned down, and encircled
Becca in his arms. He kissed her cheek and then
pressed his forehead against hers. "I'm here, baby
sister. You don't need to be afraid."

She may have heard him, but fear rose in her
eyes, even as she began to struggle and choke. He held
her tight and closed his eyes, not bearing to see her
suffer.

Strong hands pulled him away. He opened his
eyes to see Dr. Rose leaning over Becca.

"What do you think you're—"

"This isn't normal," Dr. Rose interrupted. "She's
trying to breathe on her own."

Rose peeled the tape from around her mouth.
"Becca, I need you to breathe out hard."

Becca gagged as Rose pulled out the ventilator
tube. And then Becca gasped, breathing in deeply.
"Wasn't..." Becca said, her voice rasping, "I supposed
to die?"

Dr. Rose nodded in disbelief. She turned to Nick. "It has to be Fae's blood." She turned back to Becca, then looked up at the monitor. "I don't believe it. Her blood pressure's normal, her O2 stats look good, she...looks fine. Well, according to the monitor."

"I don't feel fine. My throat is killing me." Becca pressed her hand against her throat.

"It's to be expected," Dr. Rose said.

"Bec," Nick said in disbelief. "Your hand."

Becca looked at her hand, awestruck as she lifted it in front of her face. "What happened to me?" She looked to Dr. Rose, confusion in her eyes. "And what do you mean, 'Fae's blood'?"

Dr. Rose raised an eyebrow at her and then turned to Nick. "I think you should be the one to tell her."

"Tell me what?" Becca asked.

Nick sighed, his heart trembling from relief as he looked her over. *She's still alive.* He couldn't wrap his brain around that fact. How could he explain what happened so that she would understand?

"You know those books you like to read?" he finally asked.

"What are you talking about?" she asked, confusion clouding her features.

Nick raised his eyebrows as he blinked back tears—this time tears of joy.

"You mean the paranormal ones?" she answered. "You said they were stupid."

218

Nick took a deep breath. "I guess they're not as stupid as I thought."

"I'm confused. I thought I was going to hear about why I'm not dead and why I can suddenly move. Instead, you decided to have your own little book group session?"

Nick looked to Rose for help. She shrugged.

"Maybe that wasn't the best way to start," Nick said and sighed. "What I mean to say is that supernatural creatures do exist."

"That's insane."

Nick shook his head.

"So, Fae's a supernatural creature? Did she feed me her blood?" Becca's voice rose. "Is she a vampire?" Becca's eyes were wide as she seemed to embrace the possibility. Concern spilled into her expression. "Am *I* safe to be around?"

"You're not a vampire, Becca."

"What am I?"

"You're human," Dr. Rose said. "Like your brother and like Fae."

"I don't understand," Becca said. "Fae's not...supernatural?"

"I wouldn't say that," Dr. Rose said. "She's been infused with supernatural power."

"What kind of power?" Becca asked.

"Youth," Dr. Rose said.

"She's young?"

"You've heard the legends of the Fountain of Youth, right?" Nick asked.

"Yeah, of course."

"Fae was born in the fountain," Nick continued. "And when that happened, the power of the fountain infused inside her. Her blood holds the power to restore youth."

"Are you saying, I'm younger."

"Right."

"How much younger?"

Dr. Rose stepped forward. "I'm not sure. If Fae's blood had done its job completely, you'd be approximately twenty-two years old. But her blood is currently diluted."

"Maybe I'm not twenty-two, but she's turned back the clock for me. Will I start aging again? Do I still have muscular dystrophy?"

"I'm afraid so," Dr. Rose said.

"Well, that sucks."

"Why?" Nick asked.

"Because, you doofus, I have to go through it all again."

"Not necessarily," Dr. Rose said.

Becca's eyes darted from Dr. Rose to Nick. "What? Are you going to prescribe Fae's blood to me?"

Dr. Rose looked over at Fae. "That's not a bad idea, but we have something else in mind. Fae has offered her bone marrow to you. A bone marrow transplant should make the change permanent."

"So, I'll be permanently young? Does that mean I'll never die?"

"You'll still have the risks of a normal human. If you get hit by a bus..." Rose's voice dropped off as she raised her eyebrows.

"I get it. I can still die, but I won't age. Like ever?"

"Right."

Becca sat in silence for a moment. "This is a lot to take in." She looked at Fae, and concern creased her forehead. "You'd do this for me?"

"Of course," Fae said, rising from her chair. Nick stepped in quickly and took her arm to help steady her and keep her weight off her injured foot.

"I may not be a doctor," Becca said. "But I don't think Fae's up for major surgery. She looks like she can barely stand."

"We would have to wait for her to recover her strength," Dr. Rose said. "We're probably looking at two months for a complete recovery. I'd like all the blood in her system to be her own."

"Okay," Becca said. "I can wait, but I have one more question."

"What is it?" Nick asked.

"Can I freakin' get out of this bed? I haven't walked in years. I'm still having a hard time believing I can do it."

Dr. Rose stepped up to the side of the bed. "I'm not sure you can. Fae's blood isn't at full strength. But I'm not against having you try."

Nick sat Fae back in her chair and took the position on one side of Becca as Dr. Rose took the other side.

Becca struggled to move her legs over the side of the bed. She probably wouldn't be able to walk quite yet. But just being able to move her legs was a big improvement. He just hoped Becca wouldn't be too disappointed.

Nick and Dr. Rose easily lifted Becca. She'd lost a lot of weight with her illness. He carefully lowered her down to give her a chance to try to stand on her own two feet. When her legs began to buckle, he held her up. "Sorry, baby sis."

"No, no," Becca said adamantly. "Let me try something."

She dragged one foot out in front of the other. Nick and Dr. Rose let her take the lead and step forward. Becca dragged the other foot, and once again they followed. Becca might not be walking on her own yet, but she could go through the motions. Nick was thrilled. She hadn't been able to do this in over a year.

He looked over only to see tears in her eyes. His heart sank when he saw her disappointment. "I'm sorry, Becca."

She shook her head and laughed through her tears. "You're such an idiot."

She turned her tear-streaked face toward him. "These are freakin' tears of joy, doofus."

Nick smiled, tears of his own threatening to fall.

Minutes later, they ended up standing in front of Fae. Becca's tears falling freely now. "Thank you," Becca said simply.

Fae nodded, tears in her own eyes. She rose and put her arms around Becca. "You don't need to thank me. I was happy to do it."

Nick swallowed a lump in his throat as he looked at the two most important women in his life. What started out as the worst day of his life turned out to be the best.

Life didn't get better than this.

Chapter 23

Fae knew this job would end up biting her in the butt. Nick wanted to watch her at work. He insisted she still needed a guard. It had been one month, and she was ready for life to get back to normal. Though until they caught Lafayette, life couldn't ever be normal. Still, here she was, back at work—still weak, but functional.

She certainly hoped today wouldn't be the first day of modeling in the buff. From the looks of it, Nick wouldn't be backing down. He confirmed her suspicions with his next words.

"No," he growled at Fae. "You are absolutely not going in there alone."

"I have to," Fae said, determined. "And I've already missed too much work as it is. I'm lucky to still have a job."

"And what, you expect me to grab a burger and fries and leave you unprotected while you work? What kind of job *is* this?"

"It's perfectly respectable. I provide a valuable service."

"I never thought it wasn't respectable. Darn it, Fae, what are you trying to hide?"

Fae looked down, heat rising in her cheeks. "I work for the college's art department...as a model."

Nick didn't say anything. He was smart. He knew exactly what that statement implied. Fae could imagine the condemnation in his eyes and wasn't ready to face it yet. He pulled her to a stop in front of the building, stepped in front of her, and lifted her chin up so that she had to look him in the eye.

Fae felt a jolt of surprise when she saw his expression. He *did* look unhappy, but also relieved.

"Figure drawing, right?" he asked.

Fae nodded.

"I tried to take that class when I was in college. They wouldn't let me. It was an upper-level class for art majors. I'm guessing it's the same here."

Fae nodded again.

"Listen," he said, his voice low. "I do have to admit, I'm not thrilled you've been seen naked by countless men. But I understand."

Fae shook her head

"I don't understand?" he asked.

"No," Fae stammered. "I...haven't posed nude yet."

Nick sighed and raised his eyebrow. "You don't want to do it," he said, stating her feelings.

"I'll have to," Fae said, resigned. "Eventually."

"You don't have to do anything you don't want to, Fae."

"I need the money. I tried to find something else, but I came too late. All the other jobs were taken. I couldn't even find a job flipping burgers."

"I know of a job."

"Oh, please don't tell me *you* want to hire me. I don't need a pity job."

"It's not me. It's the office. It's not much, just custodial, but it pays better than minimum wage. One of the girls just up and quit."

"How many hours? I can't miss school."

"It's after five, only twenty hours a week."

"I'd be working for the FBI?"

"You won't be an agent, but yeah. How much are you making at the school?"

Fae cleared her throat. "Fifty dollars an hour."

Nick swore. "Seriously?"

Fae nodded.

"I'm in the wrong profession."

"You'd pose nude?" Fae asked, trying her best not to imagine him shirtless and...um yeah, she wouldn't even think about the other things he'd expose.

"For fifty bucks an hour? Oh, yeah."

He gestured toward the building. "We're here."

Fae nodded.

"So, what are you wearing today?"

Fae sighed. "I'm not sure. They've been having me wear different kinds of fabrics."

"Are you clothed underneath the fabric?" he asked.

Fae frowned.

"What?" He put his hand over his heart. "I'm just asking."

"Sometimes."

He nodded. "Good to know."

Nick sat down in the back of the class and got a good look at the students. The women slightly outnumbered the men. They obviously weren't freshmen, and many were a bit eccentric—loud clothes, bright hair. Definitely members of the arts community.

The hairs on the back of his neck stood on end. Another college student stepped into the room. Nick casually glanced his way. He was a bit odd—greasy hair, filthy clothes. But there was something else off about him Nick couldn't quite put his finger on. The professor immediately stood and walked over to him.

Fae stepped in, and a hush settled over the room.

Nick's heart skipped a beat. She wore a floor-length, white dress that billowed around her hips. The neckline plunged just below the swell of her breasts.

She looked stunning—like she belonged on the silver screen in the 1930s.

Fae kept her eyes down as her high heels clicked against the wood platform. She stopped in the center and stood with her feet shoulder width apart, hands behind her back, fingers locked together. She looked up—her eyes passing by everyone in the room without pause and coming to rest where the wall meets the ceiling. She relaxed into a natural pose; she seemed to be born for this job.

He had difficulty breathing, much less taking his eyes off her, but he needed to get a look at the other students. He was surprised to see they were already busy at work with pencils flying over their pages. All except the man who had just entered.

And then Nick caught movement from the open door where Fae had come from. Another man watched her, a big man. Nick's eyes narrowed.

Who were these characters?

His phone vibrated in his pocket. He pulled it out and furrowed his brows. It was Don.

We've been ordered to bring you in.

Nick's heart skipped a beat. *Why?*

Division X isn't with the FBI. The documents they provided were...well, they weren't from the director.

Nick swore under his breath. He'd trusted Thomas, Dr. Rose...He'd trusted them all. What was going to happen to Becca? Could Dr. Rose really help her? If she were arrested, she wouldn't be able to.

Another one showed up, this time a woman—tall, sleek, with a coldness in her eyes.

Looks like a team is already here, he texted Don.

Don responded immediately. *What? That's impossible. Young is assembling the team now.*

Nick scowled, doubt and disappointment on his mind. He could have sworn Thomas was an honorable guy. And the people in this room—whoever they were—were not here for anything good. Nick caught the gleam of a pistol under the hoodie of one of the men, confirming his thoughts. Who were these characters? Could they be from Division X? Maybe they were alerted that they'd been made and now were out to silence him and Fae.

Nick looked over at Fae. She seemed completely unaware of the danger. And they were in real trouble. There were two exits from this room, and they were both covered.

Nick sucked in a breath of air when Avira stepped into the room. His first reaction was relief—Division X was here to help.

No. They are not the allies I believed them to be, Nick chided himself.

He narrowed his eyes when Avira closed her eyes and raised her hand. Black billowing smoke issued from her fingertips—no, it *was* her fingers. From her fingers down to her arms, she evaporated into a mist. In seconds, she was nothing more than a ghostly apparition. She flew around the room, brushing over the class members. One by one, they began to fall. Nick had a fleeting question pass over his mind. Why weren't the students trying to avoid her? They didn't even seem to see her.

Despite the obvious pointlessness of the gesture, he reached for his gun.

A voice snapped in his head—Avira's voice. *Don't do it. They'll see you and respond. I'll take care of them.*

She swirled around the room, passing through everyone but him and Fae. Within seconds, they were the only conscious people left in the room. The black smoke gathered and thickened, materializing into the shape of a woman. Avira was back.

Nick stood, not moving. "What did you do?"

"I just had a snack," Avira said. "They'll be fine."

"Sounds like you still haven't figured out what she is yet," Thomas said as he walked through the door.

Nick stepped over to Fae and shoved her behind his back. He pulled out his gun, cocking it and pointing it at Thomas's heart. "That's not the only question I have."

"Nick, what's going on?" Fae asked.

Thomas lifted his hand toward Avira in a gesture for her to stop as he shook his head. He turned back to Nick. "Let me guess. You found out that we're not sanctioned by the FBI?"

Nick heard Fae's intake of breath. He gave a quick nod. "Who are you? What do you want from us?"

"Believe it or not, we really are the good guys, Nick. We're an organization that has been around for much longer than the FBI. Our job is to protect the humans from supernatural creatures, and then sometimes protect supernatural creature from humans, and then always... Protect our secret."

"What secret?" Nick asked.

"Our existence," Avira said.

"And you decided to drag me into your world? Why?"

Thomas shrugged. "I've no idea. We took our lead from Jones. He's the brains of our operation. He's what you might call gifted."

"This is insane."

Thomas shrugged.

"I'm guessing you figured out who these people are," Nick said as he nodded toward the stranger lying on the ground.

"They're the reason we came today. We got a lead indicating they were coming."

"You brought Avira to take care of them. What is she, really?"

"If you put down your gun, I'll tell you," Avira said.

Nick sighed, wondering if he were making a big mistake. But seriously, he'd learned to trust his gut.

And his gut was telling him that they were telling the truth.

He lowered his gun and replaced it in his holster.

"I'm a succubus," she said unabashedly.

"Isn't that a demon that has sex with men and sucks their souls?" Nick asked.

"The only man I'm having sex with is Thomas."

Nick looked around in horror. "You sucked the souls out of these innocent students?"

"Of course not!" Avira truly sounded offended. "I merely nipped at them. No permanent harm done. I haven't eaten a soul in years."

Thomas cleared his throat.

"Well, not from a live person. And the ghosts I feed on are vengeful spirits that have lost every ounce of their humanity. I'm doing them a favor."

"But you are a demon," Nick said.

"That's a term you humans made up for beings you didn't understand," Avira said.

"You didn't hurt Dolores or Captain Abela, did you?" Fae asked as she stepped forward.

"No, sweetie. They still had their humanity intact."

Fae nodded.

"Are you talking about the people from the ghost tour?" Nick asked Fae. "You saw their ghosts?"

"Listen," Avira said, interrupting. "I'd love to keep chatting, but I think it's time we were leaving.

These people are about to wake up, and you really don't want to know what *they* can do."

Chapter 24

Fae lay in the back seat of the car wriggling into her jeans as Nick kept his eyes glued to the road. They followed Thomas and Avira going north on I95 toward Jacksonville. Nick had a tight grip on his steering wheel and a permanent scowl on his face.

Fae finished changing into her street clothes and climbed over the seat. She'd have to return the evening gown to the school when they got back. She had no idea how to explain what happened to the art professor. But right now, they had bigger worries on their plate.

"You forgot your zipper," he glanced down.

"I thought you weren't watching me change." She zipped her jeans and belted herself in.

He shrugged. "It's nothing I haven't seen before."

"You've never seen *me*."

"Yes, and it's a crying shame." He smiled as he shot her a look.

Fae shook her head at him as she held back a smile. Turning back to the road ahead, her smile faded. "Is this going to ruin your job with the FBI?"

Nick sighed deeply as he glanced at her. "From the sounds of it, my job is already screwed."

Fae's heart sank. Not only did she feel terrible for Nick, but she'd been hoping to have her own career with the bureau. She wanted to ask him about her chances now, but she figured it was not a good time to bring it up.

They got off the exit to Jacksonville. Fae looked up to the skyscrapers towering overhead and said, "Do you think Division X works out of one of these buildings?"

Nick's brows were furrowed when he shrugged. "I've no idea."

Fae's heart lightened at the hope in his voice. She wondered if he was thinking what she was thinking: that perhaps Division X was more than just some one-room operation.

That hope extinguished when they took a turn down a back alley littered with trash.

"You gotta be kidding me," Nick mumbled.

"Maybe it's not as bad as it seems," Fae said. "I mean, Avira's car is a Lexus. She can't be making minimum wage."

"That may not be her car," Nick said.

"You think she might have stolen it?" Fae frowned.

"I seriously have no idea."

Fae sucked in a breath when she saw three men leaning against a building. Their eyes seemed to glow as they passed by. No, that had to be a reflection. It *was* dusk. The glow must be caused by the shining headlights.

Nick and Fae continued to follow Avira and Thomas as they turned into a parking lot surrounded by crumbling brick buildings. When Avira parked, Fae's heart sank. She really hoped they were just passing through this dilapidated place.

Nick pulled Fae back before she could open the car door and said, "Stay close to me. And if worse comes to worse, I'll call in the FBI." Nick huffed. "The *real* FBI."

As they followed Thomas and Avira across the lot, Fae tried not to look directly at Avira. She appeared mostly human—except for the glowing skin and swirling eyes. Fae wasn't surprised to realize she was the only one who could see the inhuman side of her, but she wished others could see it too. At least then she'd know she wasn't crazy.

Thomas turned back. "Neither of you have any heart problems, do you?"

Fae shook her head as Nick asked, "Why?"

"You're in for a shock," Thomas said.

They approached a steel door. It creaked as Thomas pushed it open. A cool gust of wind laced with a sweet woodsy scent and a hint of thyme hit Fae. *At least the place doesn't stink.*

She had a hard time seeing past Thomas, but from what she could see, it looked like some kind of garden atrium. Her suspicions were confirmed when she took her first moss-cushioned step inside.

Looking around, she gasped.

Towering trees and foliage so thick you couldn't see the sky surrounded her. It looked like a forest—with trees larger than any found in the Appalachian National Forest. Through the darkness and the foliage, Fae could see several quaint cottages lit by lanterns and fireflies. This looked like something out of a fairytale book.

Fae looked back just as Avira closed the door. The brick wall surrounding it was gone. All that was left was a lone, rusty door standing in the forest. A small, bubbling brook flowed behind it where the parking lot should be.

"Where are we?" Nick's voice shook. He sounded just as stunned as she felt.

"Between," Thomas said.

"What does that mean?" Nick asked.

"We're between the world of man and the faery realm." He strode purposely forward. "Come on. We're expected."

"By whom?"

"Jones. Or here we call him Conall."

"What kind of name is Conall?"

"Elven."

Nick shook his head. "Someone needs to wake me up."

"That's what I thought when I first came here," Avira said. Fae could hear the amusement in her voice.

About a hundred paces into the forest, they came to a large wood cabin. It looked like something out of colonial times. Thomas raised his hand and knocked on the door. A woman with long, curly hair and a floor-length blue dress opened the door. She radiated youth and beauty.

"Hello, Kaare." She smiled. "Avira. Come on in. He's been waiting for you."

Nick held Fae's hand in a tight grip, and he kept her at his back when they entered.

"Hello," the woman said. "I don't believe we've been introduced. My name is Hope."

Nick paused before he answered. "I'm Nick."

"And I'm Fae," Fae said with a tentative smile. This woman *seemed* friendly.

They stepped into an open living area. The floors were made from dark wood planks, the furniture looked antique, and a roaring fire burned in a vast fireplace with a cast-iron cauldron over the flames. The lid clanked as steam escaped. It smelled amazing, like... pot roast? Her stomach grumbled in response to the tantalizing smell.

A tall, muscular man in a green tunic and brown boots stepped into the room. His eyes were just as light blue as Fae's, but the most striking thing about him were his ears. They were pointed. He looked like he belonged in a *Lord of the Rings* movie.

"Well, well." He looked straight at Nick. "Good to see you again, Agent Chase." He turned to Fae, and his eyes lit up. "Ah, so you're Fae."

Fae nodded, unnerved.

"I've heard a lot about you. I can't say I've ever met a human quite like you. It's an honor." He reached out his hand.

Fae took it, and, instead of shaking, he kissed her hand. His lips on her skin sent a jolt through her. Even after he no longer touched her, she felt a lingering...something. Power?

He turned to Hope. "Dear, why don't you make our guests some tea?"

She smiled sweetly. "I'd be happy to."

"How is this place possible?" Nick asked.

Conall gestured to the couch. "Have a seat and I'll see if I can explain."

When they were seated, Conall continued to stand as he spoke. "The world you know is only a small part of what is actually out there. At any given place, there are numerous layers of existence. You have the human world, and closest to that is the world of spirits—the place where your life force goes when you die. And then there's the realm of the Faeries—a place few humans have ever been to. Between the Faery realm and earth is what we call 'the between.' That is where Hope and I choose to live. Given the fact

I am Elven and she is human, it seemed the best option."

"Where does Division X factor into all this?" Nick asked.

"Division X?" Conall said.

Thomas chuckled. "It's what he calls the Order."

Conall raised his eyebrows and shrugged. "Division X, as you call it, is an order that has been around for a millennium. Our job is like yours—to protect and serve. We protect the innocent and generally do good."

"Do good?" Nick frowned. "I wouldn't say what you've done to me is good. I'm being hunted by my own team. My career is over. My life is screwed."

"Your sister is alive." Conall raised an eyebrow.

"Thanks to Fae," Nick added.

"And Rose will make the change permanent," Thomas said. "I'd say that's a fair trade."

Fae wasn't surprised when Nick didn't argue. How could he? Conall spoke the truth.

"I know you're not happy with us right now, but believe me, your career couldn't have taken a better turn. I'd like to offer you a job." He turned to Fae. "Fae too, though she would need training."

"You want Fae to drop out of school?" Nick sounded less than happy.

"No. I'd like her to transfer. She can finish out the semester and then make the transfer next term. We have a little-known program taught at Harvard."

240

"What kind of program are you talking about? I went to Harvard, and I never heard of—"

"You're human," Thomas interrupted. "Of course you didn't hear of it."

Fae spoke up. "I wouldn't have a chance of getting in anyway. I have no high school transcript, no real schooling before working on my GED."

"Getting in won't be a problem," Conall said.

Fae's heart leaped at the chance to go to such a prestigious university. Could this be real? "Do you think I could make it at a school like that?"

"Absolutely," Nick said. "Fae, you're brilliant."

"Which is why we want her. That, and the fact that she'll be around a long, long time. You can't beat the centuries of experience she'll have one day."

"And why do you want me?" Nick challenged. "I'm only a human, after all."

"Mostly human," Conall said.

"What do you mean, mostly human?" Nick asked, his eyes wide.

"From the level of energy I feel coming from you, I'd say you're a quarter faery. Why do you think I let you join the team in the first place?"

"Are you saying I have a grandparent that was a faery?"

"Is," Avira said. "They're immortal."

"It also explains your attraction to Fae," Conall said. "She's simply brimming with faery energy."

Fae's heart sank. Was that why he found her attractive? Could it be possible he wasn't truly attracted to her, but to the energy she emanated?

"Excuse my husband," Hope said as she handed Fae a hot cup of tea. "My husband didn't mean to offend you. For someone so smart, he can be pretty dense sometimes." This woman was very perceptive.

"I'm sorry, Fae," Conall said. "What I meant was that like attracts like in the Faery realm."

"And where does that leave me?" Hope frowned at her husband. "I'm a hundred percent human."

"I should just stop talking now." Conall looked exasperated.

Hope stepped forward and pulled Conall down for a quick kiss. "Yes, you should." She snickered.

"One thing I can't figure out, though," Nick said. "How did you fool my entire team? You show us one document, and we're ready to turn over the biggest crime scene in the state."

"A little glamour goes a long way," Conall said. "With training, you could use glamour yourself."

"So, that wasn't a real document?" Nick asked. Just a blank sheet of paper."

Nick shook his head in disbelief.

"What do we do now?" Nick asked.

"We need to take out Lafayette," Thomas said, "and until Fae learns to use her abilities, we need to give her better protection. Members of Disorder are now involved. They are much more dangerous than Lafayette."

"What kind of abilities are you talking about?" Fae asked.

"Your power to grant youth is yours to control," Conall said. "And given the level of energy I feel from you, it's likely there are other undiscovered abilities you have. You just need to learn to tap into them. I can help you with that."

Fae was both elated and regretful about her undiscovered abilities. She'd wanted a normal life, but given this new information, she probably would never have one.

"Who is this Disorder group we're up against?" Nick asked.

Conall turned to him. "They are supernatural creatures. Some were once members of the Order but have left or been excommunicated. They live to create disorder for the Order."

"What kind of protection are you talking about giving Fae?" Nick asked.

"She will need guards, and we need to strengthen the link you have with her."

"Link?" Fae asked, intrigued.

Conall turned to Fae. "You inadvertently forged a link with Nick when you kissed him."

"I wonder if that's what happened with Mike Pendleton?" Fae asked Nick.

"Sort of," Thomas said, surprising her by knowing what she was talking about. "He was all human, so the link was too much for him to handle."

"What kind of link is it?" Nick asked.

Avira spoke up, her eyes on Nick. "You remember the feeling you got when we neared the place Fae was being held?"

Nick nodded somberly.

"You felt her because of the link you have with her," Avira continued.

"So how do we strengthen the link?" Nick asked.

"You need to drink her blood," Avira said.

Fae's heart pounded in her chest. "No. Not a chance. I saw what that did to Lafayette. He was like a bloodthirsty vampire."

"Your blood won't have the same effect on Nick as it did Lafayette," Conall said. "Lafayette is human."

"What will drinking it do to me...to us?" Nick asked.

"It *will* make you younger, but more importantly, you'll be able to sense her," Conall said. "With the link, you'll be able to find her anywhere. Lafayette won't be able to hide her from you."

"There *is* another way," Avira said.

"I don't think their relationship has gotten that far, dear," Thomas said in a low voice.

"What are you talking about?" Fae asked.

"Sex," Avira said bluntly. "That would seal the bond better than blood drinking."

Fae's eyes widened as her chest constricted.

"Drinking her blood would be good enough, right?" Nick asked, eyeing her.

Fae's heart sank. It sounded like he didn't want her. Was she that unappealing? He'd rather drink blood than make love to her?

He'd said he was attracted to her, though. Why the change of heart? Perhaps now that he'd gotten to know her better, he was less than impressed. Or perhaps he'd realized that the only reason he'd been attracted to her in the first place was the faery energy.

"Yes," Conall said. "It should be enough."

Fae pressed her lips together as she frowned. "How much blood does he need?"

"Since her blood is still somewhat diluted, I'd say a pint," Conall said.

"You think I can choke down a whole pint?" Nick asked.

"That won't be a problem," Conall said.

Nick frowned at him. "Okay, let's just say I can. How are we supposed to get just a pint? Fae's blood doesn't clot. If we cut her too deep, she could bleed to death."

"We'll have to do things the old-fashioned way. Hope will stitch the wound shut."

"Does she have experience with stitches?" Nick asked.

"You'd be surprised," Conall said, tugging at the high collar around his neck.

Chapter 25

Nick stood with his hand hovering over Fae's wrist, a razor blade in his fingers. *What am I doing? Am I really going to cut Fae's wrist and drink her blood?* His stomach sickened at the thought.

"Why don't you let me do it?" Thomas asked.

Nick pulled the blade back. "If anybody is going to do it, it'll be me."

"Nick," Fae said. "It's okay. Just get it over with. I swear the anticipation is worse than the act."

He nodded and moved in again—the blade once again hovering over her wrist. He stood, his mind screaming at him not to do it. Harming Fae seemed to go against every fiber of his being.

"It looks like the link is stronger than we thought," Conall said.

"But not strong enough," Avira said.

"Nick," Fae's voice beckoned to him. "It's okay. You don't have to do it." She took hold of his wrist and carefully pulled the razor blade from his fingers. Before he could guess her intent, she slashed her own wrist. Blood spurted across his shirt.

"Oh, shoot," she exclaimed. His heart took a flying leap against his chest. "That was deeper than I wanted to cut."

"Fae," Nick growled, and then he cursed. "We have to stop the bleeding." He clamped his hand over her wrist.

Avira had a mug just below his grasping fingers and said, "I need you to let go for a moment."

"Forget it," Nick snapped. "She's going to bleed to death."

"She's not going to bleed to death. She barely nicked the artery," Avira said as she caught the stream of blood pouring from between his fingers.

"Hope," Nick shouted. "We need you to stitch it up."

"As soon as the cup is full," Hope said calmly, a needle and thread in her hand.

Nick bellowed a curse in frustration.

"I would ask you not to use profanity in front of my wife," Conall said.

"It's okay, dear," Hope said. "I can see how upset he is."

"I almost have enough," Avira said.

Hope stepped forward. "Just tell me when."

Avira nodded. Half a minute later, Avira said, "Okay, that's enough." She pulled the cup away, and Hope moved in.

"Mr. Chase," Hope said. "I need you to move your hand."

Nick hesitated, afraid to let go.

"I work fast," Hope said. "You needn't worry so."

"Nick." Conall took him by the shoulders. "She really is great with a needle. Come on. Just step back."

Nick took a hesitant step away and held his breath as he let go.

The bleeding had slowed to an ooze. "Fae's a remarkable healer," Hope said, her eyes wide. "I don't think we'll need to stitch it after all." She turned to Nick. "Just put pressure on it, and we'll check it again in a few minutes.

"Too bad," Thomas said to Conall. "I'd like to have seen your wife in action. I've heard she's quite impressive."

Conall nodded in appreciation. "That she is. After two hundred and thirty years, she still amazes me."

Hope smiled back, her countenance bright. "Why, thank you, husband." She turned to Nick. "Although the bleeding was kept to a minimum, Fae did lose over a pint of blood. I think it best we provide some nourishment and she stays to rest until she recovers her strength."

"I'm not leaving her," Nick said.

"Of course not," Hope said.

Avira stepped forward, the cup of blood in her hand. "Fae risked a lot to get you this."

Nick looked down. His stomach took a turn at the sight of the thick, dark liquid. "I can't guarantee it won't come back up."

"It won't," Avira said. "Just drink it, and then we can concentrate on getting Fae cared for."

Nick looked at Fae. Her face paled even as her eyes reassured him.

He closed his eyes and pressed the cup to his lips as he tipped it back. The warm fluid filled his mouth. He'd thought he would be gagging at this point, but the taste filled him with inexplicable joy. She was near him. He could sense her...feel her. Fae's presence was like...it was hard to organize his thoughts and feelings into something he could explain. It was like coming home to the smells of Christmas dinner after being away at college a full semester.

To him, Fae was home.

"How do you feel?" Avira asked. "Any different?"

He nodded, locking eyes with Fae. She looked down, her pale face tinged with red. She was so beautiful when she blushed.

Concern filtered in when he could feel her exhaustion. She still hadn't fully recovered from the horror Lafayette inflicted on her. And then they drained another pint of blood?

What were they thinking?

"So," Avira continued, "do you think you can find her anywhere?"

"Yes," Nick answered. Before Avira could ask any of the other questions that were brimming in her curious eyes, he turned to Hope and said, "You mentioned Fae could rest."

"Yes," Hope said, "but I think she should eat something first." She turned to the others. "You are all welcome to stay for dinner." Her eyes landed on her husband's. "Conall, why don't you get the place settings?"

Minutes later they sat down to pot roast, sourdough bread, and a leafy-green salad. Nick watched Fae closely. Hope poured her a glass of fresh apple juice. Fae took a long drink and began to nibble at the food. Nick ate but didn't even taste it; his thoughts were completely on Fae.

Her eyes met his for a moment, and then she cast them down. Nervousness radiated from her. She was worried about what he felt about her now that he'd drunk her blood.

He might be able to find me, but how does he feel about me? He acted like sleeping with me was the last thing he wanted to do.

Nick nearly choked on a potato when her thoughts came through, crystal clear. He looked up at her. The sound of him choking stunned her, and her thoughts were no longer coherent.

Nick swallowed down the vegetable. After clearing his throat and taking a drink, he said, "Conall, can I please have a word with you? In private?"

Conall raised his eyes. "Of course." He looked at the others. "Please excuse us."

Conall led him to a study filled with books.

As soon as Conall closed the door, Nick blurted, "I can hear her thoughts."

"Really?" Conall asked.

"No, I'm lying."

Conall frowned at him.

"Of course, really!"

"It's normal to feel impressions of what she's feeling."

"It's not just impressions. I can hear *exactly* what she's thinking."

"That *is* unusual." Conall raised an eyebrow.

"I'm going to have to tell her," Nick said. "Do you know what that's going to do to us? How it's going to wreck our relationship?"

"I'd wager that being able to read her mind would help in your attempts to win her affections. You'll know exactly what she likes and what annoys her."

And when she completely misread him. She thought he didn't want to sleep with her? Nothing had ever been less true!

"She won't appreciate the benefits."

"Do you really need to tell her?"

Nick huffed and shook his head in disbelief. "And what happens when she finds out I kept this from her? She's smart. She'll figure it out." Nick took a step toward Conall. "Did you know that this would happen?"

"Not exactly."

"What is that supposed to mean?" Nick growled.

"Each connection is different—the stronger the bond, the more the two are fated to be together."

"I don't believe in fate."

"But you do care for Fae."

"Which is why I'm concerned."

"You don't need to be. You two are meant to be together."

Nick frowned. "Like I said—"

"You don't believe in fate," Conall interjected. "Not believing in something has no bearing on whether or not it's true. An hour ago, you didn't believe in elves, yet, here I am."

All this talk of fate made him think about Conall's own fate. How did he end up with a human wife? "Can you hear Hope's thoughts?"

Conall raised his eyebrows. "I wish! That woman's mind is a mystery to me. But I do trust her. And I love her more than my life. I'd lose my head for that woman."

"You've been together for over two hundred and thirty years?"

Conall nodded.

"That's a long life for a human."

"I'm not without power, Nick Chase, and as long as my heart continues to beat, so shall Hope's."

"So why do you choose to live here?"

"We live here because neither of us has to hide. In the human world, I must cloak myself from the world and take on a human appearance. And in the world of Faeries, Hope would be at risk. Other faery-kind see humans as a subspecies worthy only of passing entertainment. It isn't unheard of for either an elf or faery to seduce a human and then shrug them off or even kill him or her once they tire of them."

"So, I'm the product of a faerie's romp with a human subspecies?" Nick's brows pressed together.

Conall shrugged. "Most likely."

"How did you and Hope end up falling in love?"

"It's a long story, but I learned what it felt like to be a subspecies among the humans. Hope was the one person who treated me with dignity, and in the end, she saved my life."

Nick suddenly felt embarrassed. He was confused for a moment before realizing it was Fae's emotions he felt.

"I need to get back to Fae," he said simply.

Conall nodded, and they both returned to the table.

"It's about time you two returned," Hope said. "Nick, you need to put Fae to bed, she nearly took a plunge in her stew when she started drifting off."

Thomas chuckled. "I'm afraid I was boring her with tales of my early days in the Order."

Fae rubbed the sleepiness from her eyes. "No, it was fascinating. Really. I'm just tired." *Dead tired.* Her thoughts came through. *Wait a minute. Nick's supposed to put me to bed?* Her heart took off in a sprint, and her emotions bordered on panic. *What if he wants to kiss me goodnight? What if—*

Nick experienced relief when he blocked her thoughts mid-sentence. He'd heard enough for him to think about. Her thoughts sounded like those of a woman complete innocent. A virgin. He glanced over to her. She looked away immediately, and another tinge of red stained her cheeks.

She *was* a virgin. No wonder he felt the need to move slowly with her. A surge of possessiveness rose in him. He would be both her first and last. He thought briefly of the idiot, Mike Pendleton. If he ever came near Fae again, he'd rip his throat out! And then the others—ninety percent of the male student body. They all had lust in their eyes when they looked at Fae—from her stunning eyes to her lush body. It would be even worse if she ever posed nude in that blasted art class. Nick had the insane urge to pound his fist into someone's face until they were—

At the image that surfaced in his mind, Nick was shocked out of his thoughts.

What was he thinking? He was prepared to go into a homicidal rage over just the thought. He needed to get control of himself. And he needed to get more information out of Conall—find out how to control his emotions. He'd never had a problem with jealously before. But Fae? Just the thought of her with someone else had him ready to murder someone.

Yeah, Nick could seriously injure a hormonal college student if he didn't get control of himself.

Fae leaned into his side. He could feel her tremble. His previous thoughts flew from his mind. He had no room in his head for anything other than caring for Fae in her weakened condition.

She gasped as he swept her up in his arms. She put her arms around his neck and said, "You know I can walk."

"And I can carry you." He smirked. "Looks like we both have things to be proud of."

"Smart-aleck." She grinned and lay her head on his shoulder.

Nick looked to Hope, who held back a smile.

"Where to?" he asked.

"As you walk out the door," Hope said, "it'll be the first cabin on your right. It's made exclusively for guests, so feel free to make yourself at home."

Chapter 26

Fae's heart raced as Nick carried her across the threshold of the door into the cabin. This place looked strangely like the cabin from her imagination—the daydream was crystal clear in her mind. Perhaps, this time she'd get to kiss Nick. Did he even *want* to kiss her?

She looked him in the eyes. They twinkled as he murmured, "You're so beautiful. You have no idea how much I want to kiss you right now. But I'm afraid I couldn't stop at just one kiss."

She smiled. She'd obviously misread him before. But, he was probably right. Kissing would be a bad idea. At least, it wouldn't fit with her plans for waiting for marriage.

Nick coughed and then cleared his throat. "You mind turning on the light?" Nick asked, still sounding a bit hoarse. "I seem to have my hands full."

"You can put me down, you know," Fae said, slightly breathless.

He raised his eyebrow. "That's a less desirable option."

Fae chuckled. "I have to be getting heavy."

"Not at all."

She found the switch on the wall and flipped it.

Warm light spread over a quaint living area with a kitchen off to the side. Bulging logs lined the walls of the room, lit with the glow of lamps. In front of them sat a plush, brown leather couch with matching love seat. Between those stood a square, glass coffee table. The pane rested atop a stout, gnarled trunk that broke into three branches reaching up to kiss the glass. A cobblestone fireplace was the icing on the cake in this cabin. A stack of wood sat ready beside it. Fae could smell the lingering scent of burnt maple.

"Wow," Fae breathed. "This place is great."

Nick nodded appreciatively as he blew out a quick breath and looked around. His eyes lingered on the opening to a hallway. "Let's get you ready for bed."

He finally let her down to rest on her own two feet and led her into the hall. He flipped on more lights as he went. There were two bedrooms that looked nearly identical on one side of the hall, and on the other side, a bathroom, a linen closet stocked with towels and bedding, and then there was a laundry room toward the end. At the very end of the hall stood a door. It held a rectangular window through which Fae could see slashes of tree trunks in the darkness.

Nick took her arm and lifted it as he looked her over. The slash on her wrist was completely gone, but she still had smears of blood down the entire length of her arm and crimson splatters across her shirt and jeans. It looked like she'd survived a murder attempt.

She looked over at him, and he looked worse than she did.

"We should probably clean up," she said.

"Yeah," he said, his voice tight. He dropped her arm and stepped away. "Why don't you go on in the bathroom and strip down? I'll get our clothes in the wash while you shower. Hopefully, this place has enough water pressure to handle it."

Fae nodded, trying not to think about them both naked in the same house. She stepped inside, carefully locked the door, and peeled off her clothes. Looking at her pink, lacy underwear, she considered a moment holding on to those. Did she really want him to see them? She truly *did* need them washed, though. She couldn't stand the thought of showering and then putting on used underwear. Besides, she'd be a fool if she thought Nick had never seen a women's bra and panties before. She settled on rolling them inside her shirt and jeans.

She stood, working up the nerve to hand them to Nick.

Fae jumped at a light rap on the door. "You ready to hand over your clothes?" Nick's voice filtered in. She had a sudden image of Nick standing completely in the buff outside the door.

Fae swallowed. "You're still dressed, aren't you?"

"Don't ask questions you don't want answered, Fae."

Oh, good grief!

She pressed herself behind the door as she unlocked it and squeezed her bundle through the crack. He took it and said, "Thanks." She could swear she could feel him smiling, amused by her behavior.

Moments later, she was covered in lather and standing in a hot shower. The water pressure seemed fine and the water heater worked perfectly. Fifteen minutes later, she turned off the tap and toweled off.

Smacking her lips, she wished she could brush her teeth. Perhaps...

She looked in the drawers under the sink and smiled in relief. It was stocked with everything she'd need—brand new toothbrushes, toothpaste tubes, hairbrushes, and razors—everything still in their store packaging. Breaking out the new items, she commenced ridding herself of the film that covered her teeth.

Looking up at the mirror, she used her hand to clear the fog off the glass. Then she brushed out her hair, parted it, and braided it down the sides. She looked at the end-result and sighed. She didn't have a speck of makeup on her face, but she looked otherwise put together—except for clothes. Those would take a while.

It wouldn't do for him to see her in the nude, she thought as she looked herself over. She'd have to leave the bathroom clad only in a towel.

She could do this.

Maybe.

Oh, good grief. She was a twenty-two-year-old woman! She could absolutely do this.

Wrapping the towel tight around her chest, she stepped into the hallway and gasped. Nick moved toward her fast, his muscled chest at eye level to her. She looked down quickly, relieved to see he had a towel hugging his hips.

"I hope you saved me some cold water," he muttered as he brushed by her.

"Um, yeah. There's plenty of...did you say cold water?"

He didn't slow down to answer her, but entered the bathroom immediately and shut the door behind him. Before she even left the hall, she heard running water.

Stepping into the first room she came to, she eyed the bed with a deep longing. Draping the towel across a chair, she stepped to the dresser. There couldn't possibly be...

She opened the drawer and smiled. Hope thought of everything. Fae ruffled through a few nightgowns and brand new underclothes and found her size. She pulled off the tags, slipped into them, and sighed happily.

She could now go to bed.

Chapter 27

The murmur of a voice roused Fae from her slumber. She opened her eyes to darkness. She could just make out her bedroom door—ajar. Nick must have opened it.

Her heart thumped hard in her chest when she heard again what must have awakened her. It was a voice—not so much heard by her ears, but something she *felt*. Someone called for her.

Should she wake up Nick?

No. There was something familiar about that voice. Something that told her she had nothing to fear.

Fae pulled the covers away and got up. Where was it coming from?

She wandered to the window and pushed it open. The voice was louder, but still, she couldn't quite hear what it was saying.

Fae tip-toed through the cabin and opened the front door. Goosebumps rose on her arms as cool air breezed over her exposed skin. She stepped outside, closed the door carefully, and then turned to look at the forest. It glowed, lit by the unseen moon above the trees.

She turned toward the sound and began to walk down a path, her bare feet padding over the hard, cool flagstones. Perhaps she should have put on her shoes. She dismissed the possibility of returning for them.

She didn't want to chance waking Nick. She had a feeling he wouldn't be enthusiastic about her wanting to take a midnight stroll in the woods.

The path meandered through the giant trees as the sounds of insects chirped around her. It sounded like crickets lived in the "between" too. Fae continued to walk for a long while, and the voice grew louder. It wasn't really speaking; it sounded more like singing.

She was almost there.

The sounds of water drowned out the sounds of the insects. *There must be a river nearby*, Fae thought just as she stepped into a clearing.

Bathed in moonlight stood the most beautiful scene Fae had ever laid eyes on. A fountain sat on top of a hill. Stone steps at her feet led up to the structure. Water flowed over the side of the fountain, as if someone had been filling it and left the water running too long. The water continued its flow down the steps and seeped into the mossy ground at her feet.

Sloshing through the water, Fae made her way up the steps. Even though the air around her felt cold, the water warmed her feet. When she got to the top, she gasped at the breadth of the fountain. It was the size of a swimming pool, brimming with water that spilled over the side.

The singing stopped, and then a voice spoke, filling her with inexplicable joy. *Fontaine. You've returned to me.*

She'd heard this voice before, but couldn't quite place where.

Come join me in the water.

"I'll drown," she said.

There was a warm chuckle. *You won't drown, my child. You are born of my waters.*

"Who are you?" Fae asked, uncertain whether she should be terrified or not.

I am the Lady of the Fountain.

"Is that kind of like the Lady of the Lake? The one in King Arthur's legend?"

You speak of Freya, my sister. My name is Ester.

Fae looked around at the forest of the Between and wondered if this was the place she was born, and not the bayou in Florida. Could her mother be buried around here?

This is not my original home, Ester said, as if she could read Fae's thoughts. *I have been moved twice in my lifetime. My first home is in a place you call Ethiopia. I lived happily there for many centuries. But then I was stolen from my home and brought to the Americas. For many years, I was kept safe by my guardians, but then one betrayed me and wished to exploit my powers. I did not allow him to use me to further his evil designs. But then I was left alone—until a man named Conall found me and brought me here.*

"Why didn't he return you to your home in Africa?"

The elf informed me that my home had been corrupted and I would not be safe there.

"I'm really sorry."

Don't worry over me, child. This place is wholly adequate.

"That's good to hear." Fae paused, the question she'd been dying to ask on the tip of her tongue. Finally, she asked, "Do you remember my mother and father? Do you know where I can find them?"

I'm sorry. Where they are, you cannot go. Your mother's heart ached from the loss of her husband. Her despair so poignant, it awoke me from my slumber. I tried to do what I could to comfort her. I attempted to use my power to lighten her aching heart. But, my influence was greater than I expected. Most humans cannot hear my voice, most are not even touched by it, but your mother not only heard me, she ran to me. And when she approached, my guardians perceived her as a threat and destroyed her. I am truly sorry. I never meant for that to happen. A woman such as her did not deserve to die. The least I could do to make amends would be to save her child.

Fae's heart sank. She truly hoped that Brigitte had been lying and her parents were alive somewhere. Fae could feel the remorse emanating from the fountain and felt the need to comfort Ester.

"You did save me."

Yes, I did.

Holly Kelly

"Thank you," Fae said.

You *are welcome, my child.*

Fae reached out her hand and touched the water. Her spirits immediately lightened. The water took on a green glow as a breathtaking face appeared just below the surface, haloed in long, black hair. The Lady smiled at her but remained beneath the water.

"So, you can grant youthfulness?" Fae asked.

Or take it, from anyone that touches my waters.

"What happens when they drink?"

They are not meant to drink. That is a theft. Youth stolen without permission. For most, the punishment is immediate—madness.

An errant leaf drifted and landed on the surface of the water. Fae expected it would float, but it didn't. It dropped like a stone. This water wasn't like any other she'd seen. Fae wondered what those waters had done to her.

The waters did nothing to you. I gave you my power. I saw what Lafayette had planned from the beginning. I could not stop him from destroying my guardians, but I could keep him from succeeding in his quest for eternal life. So, I gave you my power—leaving me weak and powerless. That act accomplished two things—it kept the power from Lafayette, and it saved your life.

"Are you still powerless?"

No, my dear. The Between is rich with power. I am now fully restored.

"That's good to know, but I'm sorry to tell you that Lafayette must have found out what you did. He came after me. He got his youth back."

That is unfortunate. I only meant to protect. Instead, I cursed you.

"I wouldn't call eternal youth a curse."

It can be. There is no fear as universal as the fear of death. Men will kill to stop it. They will do the most heinous and terrible things to avoid it. And giving you the power to grant eternal life will make you forever a target. Now, I would ask you again, will you please join me in my fountain?

Nick awoke with a start and leaped out of bed. He raced to Fae's room and flipped on the switch to confirm what he already knew.

She was gone. It wasn't just a dream. Fae was at the fountain.

Nick burst through the cabin door and hit the path at a run. He knew exactly where he was going, having traveled there just minutes before in a dream. The so-called Lady of the Fountain wanted Fae to take a plunge in the water. Nick didn't know what that meant for Fae, but the possibilities were terrifying.

The fountain came into view, towering above him. He could see Fae at the top, climbing over the side of the fountain and entering the water. He took the steps two at a time as he raced to get to her in time.

"Fae, don't do it!" he shouted. "Get out of the fountain!"

She heard him and turned back—her eyes wide in surprise. And then he felt a tug at his feet. No, not his feet, Fae's feet. The Lady pulled her down.

Fae clutched the side of the fountain to stop her descent. Then the Lady pulled harder. The stones scraped against Fae's arms as she did her best to hold on.

You let him drink your blood?

He heard the familiar sound of the Lady's voice through Fae's mind. She sounded angry. *That was a mistake. Human connections only lead to misery. He can't be trusted. Stay with me. I will keep you safe for all eternity.*

"No," Fae shrieked. "I didn't know you planned to *keep* me here." Fae's grip slipped just as Nick got to the top.

He ran to the fountain as Fae plunged beneath the surface. He grabbed her outreached hand, and his body slammed into the stones as the creature pulled Fae down. This Lady was strong. Nick was half surprised that Fae's shoulder wasn't yanked from its socket.

Nick pulled with everything he had in him. Fae cried out in pain, making his heart clench and his adrenaline to spike.

Her face broke the surface, and he continued to pull, grabbing at her shoulder and then wrapping his arm around her body as he tore her from the water. When at last her feet were free, the resistance disappeared and they flew back, landing in a heap at the precipice of the descending steps. Fae turned away and coughed the water from her lungs. When she'd gotten rid of most of the liquid, Nick's arms circled her.

"I trusted her," she gasped between coughing jags. "I can't believe...she planned to keep me there...forever. She's no better than Lafayette." She turned around in his arms to face him.

Nick enfolded her in his embrace. They were both shaking, and Nick found he couldn't speak. He'd just had the scare of his life.

He'd almost lost her.

Nick could hear the Lady saying some very unladylike things. She was furious with him. He could care less how that pond scum felt. She may have saved Fae's life, but that didn't erase the fact she wanted to keep her prisoner.

Nick swept Fae up in his arms and carried her down the steps to the forest below. Fae shook her head where it lay against his shoulder and said, "I'm sorry, Nick. I shouldn't have come here on my own."

He sat her down on her own two feet.

"Fae," he said and paused. When she looked at him, he continued. "I'm just glad to have you back." He looked at her full, wet, quivering lips and leaned over, capturing them with his mouth. Kissing her now was a strange, elating mixture of feelings—both his and hers. The adrenaline in their systems fed their desire, and Fae moaned as she clutched his hair and wrapped her leg around him, driving him mad. She was too innocent to realize the effect her actions were having on him. He continued to make love to her with his mouth as his hands wandered the curves of her waist and down her hips, grabbing onto her leg and pulling her into him. He wanted this woman like he'd never wanted any other. He felt he would literally die if he didn't have her.

When he considered finding a patch of soft ground to strip her of her wet clothes, he stilled. *What am I doing?* A heartbeat later, he growled as he pulled away.

Fae had planned to wait until she was married before having sex—heaven help him. Though the way she responded to him, he knew she wouldn't resist his advances now. Still, there was no way he'd take her here on the forest floor. He loved this woman. He'd walk through red hot coals for her. And if he'd do that, he could find it in himself to marry her before he made love to her.

He sighed over the impossibility of what he had decided. Before he could lose his nerve, he looked her in the eyes and said, "Marry me."

Fae blinked, stunned, her face still streaming with water. She was drenched and shivering. And here he was, proposing to her.

"Did I hear you right?" Fae asked.

Nick cracked a smile. "I wouldn't have believed my own words either if I hadn't been the one to say them." He swallowed as his smile faded. "The link we have now...I can feel your emotions, hear your thoughts."

Fae's eyes widened.

"I know you feel the same way I do. You love me, and I love you, Fae. From the moment our eyes first met, I've loved you. And I know I always will. Conall told me we are fated to be together. I'd never believed in fate before, but it makes sense. I feel such a strong connection to you. Even before I drank your blood, I felt it. So why should we fight fate?"

He lowered down on one knee. "I'm sorry I don't have a ring to offer yet, but I'm asking you, Fae. Will you marry me?"

Fae chewed on her bottom lip, her eyes wide. She searched his expression, trying to determine if he was serious. Finally, the shock melted into a smile, and tears sprang to her eyes. "You're serious?"

He sighed. "I've never been more serious."

Fae nodded as she touched her fingers to her lips. "Yes. I will."

Nick grinned as he rose from his knee and swept her up in his arms. He kissed her again and was filled with such joy and happiness he thought he might burst. He wasn't sure where Fae's feelings ended and his began, but he was too happy to care.

Chapter 28

Lafayette sat in silence as three idiots sat around his kitchen table and argued.

"I swear," Hunter snarled as he slammed his coffee cup down. The liquid sloshed onto the table. Even in his human form, this shape-shifter acted like a grizzly bear. "If I see Avira again, I'll tear her arms off."

"Not if I get to her first," Lavinia said. The tall, bony witch was all sharp edges and angles—not just her body, but personality too.

Lafayette's temper began to rise. It had been a mistake to ask them to help. These clowns thought they were the ones in charge. He'd just need to set them straight. "You three had a simple task. You were to bring me Fae Miller."

"Don't you even start with us," the witch snapped as she pointed her long finger at him. "You might've brought us in, but you don't own us. You're lucky we are letting you participate."

"Yeah," Theon said. Lafayette had no idea what kind of supernatural creature Theon was, but he looked like someone who spent his life living in his mom's basement playing video games all day. A typical nerd.

What was he thinking? He thought by bringing in supernaturals, he would gain the upper hand. But abilities didn't outweigh brains, and Lafayette stood head and shoulders above them in that department.

"I'll tell you what's going to go down," the witch said. "We're going to follow the girl. Watch who she interacts with, and if other members of the Order show up, we kill them—plain and simple."

"I hope Conall makes an appearance," Hunter said. His meaty hand wiped his mouth. He looked like he was practically salivating over the possibility of coming face to face with him.

"You wouldn't last three seconds against Conall," Lavinia said, scowling.

"I don't care about what you do with the Order members," Lafayette said, "but the girl is mine. No one is to harm her."

"You still haven't told us why she's so important to them," the witch said. "I don't know how we can work together if we can't trust one another."

Yeah, right. These imbeciles trusted no one. This was just another feeble attempt to get information from him. "I've already told you enough. I want her, plain and simple."

"Where's your bathroom?" Hunter said, lumbering to his feet. Lafayette wasn't surprised he had to go. He was on his fifth cup of joe.

Lafayette shrugged toward the hallway. "Last door on the left."

"But why do you want her?" Lavinia asked, undeterred.

"Listen," Lafayette said. "She's one hundred percent human, nothing special, other than she's the adopted daughter of someone who betrayed me. And *you* told me what her boyfriend is. A—"

"Yeah," she interrupted. "He's got some faery blood in him. But that still doesn't explain why the Order would go out of their way to protect them."

"How should I know?" Lafayette said. "Maybe Nick Chase has family in high places. Perhaps his grandmother is a member of royalty in the Seelie court. I don't care what he is, I want the girl. I have special plans for her."

"She *is* pretty hot," the Theon said, raising an eyebrow.

"Hey," Hunter shouted from down the hallway. "Did you know you have a dead girl in your freezer?"

Lafayette rose to his feet, fuming. "What are you doing in my freezer?"

"I smelled the blood," the bear answered.

Lafayette looked from the witch to the nerd, gauging their reaction. He paused at the nerd. His eyes were wide as he licked his lips.

"Can I have her?" Theon said, drool pooling at the corner of his mouth.

"She's frozen solid, you idiot," the witch said. "You'd break your teeth."

"What are you?" Lafayette asked the kid before he could censor himself.

"You wouldn't have to ask that if it weren't for me," the witch answered. "My magic keeps him fresh."

Lafayette frowned in confusion.

"Let's just say," Lavinia said," brains are at the top of his list of favorite foods."

Lafayette took a step back and grimaced. "Zombie."

The zombie-nerd rose to his feet, glaring at him. "I'm getting tired of your condescending attitude. The difference between you and me is only one bite. One bite, and you'd be just like me. So, I'll make you a deal. Stop insulting me and my friends and let me have the dead girl, and I won't feast on your flesh. And believe me, I won't leave enough for you to come back and torment us."

"You do know that if you kill him," the bear said as he returned, "you won't get paid, right?"

The zombie turned to the bear and glared. "Shut up."

The witch chuckled and said, "It didn't even cross the newbie's mind. Not that zombies are much concerned with money." She stood, an evil glint in her eye as she smiled at Lafayette. "I do have to say, money is not the motivator for me either, and I'm done with you too. I appreciate you giving us an opportunity to strike against the Order. And because of that, I'll let you leave alive. Forget the girl. Don't show your face around here again, and you won't face my wrath."

The three of them stood over Lafayette as he sat, fuming.

"I still get the dead girl, right?" Theon looked over at the witch with excitement in his voice.

"This is my house," Lafayette said, stunned at the turn of events.

"Not anymore," the witch said, sneering as she stepped toward him, her fingers sparking and crackling as electricity danced over her raised hand.

Lafayette leaned back and frowned. "Can I at least take my backpack?"

When the witch nodded, he stepped over to where it was propped. He leaned down and reached in. When he stood up, his hand flashed forward. A curved blade whistled through the air and stuck into the wall behind the witch's back. Her eyes widened in shock. Her head rolled off her neck and landed with a thud on the wood floor—followed by her lifeless body.

"That never gets old," Lafayette said, smiling, and then turned to the other two as he clutched two more shuriken blades in his raised hands. "Do you two want me out also?"

Hunter shook his head vigorously. "No, not me. I'm in this for the money. You pay me, and I'm happy."

The nerd couldn't keep his eyes off the witch's head bleeding on the floor.

"What about you, zombie?" Lafayette snarled. "You still want to take a bite out of me?"

Theon gave him a quick glance and then turned back to drool over the head. The eyes were blinking as her mouth gaped open. The witch's head was still alive!

"No, not me. I'm totally on board. If..." Theon paused as if fearful of Lafayette's response.

"If what?" Lafayette said, astonished.

"You let me have it," he gestured to the severed head, "I'll do whatever you ask." The witch's eyes widened in horror.

Lafayette blew out a breath in equal parts relief and disgust. "Like I care."

Chapter 29

Nick approached the FBI field office with Conall at his side. "Are you sure this is going to work?" Nick asked.

Conall smiled. "Of course I am."

Gaping mouths and wide eyes greeted his arrival. Don paled when he looked up.

ASAC Young poked her head out of her office. A big smile spread across her face. "It's you."

"In the flesh," Nick said.

"You do realize we have a warrant for your arrest, don't you?" Young said, sauntering up to him.

"Not anymore," Conall said, stepping forward. "The charges have been dropped, and Agent Chase has been cleared of all wrongdoing."

"And you are...?" She raised an eyebrow.

"Executive Assistant Director John Jones."

Young swallowed a gasp. "I'm sorry, sir, I didn't recognize you at first."

"Obviously." He turned to Nick. "I'll be waiting out here when you're ready."

"Yes, sir," Nick said, suppressing a smile. He stepped into his office with Don at his back, pulling the door shut.

"Okay, Nick," Don said, "you've got some explaining to do."

Nick sank into his chair and leaned back. "Division X has friends in high places."

"This is all completely insane." Don's brows pressed together as he shook his head. "You have to tell me; how did they fool everyone with the letter from the director? I've gone over it a million times in my mind. I saw the note. I remember clearly what it said. How in the world did they do it?"

"You wouldn't believe me if I told you."

Don huffed. "I guess that's all the answer I expected." He stepped over and sat down on Nick's desk. "Listen, I've been blaming you for shutting me out."

"I kind of figured as much," Nick said.

"But I was wrong," Don said. "I'd do the exact same thing in your shoes. I'm sorry for the way I've been acting."

"Hey, I really wish I could include you in this. But I can't."

"I understand," Don said. "I don't like it, but I understand."

"There is something I *would* like to include you in."

"And what's that?"

"My wedding. I need a best man."

Don's eyes widened. "You're kidding me."

"I wouldn't believe it myself if I hadn't been the one to propose."

"I'm guessing you're talking about Fae. What about your class? I thought you weren't supposed to date—much less marry—your students."

"The semester is almost over. We're waiting until it ends. That'll give us a couple weeks for our honeymoon."

Don narrowed his eyes as he studied Nick. A slow smile crept across his face. "She's making you wait, isn't she?"

Nick pressed his lips together into a fine line.

"She is! I've heard there were girls like that. So, you're getting married just so you can—"

"I'm getting married because I love her," Nick interrupted. He could see a million questions, comments, and smart remarks in Don's expression, but he simply shook his head in disbelief. "Well, I guess all I can say is congratulations, then."

"Thanks," Nick said, wishing he didn't have to break the other news he had to Don. "And..."

"You're leaving," Don said.

Nick nodded.

"I figured as much when Agent Thomas said he'd wait here till you're ready. And I can't say I'm surprised. I am glad you're leaving for another position and not for prison time."

"Yeah, me too," Nick said.

"You need some help packing up?" Don asked.

"Sure," Nick said.

"I'll grab some boxes."

It took all of fifteen minutes for them to gather Nick's possessions and pack them into two large boxes. Nick never was one for collecting stuff. They picked up the packages, and Don opened the door for them to leave.

"And the police are doing nothing!" A young attractive woman spoke to a very irritated ASAC Young. Conall, on the other hand, had a clear expression of pity.

Young turned to the closest agent. "Sanchez, can you handle this?"

Sanchez looked at the woman, raised his eyebrow, and said, "Sure."

Nick approached.

"Like I told your boss, my sister has been kidnapped." The woman was clearly upset as she spoke to Sanchez. "I have a name: Marcus. He's about six-foot-three inches, a hundred and eighty pounds, in his early twenties, with a crew cut. He drove a black 1966 Chrysler Windsor. I didn't see the license plate, but how many '66 Windsors can there be in Jacksonville?" Sanchez led the woman away.

Nick smiled at Young. "I guess this is goodbye, sweetheart." He got the exact reaction he'd expected from the endearment—contempt.

"I'd say it's been a pleasure working with you, Chase. But," Young looked over at Conall and bit off her retort. "Well, anyway, good luck."

Nick huffed. "Thanks." Less than a minute later, he was a free man.

"They even went through my underwear drawer!"

Fae listened attentively. Morgan sat cross-legged on her bed in their dorm room. "I mean, did they really think they'd find clues of where to find you among my bras and panties? I know you want to be one of them someday, so I hope you won't be offended by me saying, the FBI are total idiots!"

Fae opened her mouth to speak, but Morgan went on.

"They said Nick was a wanted man and probably kidnapped you. I was like, no! He would never do that. But they didn't listen to me. Why does no one ever listen to me?"

Morgan didn't pause for a response but continued to talk. "They interrogated me for two hours and they still didn't hear a word I said. I mean, I had plenty of arguments proving that Nick was innocent. I guess they believe me now, but I doubt I'll get an apology from—"

Morgan gasped and Fae jumped in response. "What in the world is that?" Morgan asked. Her gaze locked on Fae's hand. Morgan scrambled off the bed and took Fae's hand in hers to lift it up and inspect it.

Her eyes rose from the icy diamond on Fae's finger to her face. "You didn't..."

"Didn't what?" Fae asked.

"Get engaged, of course! You and Agent Chase?"

Heat rose in Fae's cheeks as she nodded. "Yeah, he proposed."

"I can't believe it!" Morgan said. "Why didn't you tell me? When's the day?"

"Three days after finals."

"No kidding!" Morgan said. "And how are you going to plan a wedding during finals?"

"Nick's sister is handling everything," Fae said.

"I thought she was dying," Morgan said.

"They found out she really didn't have Muscular Dystrophy. What she had is treatable, and now she's pretty much fully recovered." Fae spoke the lie convincingly—though Morgan was easy to fool. Fae was only slightly saddened that she could no longer keep the promise she'd made to herself. Lies would be a big part of her life from now on. But at least these lies were meant to protect instead of deceive.

"Oh, my gosh, that's freakin' amazing!" She dropped Fae's hand and plopped back down on the bed. "So how did he propose?"

Fae smiled at the memory. "He didn't plan it ahead of time, it just sort of happened. I fell into a fountain and he had to fish me out. I guess that kind of scared him, and that's when he did it. He asked me then and there to marry him."

"So, he saved your life and then popped the question?" Morgan's face lit up.

"I guess you could say it that way."

"That's holy freakin' awesome!"

Fae completely agreed with Morgan.

"So, you went ring shopping after?" Morgan once again got off the bed and took her hand to look more closely at the ring. "That's a big diamond. I know I'm not supposed to ask, but I have to know. How much did it cost?"

"I don't know. The place we went to didn't have price tags, and Nick wouldn't say. He just told me to pick out the ring I liked. I tried to pick something more conservative, but he could see right through me. He wouldn't let me settle for something just because it looked less expensive. Somehow he could tell this was the ring I liked."

"Wow it really is gorgeous. The diamond isn't so big that it's gaudy, but it's definitely got some karats to it. And the setting is stunning! The pillow cut is my favorite and with all those little diamonds around it.... It's perfect!"

"That's what I thought," Fae said with a smile. She glanced up at the clock and sighed. "I'm sorry. I wish I didn't have to go, but my boss is expecting me. I'll have to tell her I've decided to quit."

"Oh, good," Morgan said. "You looked like you were going to have a nervous breakdown every time you went into work. I guess you aren't the bare-it-all-to-the-world kind of girl."

Fae shook her head and smiled. "No, I guess I'm not." She stood to leave. "I'll be back after I talk to Ms. Kline. I have a lot of work to make up."

"I'm surprised you can keep up. It seems like you've missed more school than you've attended."

"Yeah, well," Fae said. "I can't say it's been easy."

"I do have to say," Morgan said. "I'm going to miss having you as a roomie."

"Me too."

"Yeah, right." Morgan smirked. "You'll be married to Mr. Hottie. You're not going to give me a second thought. At least I wouldn't. Not if I had someone with that much raw sex appeal in my bed. That reminds me. Have you two...?" Morgan wiggled her eyebrows.

Fae's face burned as she shook her head.

"Seriously?" Morgan's eyes were wide. "I may have to rethink my strategy."

Fae was chuckling when she stepped out the door. The two Division X agents that had been shadowing her all day turned at her approach. The taller of the two—the one with fangs—eyed her curiously. *Had they been listening?*

"I don't know why you two are following me around," Fae said. "I can't very well be bait when there are two sharks hovering close by, ready to defend me."

"Agent Jones said we're to guard you until you've spoken your vows," the taller agent said.

"Yeah, I guess me getting kidnapped would throw a wrench in the wedding plans."

He nodded.

Curious eyes were on her as she walked across campus with the two big men in her wake. She swallowed down the lump in her throat when she saw the dean. She'd heard he kept his job but received a stern reprimand and a warning to leave her alone. He glared at her for a moment, and then turned his eyes down to the ground, spun around, and walked away.

Turning toward the arts building, she felt a jolt when she saw a young man, probably a student, with dark hair on the greasy side. But there was something off about him; something she couldn't quite place. She glanced back at the two agents at her sides. They didn't seem to notice him.

Maybe she was overreacting.

The kids blew by her without pause and headed in the opposite direction.

She was definitely overreacting.

Stepping into the arts building, she was greeted by Ms. Kline's apologetic expression. "Fae, I'm so glad to see you're all right."

"I'm fine," Fae answered. "Really, I am."

Ms. Kline looked briefly at the two agents and then turned back to Fae with a sigh. "I just need to say it outright. I'm sorry to say, we've had to replace you. I just couldn't leave my students hanging. You've missed so much work."

"No," Fae said. "It's okay. I was coming in to tell you I needed to quit. I was willing to work until you could replace me, but I'm relieved that you've got things covered."

The relief in Ms. Kline's face was apparent. "I'm so glad. I didn't want to be the one to make your life any worse than it has been. I swear I've never seen anyone with more atrocious luck."

"It's okay," Fae said. "You've been more than accommodating to me. I couldn't have asked for a better boss."

Ms. Kline smiled. "You really are a sweetheart. I wish you all the happiness you deserve. And once things are settled down in your life, I'd be happy to rehire you."

"I appreciate the offer, but I don't think modeling is for me."

"Modeling may not be for you," Ms. Kline said, "but you are exceptionally good at it."

Fae thanked her again and left. The relief she felt overwhelmed her. No nude posing for her—ever.

Chapter 30

Fae stepped back into her dorm room. Morgan was nowhere to be seen.

Fae sat down at her desk and pulled out a stack of assignments. Hours later, she was nearly done. She glanced up at the clock. 11:39 PM. Where was Morgan?

She probably met up with a boy. If Morgan was anything, she was predictably boy-crazed. She'd just better be safe. Some of the boys on campus didn't play nice.

Fae texted Nick. *I got nearly all my work done. I'm dead tired, so I'll finish the rest tomorrow.*

His return text came seconds later. *Good night, Princess. I'll see you in the morning. Love you.*

Love you, too, she replied with a smile.

The next morning Morgan still hadn't gotten back.

Fae sent off a text to check in on her. *Are you okay? You didn't come back to the room last night.*

Her text came several minutes later. *Spent the night with a boy named Theon. I'll give you details later.*

Theon? Who was Theon? And she slept with him already? Even Morgan wasn't usually that quick to hop in bed with someone. Theon must be something special.

Fae showered and took her time with her makeup. She wanted to make an impression on Nick when she walked into class. They'd agreed to play it cool. Nick didn't want any trouble for her, and being engaged to the professor might make the administration think he could possibly be showing favoritism. She just had to get through this semester, and then she'd be done with this school.

Conall had worked fast with Harvard. She was already admitted and ready to start class next semester. She wouldn't have to worry about squeezing into their dorms, she'd be living off-campus—with her husband. That freaked her out just thinking about it. She and Nick still had to find a place, but that should be easy enough. Fae had discovered something not completely surprising.

Nick was loaded.

His father had been the CEO of some big international corporation. And when he and his wife died, they left Nick and Becca with equal shares of tens of millions of dollars. Fae knew she should be ecstatic about it, but truly it made her feel less than adequate. She had nothing to contribute but the clothes on her back.

Of course, she provided eternal life to him and his sister. So maybe it did balance out.

Fae walked down the familiar hallway to her Criminology class and got a lump in her throat. She'd only been there one semester, but she felt nostalgic.

This would be the last time she walked through this hall. Stepping over to the vending machine, she got her daily Coke.

Nick's eyes rose to her as she walked into class. A hint of a smile lit his face, but he kept his composure—just like he said he would. The two agents melted into the background.

Fae sat at her desk, took a long drink of the fizzy cola, set it at the edge of her desk, and took out her notebook.

"Well, class," Nick said. "I have to say you've made this semester much better than I expected. I'm truly impressed by the caliber of students this college has. I swear Harvard has nothing on you."

A figure brushed by her desk, knocking a paper of hers on the floor. She leaned down as he mumbled an, "Excuse me."

Fae wondered briefly if Nick were reading her thoughts. No. Probably not. He said he'd gotten much better at blocking her, and he'd probably find it too distracting during a lecture to listen to her idle thoughts.

Fae took another drink and coughed. Was it her, or did the drink taste a little off?

She listened to Nick's lecture and tried to be attentive. She focused on his mouth. He sure was smart, and the things he said were brilliant. But the way he kissed... that was magical!

His eyes briefly met hers, and she could feel her face heat. *Did he hear me?*

Fae's phone vibrated. She shouldn't look at it, but she was beginning to worry about Morgan. She still hadn't seen her.

Fae pulled out the phone and discreetly looked down at the screen. It *was* from Morgan. She opened the message.

Hello, Fae. This is Lafayette.

Fae's heart dropped to the pit of her stomach. This was the man who killed women. He'd killed two already. What was he doing with Morgan's phone? Fae began to shake as she read the rest of the message.

I have Morgan. If you want to see her again, you need to lose the agents. I have people watching you. If you so much as try anything funny, I will know. And then I'll return Morgan to you in pieces. Understand?

She replied. *Yes. But if I come to you, do you promise to return Morgan unharmed?*

I give you my word, was his reply.

She had no doubt Lafayette would make good on this threat. She really hoped she could trust his word. Who was she kidding? She couldn't trust the word of a murderer.

She wanted to look around for the face of a stranger, but she didn't want to make the agents suspicious. Nick already had to know. He would have picked up on her distress. She hoped he wouldn't interfere. Still, she needed to lose the agents. But how?

They stuck to her like glue. They even waited outside the hall when she went to the bathroom. Her best bet would be to wait until class was out and the halls were packed. She could possibly lose them in the crowd.

For the rest of class, Fae only half listened to the lecture—or rather, the review. She heard enough to know that Nick could really play it cool. His lecture didn't sound any different. He *had* to be worried about her. But he was smart. He'd figure out a way to keep her safe *and* save Morgan.

Finally, the class let out. Nick continued to act as if nothing were wrong as he spoke to students at the head of the class. Fae casually made her way to the hall. She had a semblance of a plan to enact.

As she stepped into the flow of students, she looked up and gasped. She pointed her finger at a blond student who looked to be in a hurry and said, "Lafayette," as she backed into one of the agents. "That man's Lafayette."

The agents paused long enough to tell her to stay with Nick, and then they were after the student. Fae didn't waste any time but ran in the opposite direction. She hoped they weren't too hard on the poor, nameless kid.

In minutes, she was out the door. A dark-haired man stood directly in her path as she tried to side-step him to get to the school entrance. He didn't let her, though. He stepped over to once again block her way.

Fae skidded to a stop and looked up. She recognized him immediately. He was the nerd she'd seen before—the one with the greasy black hair.

"Hello, Fae," he said as she met his eyes. A chill ran down her spine.

He was dead!

There was no light in his eyes. It was like staring into the eyes of an animated corpse. Where did these people come from? Her whole life, she'd never come across a supernatural being, and now everywhere she turned, she saw glowing eyes, sharp fangs, and pointed ears.

She glanced around briefly, wondering why she was the only one who could see how incredibly...*wrong* he looked. No one else seemed to notice him. They were actually staring at her instead. It really sucked being the only one to see what these people were.

"Lafayette is waiting for you." He turned and walked away.

Fae silently followed him. *Nick, you'd better have a plan. I really don't want to be locked in a dungeon again, and I absolutely will not see Morgan chopped into pieces!*

Nick gathered up his things as the last of his students filtered out the door. His phone vibrated. He pulled it out and checked the screen.

It was Miller—one of the men guarding Fae.

"Yeah," Nick answered.

"We have Lafayette," Miller said.

"You're kidding me." Nick breathed a sigh of relief. "When?"

"Just now," Miller said. "Fae pointed him out."

Nick's brows pressed together as his heart sank. If Fae *had* seen Lafayette, he should have felt it. In fact, he hadn't felt her in a while. Of course, he had thrown up a loose block so he could concentrate during class. But he should have felt something that substantial.

He closed his eyes and reached out to her.

Nothing.

He should be feeling something—even if it were boredom. He clenched his hands as rage rose in his chest and escaped in a growl. "That's not Lafayette," he said as he rushed out the door. "Tell me where you are."

Minutes later, his suspicions were confirmed. The kid they had handcuffed was a student he'd seen float around campus all semester—a kid who now looked like he was about to vomit.

Miller stepped up to Nick. "You sure this isn't Lafayette? He does look like him."

Nick met his eyes and scowled.

"Okay, okay," Miller conceded. "But why would Fae say he was?"

"Because someone got to her. She has a kind, self-sacrificing heart, and Lafayette is using that against her." Nick pulled out his phone and dialed Fae's number. It rang until it reached her voicemail. Nick gripped the phone tight in his hand. He was hoping Lafayette would answer. He left a message for him anyway.

"Lafayette, this is Agent Nick Chase of the Order. I know you have Fae and I'm willing to make a deal. Release her unharmed and I won't pursue you. I'll let you live your unnaturally long life in peace. But, if you don't release her, or if she's harmed by you, I will hunt you down and kill you like the dog you are. And it won't be quick. I'll make you suffer. You will scream for me to end you by the time I let you die. I swear on my life."

Nick swiped the phone off.

"Wow," Miller said. "That was disturbing. You sounded convincing. If I didn't know better, I'd say you were serious."

"I was."

Miller shook his head. "There's no way Thomas will let you follow through on your threat. We don't work that way."

Nick turned to him, grabbed him by his shirt, and yanked him to his chest so they were nose to nose. "I don't care what Thomas, Jones, or anyone else says," he snarled. "That monster has the woman I love.

If he lays a finger on her, if she gets so much as a bruise from that maniac, I'll kill him!"

Miller nodded. "Okay, okay. I get it. Now let me go before you get hurt."

Nick noticed Miller's eyes were glowing red. He'd almost forgotten that with the Order, he dealt with supernatural creatures. But with the threat Fae faced, Nick couldn't care less what kind of creature he was. Still, he let Miller go.

Nick met the other agent's eyes. This guy's expression held nothing but understanding.

"You married?" Nick asked.

"Yeah." He gave a quick nod.

"Do you think I'm out of line?" Nick asked.

Davis shook his head. "Absolutely not. If anyone touched my wife, I'd string him up by his entrails."

"Exactly," Nick said.

Miller frowned. "You guys are both crazy."

"Just wait. When you fall in love with the right woman, you'll feel the same way."

Davis unlocked the handcuffs. "Sorry, kid. You're free to go." The young student rubbed his wrists for a moment, grabbed his backpack, and then took off running.

Miller wasn't deterred. "First of all, I don't plan on settling down. And second of all, even if I do, my job will *always* come first."

"I believed that lie once too," Davis said.

"We've wasted enough time," Nick said. "Let's get back to headquarters. I need to talk to Conall."

Chapter 31

Fae decided that the worst part of riding in the trunk of a car was not knowing where in the world she was going! Nick wouldn't be able to tell by reading her thoughts either. But, didn't Conall say Nick would be able to find her anywhere?

He'd better!

Fae had finals she absolutely couldn't miss.

She had a flash of guilt. Finals were the least of her worries. Who knew how much time Morgan had? Lafayette had given his word not to harm her, but he was a murderer. If anything happened to Morgan, she'd never forgive herself.

Finally, after what seemed like hours, they slowed, but then they were bumping over... a dirt road? It felt like she was going home, back to her and Brigitte's place in the Bayou. At the thought of Brigitte, Fae's heart sank. Lafayette had killed her too. Fae swallowed the lump in her throat and pressed her eyes shut against the stinging tears.

She'd never had time to properly mourn Brigitte. If she died, she never would.

No. Nick will save me.

Finally, they stopped. Feet crunched against gravel as they approached the trunk. Seconds later, it opened, and blinding light caused Fae to blink. Finally, Lafayette's face came into focus. He smiled brightly.

"Well, well, my dear. It's good to see your pretty face again."

Fae began to tremble as she remembered the last time she'd seen him. "Where's Morgan?"

"Oh, your pretty little roommate? She's fine. I didn't put a mark on her, and I won't, as long as you don't give me any reason to."

"I want to see her." Fae's voice trembled.

"Oh, rest assured, you will be seeing her, but first, you have a punishment to endure."

"Punishment?" Fae's blood turned to ice.

"I can't let your previous escape go unpunished." Lafayette spoke calmly. "You need to be taught a lesson. I can't have you running off on me at every turn, now can I?"

"What kind of punishment is it?"

"Your adoptive mother would be familiar with it. Did she tell you what the guard did to those who betrayed us?"

Fae shook her head.

"Well, you're about to find out." Lafayette dragged Fae from the trunk. The edge scraped and bumped across her stomach and legs.

"Hey! I can get out on my—" Her words caught in her throat when she came face to face with a grizzly bear. He seemed to be glaring at her, but bears didn't glare.

Lafayette wasn't fazed by the enormous wild animal, but continued to drag her beyond the house and out to a forest.

She saw the old well a moment before he picked her up and dropped her into it. A scream tore from her throat as she plummeted down, her hands reaching out and brushing against the stone side on her descent. Pain exploded across her body as she slammed against the hard ground below.

Lights danced in her gaze as she turned her head up, attempting to draw a breath. Lafayette slid a metal grate over the hole. She could hear a drill in short bursts. He locked it down with bolts.

After several long moments, Fae finally started breathing again, and her panic turned to horror. *She was trapped at the bottom of a well!*

"Make yourself comfortable, Fae," Lafayette said. "You'll be down there for a while—I'd say at least as long as the days of freedom you've had."

"That's two months!" Fae gasped.

"I know it's two months," he bellowed in anger. "I've suffered each day of it—not knowing where you were. Not knowing if I would ever find you. I faced death once again—something I swore I'd never do. I will make you suffer for the pain you put me through. I'd say it's an eye for an eye."

"An eye for an eye?" she yelled in disbelief. "But you weren't trapped at the bottom of a well! I did nothing to you but gave you youth. How is this even comparable?"

Lafayette didn't respond. Was he still there?

"Fae?" a familiar, shaky voice called out.

Fae's heart sank as she turned to see Morgan's ghostly white face.

"Fae?" Morgan said. "You're here! I know I should be horrified about that, but I'm so freakin' glad to see you." She sighed. "I didn't think I'd see you, or anyone else I cared about, ever again." Tears streaked down Morgan's face as she visibly shook.

"It's okay," Fae said. "Nick is coming." Fae took a step toward her friend. Morgan looked like she needed a hug—she was shockingly pale. What did Lafayette put her through?

Lafayette's laughter came from above, and Fae froze. "So you *are* counting on him to find you." *Oh shoot, he's still there.* "I'm happy to say we've broken the bond. You'd think someone who drinks as many cokes as you do would notice when it's been tampered with. And Nick wasn't any better. Of course, coffee masks the taste much better than Coke."

"You're lying," Fae shouted, even though she knew he spoke the truth. Her drink did taste a little off. She pushed the thought to the back of her mind. The truth was just too horrifying to consider.

"You'd like to think I am. If the Order had any brains at all, they would have known how easily it is to break the bond. Well, I've got things to do, plans to make. I'll check on you in a week. That'll give you time to think about life's consequences."

At those words, she could hear his feet crunching the gravel above. This time he really was leaving, and not only was she trapped here, her most loyal friend was, too. Fae's throat constricted as she tried to draw a breath in.

"Fae, settle down," Morgan said. "You're having a panic attack."

Fae shook her head. She had no idea if she was or not. She'd never had a panic attack before.

"Yes, you are. I know what I'm talking about. Come on, hold your breath and then breathe out slowly."

Fae did her best to do what she said. It wasn't easy.

"Okay, now do it again."

Fae found the tightness in her chest dissipating. When she finally breathed easier, she calmed down.

"He'll never find us," she said, dejected.

"Are you kidding me?" Morgan asked. "Nick is an FBI agent and he loves you. He's going to find you. You have to believe that, Fae."

Fae looked up at her, wanting so much to believe.

"He found you before," Morgan said. "He'll find you again."

Fae nodded. She squeezed her eyes shut and said a little prayer. *Please, let Nick come. And please let it be before someone else dies.* She opened her eyes and looked at Morgan, in awe at her demeanor.

"How can you be so calm?" Fae asked.

"Oh, believe me, I wasn't before I..." Morgan hesitated.

"Before you what?" Fae asked.

She looked away and shrugged. "Before I realized that no good would come of freaking out."

Fae nodded. "So how do we get out of here?"

Morgan shrugged. "I don't know."

Fae looked up at the steel grate. "There's no getting that thing off, I'm sure. Are there any loose stones? Maybe we can dig our way out." She walked up to the side of the wall and tried to wedge her fingers through a crack.

"Even if you could make an opening through the limestone," Morgan said, "we're pretty far down. You'd have to do a lot of digging to get to the surface. Not to mention, you'd have to do it with your bare hands. I'd say that's close to impossible."

Fae looked up at her friend. She'd never seen Morgan in this state. She may be calm, but there was something disturbing in that calmness. Morgan spoke more slowly, and the pep that had always brightened her face and drove her unending optimism was gone. Fae frowned, even more determined to get them out of this. She needed to not only save her friend's life but her spirit as well.

"Then," Fae said, "I guess I'll have to climb to the top and see if there's a loose stone there."

Morgan frowned back at her. "You're lucky you didn't break your neck when Lafayette pushed you down here. If you fall again, I doubt you'll be so lucky."

"Well, then, I guess I better not fall, right?" Fae attempted to smile.

Morgan cracked a weak grin. "Right."

Fae looked up and saw one of the stones jutting out—a perfect hand hold—just out of her reach. "Okay, roomie, I just need a little boost."

Morgan shook her head as shock and despair spread like a shadow across her face. She took a shaky step back. "I can't."

"What do you mean, you can't? Of course you can. I really don't weigh that much."

"You don't understand," Morgan wailed. It looked like her calm façade had cracked. Morgan stood still for a moment as if trying to gather some courage. Finally, she took a step forward and raised her hand. It trembled as she reached out to touch Fae's face. Just as Fae expected to feel Morgan's fingers brush her cheek, an icy coldness washed over her.

"I'm already dead."

Chapter 32

Fae staggered back, feeling like she'd had the wind knocked out of her again. "No... you can't be."

"Dead?" Morgan said. "Oh, believe me, I am."

Hot tears filled Fae's eyes and streamed down her cheeks. "But I came here to save you."

"I know."

"This is all my fault," Fae sobbed.

"No," Morgan said. "It's absolutely not your fault. Lafayette's the one to blame, he and those two other freaks who did nothing to stop him."

"How did you..." Fae began, but couldn't seem to finish her question. Did she really want to know how Morgan died? Could she handle the answer?

"I died quickly," Morgan said. "But that's all I'm going to say about it."

Fae nodded. It had to have been bad enough dying. She didn't want to force Morgan to relive her experience.

"Okay so," Morgan began. "Jenny and I have been working together on a few things."

"Jenny?" Fae asked, still blinking through tears.

A beautiful, young blonde materialized in front of her. "Hi," she said as she smiled sweetly and fluttered her fingers in a wave.

"You're a ghost too?" Fae asked, even though the answer was obvious.

"Yeah."

"As I was saying," Morgan continued. "Jenny and I have been practicing channeling our energy and—"

"It's a lot harder than it seems," Jenny interrupted.

Morgan shot her a glare. "Yes, it is, but with this limestone well, we've found we can do a lot more. In fact, we can even move things. I think together, we might be able to loosen the screws holding down that grate."

"I don't know..." Jenny began.

"Shh!" Morgan said. "Just shut up, okay? It's not like we have a lot of options."

Fae wiped away more tears. "I'm still having a hard time dealing with the fact that you're dead, Morgan. And Jenny, did Lafayette, um...?"

"Kill me too?"

Fae nodded.

"Yeah." She glanced at Morgan with sadness in her eyes. "We're both trying to not think about it."

"How can you ignore something like that?" Fae asked, looking from one to the other.

"Being dead is not much different than being alive," Morgan said. "Only people can't see or hear you. I was pretty shocked when you saw me so easily."

"Apparently, I can see a lot of unusual things," Fae said, and bit her lip.

"Like what?" Morgan asked.

"I'm not really supposed to talk about it," Fae said.

"Who am I going to tell?" Morgan said. "I'm dead."

"You have a good point." Fae blew out a breath.

"Well?" Morgan coaxed.

"Well...," Fae said hesitantly. "I've seen elves, succubi, shapeshifters, and who knows what else."

Morgan stood stunned, for a moment not uttering a word. "Um, Fae? Are you sure you didn't hit your head on the way down this well?"

Fae huffed a laugh. "I'm sure. I'm not what you'd consider normal."

Morgan gave a weak smile. "I'm starting to realize that."

"Shut up," Fae said as she playfully pushed Morgan—only to have her hand slip though her like she wasn't even there. Oh, right. Morgan was a ghost. "Sorry," she muttered.

"Okay, Jenny," Morgan said, ignoring Fae's blunder. "We've wasted enough time already. Let's get Fae out of here before the Lafayette comes back and kills her too. Fae *needs* to stay alive. She's about to get married to a smokin' hot FBI agent."

Morgan and Jenny could get the screws off much more easily than Fae could climb the side of the well—which really wasn't saying much. Climbing the side of the well was nearly impossible. Fae held on, suspended by the tips of her fingers and tips of her toes. *What in the world was I thinking?*

She chanced a glance down. The light had faded fast. She could no longer see the bottom of the well. It looked like a black abyss below her, ready to swallow her up in its depths. She looked up. She was nearly there, but she had never felt so hopeless. She could barely hang on. How on earth would she be able to push the grate off?

"Come on, Fae, you can do it," Morgan cheered as she floated above.

"Oh, really?" Fae replied. "How? 'Cause if you know a way for me to do it, I would really like you to tell me."

"You just need to..." Morgan said as she floated around Fae, examining the rocky wall Fae hung from. "Well, maybe...Gawd, I don't know! Maybe you should have climbed up the other side."

"You are so not helping." Fae's fingers were burning like the fiery depths of hell, and she had no idea how much longer she could hold her position. Probably not long. "Maybe escaping like this was a bad idea. If I could overpower Lafayette when—"

"No way," Morgan shouted. "You need to stay far away from him. I know I'm stating the obvious, but there's something seriously wrong with him. And he's dangerous. Even the big, burly guy twice his size is afraid of him. And he..." Morgan's voice shook as her words dropped away.

"You don't have to talk about it," Fae said, her fingers beginning to slip. She pushed up on her toes to adjust her finger grip.

"He's a monster," Jenny said. "And the kid...I don't even want to think about what he did to that witch—to her body. Even as a ghost, I feel physically ill thinking about it."

Fae's stomach soured. Could things be worse than she'd thought?

"We will get the grate off," Morgan said, obviously trying to sound confident, though she didn't even come close to succeeding.

"But," Jenny began.

"Shut up," Morgan shouted. "We *will* get this grate off!"

"Okay," Jenny said. "You don't have to get snippy."

It was difficult to see how hard they were trying. They didn't use their hands to push the grate. She didn't know what in the world they were doing. It looked like they were simply staring intensely at it. The grate shook but didn't move from its place. Morgan narrowed her eyes further and, though she couldn't be sure in the darkness, Fae could swear she saw a gleam of sweat drip down Morgan's temple. Did ghosts sweat?

"I can't..." Jenny groaned.

"Yes, you can," Morgan growled through clenched teeth.

The high-pitched sound of scraping metal made Fae cringe. And then there was a deep thud. Looking up, Fae could see only clear sky. The grate was gone.

She didn't waste any more time, but quickly climbed her way up and out of the well. Sinking to the ground and heaving air into her chest, she gasped out a thank you.

"Don't thank me," an unfamiliar voice said. Startled, Fae looked up to see a glowing figure in a black dress. Morgan and Jenny were standing at Fae's side, looking just as shocked as Fae felt.

"Who are you?" Fae asked.

"I'm someone who would rather kill you than look at you." The woman shook her head, and Fae's stomach took a turn. The stranger's head seemed to wobble. She reached up, as if to steady it, but not before Fae caught sight of light peeking through a crack in the woman's neck. It looked like she'd been decapitated. "I didn't help you out of any sympathy I felt. But there is one person I hate more than pathetic do-gooders like yourselves. And he wants to keep you locked up in that well. I plan to make the rest of his short life a living hell. Helping you helped me. Now go on. Run, get help. Let the Order catch him. But you better do it soon, Lafayette heard the commotion and is coming out to investigate." At those words, she disappeared.

Fae jumped to her feet and took off running toward the woods. Morgan kept pace at her side. Fae was surprised to see Morgan's image grow transparent in the darkness.

Morgan confirmed her suspicions when she said, "You won't be able to see me for much longer—there's not enough limestone out here—but I have to tell you something."

"What?" Fae said as she started to get winded. Too bad she wasn't a runner. She needed to put as much distance between her and Lafayette as she could before night fell completely, but it was already hard to navigate in the forest among the shadows.

"As soon as you can, bring the FBI back here. I don't want that kid..."

Fae looked at her curiously when she hesitated. "The nerd?"

Morgan nodded.

"So, what, you don't want him to get hurt? He doesn't seem like your type, Morgan."

"No," Morgan gagged. "That's so disgusting. I just don't want him..."

Fae looked at her when she paused.

"Eating me," Morgan finally said.

Fae gasped and stumbled. She caught herself and stopped to turn around.

"Don't stop," Morgan shouted. "Keep going."

Fae returned to running, dodging trees and vines as she moved. Thunder rumbled in the distance. *Please don't let it rain.* "So, he..." She couldn't bring herself to say it.

"Ate the witch—the one who helped us back there," Morgan said. Fae once again felt sick. "Well, he's still working on her. When he's finished, I'm sure either Jenny or I will be next. Right now, I still look pretty good, so it'll likely be me. Jenny's frozen solid."

"She's in the freezer?"

Morgan frowned. "Yeah."

What had Morgan seen? "Okay, I promise." Fae swallowed back bile. "I won't let him take one bite out of you."

Morgan smiled weakly. "Thanks. Oh, and before I forget. I painted you a wedding present. It's wrapped and hidden in the back of my closet."

Fae fought back tears. Would she ever see Morgan again? What was going to happen to her? Captain Abela and Dolores had been haunting the fort in St. Augustine for over two hundred years. Would Morgan have the same fate? If only Fae could save her like she saved Becca.

Fae glanced over at Morgan, shocked to see she was nearly gone—just a shimmer of her remained. They must be getting far away from the limestone. Fae stopped and turned to take one last look at what was left of her friend. "I'm going to miss you, Morgan. I couldn't have asked for a better roommate or a better friend."

There was just the faintest chuckle, and a whispered phrase, "You got that right."

Morgan's image dissipated when Lafayette's red, snarling face blasted through it.

Chapter 33

"What do you mean there's no way to track her?" Nick snarled.

Thomas turned to his team as the last of them filtered in. They had taken over one of the college's offices, much to the surprise of the night security guards. Well, they were surprised for a moment before Miller worked his vampire mojo on them. Now they were going about business as if Thomas and his team weren't even there.

Thomas ignored Nick's question and said, "I want the entire campus in lockdown."

"I don't know how I'll get the guards to agree to that," Miller said. "It's one thing giving their minds a nudge; what you're proposing would take much more power than I have."

"Tell them the students are in danger. Tell them there's an armed man on campus. I don't care what you tell them! I want every entrance and exit covered, I want this campus searched, I want students questioned, I want to know exactly where Lafayette is, and I want him and every one of his cohorts brought in, dead or alive."

All eyes widened and several jaws dropped.

"You have your orders," Thomas said. "Now you're dismissed."

The group dispersed, and Thomas stepped up to Nick's side. "You're with me. We're going to search Fae's room."

Nick nodded and kept pace with Thomas as they walked under the glow of the sidewalk lights, heading across campus. He could feel the tension rolling off Thomas. Something was seriously wrong.

Minutes later they were standing in Fae's room.

"I'm just guessing here," Nick finally said, breaking the silence, "but what you did back there was way beyond protocol. What happened?"

Thomas's lips were pressed together in a thin line. He pulled out his phone and showed him a text.

Hello, Agent Thomas. Or should I call you Kaare? I have someone that might mean something to you. We couldn't help but notice that she is reeking of your scent. A succubus is a strange mate for a cougar, but who am I to judge?

Knowing your kind mates for life, I'm guessing that you're ready to rip my throat out about now. Am I right? Well, I'm offering to let her go unharmed, if you deliver up to me Nick Chase—dead. Oh, and if you have any second thoughts about giving in to my demands, I have your woman chained outside in a clearing. So, that would mean you have till sunrise.

Text me when the agent is dead, and I'll tell you where to meet me.

Nick swore. "I'm hoping you aren't thinking of giving in to his demands." He frowned when Thomas didn't give a quick dismissal.

"We need to find them before the time is up," Thomas said.

"What happens to Avira at sunrise?"

Thomas swallowed. "She dies."

"We need to get to her before then."

"Way to state the obvious," Thomas sneered.

"Doesn't Conall have a way of tracking Fae?"

Thomas shook his head. "Your bond with her *was* our way to track her."

"How did they break it so easily?"

"Lafayette has been a guardian of the Fountain of Youth for a long time. I guess he learned a thing or two."

"Yeah, and your guards screwed up."

"They did their job."

"One of them should have stayed with Fae." Nick narrowed his eyes.

"Yes, one should have." Thomas rubbed his eyes as if he were fighting off a headache. Nick pulled up a chair and opened Fae's laptop.

"What are you looking for?"

"Cell phone records. I know it's wishful thinking, but maybe I can track Fae and Morgan." Nick's fingers flew over the keyboard.

"Morgan?"

"Fae said she was worried. She hadn't seen or heard from her roommate since yesterday afternoon. I'm guessing Lafayette used her as bait. Ah, here we go."

"You got the cell phone records already?" Thomas stood, looking over his shoulder.

"I got Fae's, but that was easy. I know all her passwords. It'll take a few more minutes to get Morgan's."

A moment later, Nick said, "Got it."

Nick and Thomas both read the texts, and Nick's blood began to boil. It was just as he suspected. "I knew it. But..." His fingers flew over the keyboard, and the screen he wanted popped up. He cursed loudly. "Either Lafayette has turned off the GPS locator on both their cell phones, or they're in an area so remote, it doesn't get service. They dropped off the radar about sixty miles south of here. But knowing Lafayette's tendency to send us off on wild goose chases..."

"Yeah," Thomas said. "They could be anywhere. Is there no other way to track them? You don't have any hacker trick?"

"No."

Thomas paced the floor. "Let's go over what we know. We know Lafayette's running around with Lavinia and a couple other Disorder members—one a known shifter, and the other we're not sure of. He looks like a new recruit."

"Who's this Lavinia?"

"She's a nasty witch. Conall has a long history with her—not a good one. She's worse than Lafayette. And she's powerful. She has to be the one who subdued Avira. None of the others are powerful enough."

"So how do we find her?" Nick asked.

"That's an age-old question. The Order has been trying to catch her for over two hundred years."

"We need to find them today." Being surrounded by everything Fae had owned, everything she'd touched, and even her lingering smell... It drove him mad that she wasn't there with him. That she wasn't safe.

"Our best bet is finding Lafayette," Thomas said.

"Okay." Nick tried to force himself to think analytically. "Let's go over again what we know about Lafayette. His real name is Demarquis Lafayette. The one alias we've found is Marcus DeCruise. He's about six-foot-three, a hundred and eighty pounds. He has blond hair, crew-cut style." The familiarity of the description hit him with great force. He swore as he pounded his fist against the desk. "I'm such an idiot!"

"What?" Thomas said, his eyes wide.

"I need to go back to the FBI," Nick said as he packed up his computer.

"In the middle of the night?"

"I just need to talk to one person."

"Why? What resources could this person have that we don't?"

"A witness."

Nick and Thomas made their way up a flagstone pathway to a small beach-front, clapboard home. It was midnight, but every light in the house was on. The crisp, salty-sea air blew over them as they stepped up onto the porch. This was the address Sanchez had given them.

Even before they knocked, the door flew open, and a familiar face appeared. "You found her, didn't you?" the woman said with a mixture of hope and anguish.

"Olivia Harris?" Thomas said.

She nodded as she chewed on her bottom lip. "Did you find my sister? Is she still alive?"

"May we come in?" Nick asked.

She pulled the door open and stepped back.

The place was neatly decorated with bright, cheerful colors and lots of throw pillows.

"Ms. Harris," Thomas said. "We have a few questions to ask."

"I'm not answering a single question until you answer mine. Is my sister still alive?"

"We don't know," Nick said.

"But I thought you found her?"

"Not yet," Thomas said. "But we suspect who she might be with."

"He's a killer, isn't he? I let her go home with a murderer."

"What makes you think that?" Nick asked.

"Well, I don't know," she snapped. "How about the fact that she never came home?" Her voice rose in volume until she shouted.

"Calm down, Ms. Harris," Thomas said.

"Calm down?" She continued to shout. "How am I supposed to calm down? You don't know whether she's dead or alive."

"Your best bet of finding your sister," Nick said, "is to keep your cool and help us figure out where she's being held."

Olivia sank into a seat and dropped her face into her hands. "So, you know who has Jenny. It's Marcus, isn't it? I let her leave with a criminal."

Thomas sighed. "His full name is Demarquis Lafayette. Most call him Lafayette, but he also uses the alias Marcus DeCruise."

"Who is he? What kind of monster took my sister?"

They hesitated to tell her, especially seeing how fragile she was.

"Please, just tell me the truth." She raised her pleading, teary eyes to them.

"He's a disturbed man, but he's not a killer," Thomas lied. "He's abducted women before, but he keeps them alive, if that makes you feel any better."

Nick suppressed his reaction. He was shocked that Thomas was outright lying to this poor woman.

Tears brimmed in Olivia's eyes as relief flooded her face. "Are you telling me the truth?"

"I would never lie about something like this," Thomas said with sincerity in his voice. This guy was an amazing actor.

For the next half hour, they drilled her for information. She answered readily, even eagerly, with a light in her eyes and hope in her voice. When they finally left, they had some real leads.

"I don't know if I agree with your methods, but I'm so sick with worry over Fae, I'm not going to lecture you."

"I'm not proud of what I had to do," Thomas said, "but we only have until sunrise. And you saw how messed up Olivia was. If I had told her the truth, we would have gotten nothing more out of her. She'll have to deal with reality soon enough."

"What chance do you think Jenny has of being alive?"

"Slim to none."

Nick didn't want to ask about Fae's chances. Was he living in denial about Fae's fate? He hoped beyond hope that he wasn't.

Chapter 34

Fae awoke with a pounding in her skull. Raising her head, she tried to get her bearings. She sat on the ground, leaning against a post. A familiar scent surrounded her—a mixture of dust and old animal stalls. She opened her eyes to darkness that was pierced by a sliver of moonlight coming through a barn door. She tried to move, only to find that she wasn't just leaning against a post, she was tied to it.

"Hey," she shouted, her voice driving like a nail into her head. Lafayette must have hit her hard to give her a migraine as bad as this one. Nausea rose in her stomach, and she fought it back.

"And beauty awakes." Lafayette's voice filtered in as he stepped through the door, carrying a lantern.

Fae blinked back tears. She absolutely hated feeling helpless. "What are you going to do with me?"

"I can't say how much you disappoint me." He frowned at her as he set the lantern on the table beside her. "I'd learned so much about you, Fae. I thought I knew you. How kind and self-sacrificing you were. I guess you're only self-sacrificing when you think your knight in shining armor will save you."

"What are you talking about?"

"You ran away and left your dear friend Morgan," he said with a raised eyebrow. "I thought your concern would be primarily for your friend."

"Morgan's dead," Fae said, her voice hollow.

Lafayette blinked in surprise. "Now that's just not true."

"You're lying," Fae said.

"What happened to that trusting soul you used to have?"

"I've never trusted you."

"Well, you can trust me on this." He turned to glance behind him. "Morgan, come in here and tell your roommate you're alive."

Fae's heart dropped when Morgan walked into the room. Her face was bruised, her clothes tattered, and there was no ethereal glow. This was no ghost.

Morgan turned her eyes on Fae, and Fae's stomach twisted in a knot. She was looking into the eyes of a corpse.

"Get her away from me," Fae snarled.

"Interesting." Lafayette took a step toward her. "Tell me what you see."

Fae turned to him, anger boiling under her skin. "I see a walking corpse."

"The term is zombie," Morgan said in her familiar, haughty voice—the voice she used when talking about people she didn't like. It felt so wrong hearing that voice coming from a corpse—even a corpse that looked like Morgan. She narrowed her dead eyes at Fae. "And the way you're looking at me tells me you have a problem with zombies."

Was she serious?

"There's nothing wrong with who and what I am," Morgan said. "I'm still the same me, I still have the same hopes and dreams. I'm still a beautiful person inside and out."

Fae looked on in distrust. This couldn't possibly be the real Morgan. Her spirit floated around somewhere. But perhaps there was enough of the real Morgan left in there—locked inside her brain—that she may be telling the truth. Morgan continued to ramble on in her usual way, so much so that Fae wondered if a part of her friend *was* still in there.

"You still don't believe me, don't you?" Morgan asked Fae.

"I...I don't know."

"Well, you know what? I don't think I like you anymore." She turned to Lafayette. "Can I have her? That guy in there just doesn't taste right, and his screams are really getting on my nerves!"

Fae's stomach heaved when she realized what Morgan meant. No! That wasn't Morgan. That was simply her animated corpse. Fae pushed back the bile that rose in her throat and said, "But I thought you were the same old Morgan. Morgan never would have...done what you're doing."

"Excuse me. Did you not hear the part about me being a zombie? I swear no one listens to me!" She turned back to Lafayette. "So, what do you say?"

"If you'd started on Theon's brain like I told you," Lafayette said, clearly irritated. "He wouldn't be bothering you."

"Have you ever tried to get into someone skull? It's harder than it looks. I tried banging it against the floor, but that didn't even crack it. And then I tried—"

"Do you have to ramble on so much?" Lafayette bellowed, his voice rising until he roared in anger. "I swear, I should have kept Theon and had him finish you off. I still might if you don't shut up!"

Morgan snapped her mouth shut as she nursed what looked to be a bite mark on her arm. Her lips were quivering as she turned on her heels and bolted out the door.

Lafayette breathed heavily, then seem to relax. He turned back to Fae, smiled weakly, and sighed. "As you see, Morgan is still alive, as agreed."

"You make me sick," Fae said.

"Yeah, well, you make me young. And as long as you continue to keep me young, you and I are stuck together." He stepped forward and crouched down next to her. "Listen, I'm sorry about Morgan. I'm sorry about a lot of things I've done lately—locking you in a dungeon, throwing you down a well, killing your friend. I truly don't know why I've been acting so crazy. I'm not usually like this. But I'm trying to make things right. I thought by bringing Morgan back, it would go toward making restitution to you. I thought it would fix things. I think it still can. I'm sure she'll come around. Theon acted pretty normal in his nerdy kind of way, so I'm sure Morgan—"

"Are you talking about the guy Morgan is eating?" Fae interrupted.

Lafayette blushed. "Um, yeah. Sorry, that didn't sound right, did it?"

Is this guy for real? "Listen," Fae said, "if you really want to make restitution, I know exactly what you can do. Let me go."

He shook his head. "You're asking the one thing I absolutely cannot do."

"Why not?" she asked.

"What if I can't find you again? I'll die."

"Yeah, maybe in fifty or sixty years. Everyone dies sometime."

"No. Not me. I refuse to die. I refuse to disappear into nothingness."

"You're not going to disappear. Don't you believe in life after death?"

"Do you think my fate would be any better? If there were life after death, I'd be going to hell and I'd burn for eternity for what I've done."

"You can't know that."

"And you can't know any of it. You don't understand. You've never had to look at the face of death and wonder. You're immortal."

"That's not true. I may not age, but I can definitely die. You almost killed me yourself when you drank my blood and left me in that dungeon."

"You're lying. I know about your ability to heal quickly."

"That ability comes from my blood, which you drained—leaving me vulnerable."

"I...I'm sorry. I didn't mean to do that."

"You're only sorry you almost lost your blood supply."

"Yes. And I won't risk it again. I've got the bear working on your next home. And this time, I'm keeping you close." He squatted down and brushed his fingers across her cheek.

Fae jerked back. "What are you talking about?"

"I'm keeping you right here. In the well. I'll just fill it with water, bolt a steel door down, and put you in. We've got a filtration system and everything. This will be a much better home for you than that dungeon."

"You're crazy!"

Lafayette pulled out his phone and swiped the screen. "Probably, but Hunter is getting it...ready..." His voice dropped off as confusion spread over his face. He furiously tapped his screen, and horror spread across his face. He burst into rage and a string of profanities poured from his mouth. He stepped toward the doorway and bellowed, "Hunter, I need you to come here now!"

Minutes later, a huge man stepped into the lamplight. "What is it, boss?"

"Did you use my phone to text anyone?"

His eyes widened in surprise. "No, of course not."

Lafayette glared at the phone in his hand. "It had to be Theon."

"What did Theon do?" Hunter asked with a hint of regret in his eyes. Fae wondered how he felt about Morgan eating the nerd. From what she saw, she thought he might not appreciate it. Perhaps Theon was a friend of his. She might be able to use that to her advantage.

"He texted Kaare and offered him a trade! The FBI agent for Avira." Lafayette dragged his fingers through his hair. "At least he asked for a dead FBI agent. That's one less person I have to worry about."

Fae's heart took off on a sprint. Would Thomas really kill Nick to save the woman he loved?

"But we don't have Avira," Hunter said.

"You don't think I know that?" Lafayette snapped. "Theon was probably after a snack. That kid has a ravenous appetite."

"Had." Sadness darkened Hunter's face.

He did like the zombie nerd.

Lafayette's eyes widened.

"Morgan found the sledge hammer," Hunter said.

Fae felt sick again. This whole situation sickened her. "That's not Morgan," she said.

Hunter turned a glaring eye on her. He looked livid. As if all this was her fault! She didn't ask to be ripped out of her world and taken here. And Morgan didn't ask to be murdered and her body brought back soulless and craving human flesh.

Lafayette didn't even acknowledge that she had spoken. "Theon deserved to have his head bashed in," Lafayette said. "Do you know what Kaare is capable of? And he thinks we have his mate! He's going to be tearing apart every lead until he finds us."

"And you don't think Nick isn't already doing that?" Fae asked.

Finally, Lafayette turned to frown at her. "Agent Chase can't decapitate me with a swipe of his claw or eat me while I'm alive and screaming. A werecougar can and will do that—especially when his mate is threatened."

"So, what do we do?" Hunter asked.

Lafayette narrowed his eyes. "We move forward with our plans. There's no way they can trace this farmhouse to me. I left no leads, no trail. We should be safe." They stepped out the door and started back to the house. "How soon before it's ready?"

"It's nearly done. Putting on the cover should be easy enough, and then we'll just need to fill it with water and turn on the filtration pump."

"As soon as it's ready," Lafayette said, "put her inside and..." their voices trailed off.

He's going to trap me in that old well and fill it with water? "Oh, no you won't." Fae pulled on the rope tied around her wrists, but the harder she pulled, the tighter it got. Finally, it was so tight that she couldn't feel her fingers. She looked around in a last attempt to find a way to escape. Lafayette had left the burning lantern. It didn't help her though. There was absolutely nothing within reach.

Where were her ghosts when she needed them? "Morgan? Jenny? Where are you?" she whispered loudly. Maybe they were still at the well. They had a hard enough time removing the old grate. A steel door would be impossible. This situation in the barn provided her best chance for escape.

"Morgan! You can't leave me here like this!" She hoped to see their glowing faces any moment, but they didn't come.

A darkened silhouette stepped into the doorway. Morgan stepped into the lamplight as she entered the room. Blood covered her smiling mouth and dripped down her chin. "You called?"

Chapter 35

Nick sat at his former boss's desk, furiously searching through this year's auto sales of '66 Chrysler Windsors. There were a good number of them, but none around the area where Jenny was kidnapped.

Thomas paced the floor and once again stopped to glance at the clock. "It's six o'clock, we have—"

"An hour and thirteen minutes. I know."

Nick turned his focus back on the case. Perhaps the car wasn't bought but stolen. Nick started a new search. Results popped up immediately. Young had a wicked fast computer. "Ah ha!" he shouted.

"What?" Thomas said.

"I've got something. There was a report of a missing black '66 Winsor fifteen miles from the location of the kidnapping, and it so happens the theft occurred the day before Jenny disappeared."

"But if it's stolen, how do we find it?"

"I haven't gotten that far."

Thomas swore. "We have to find it before sunrise."

"I know." Nick's fingers flew over the keys. "Let me just check a few things." A strange pattern emerged as he searched reports in and around the area where the car was stolen. "This is odd. There was a missing person's report that was never properly followed up on."

"So?"

"Apparently, the person who reported it turned up dead the day after the report. The police didn't put two and two together because the man filing the report lived two hours away and died of so-called natural causes—a heart attack."

"A heart attack doesn't sound strange to me."

"The man was twenty-five."

"So, he was young. That's not unheard of."

Nick dug deeper as he pulled up related files. "And here's another strange coincidence. The man who was reported missing signed over the deed to his house to someone named Mark Hansen. But it happened just two days before the man disappeared."

Thomas breathed a curse. "Mark? Marcus? That can't be a coincidence. I think we're looking at another alias. Where is the home located?"

"Sixty-eight miles south from here."

Thomas grabbed his jacket and jogged toward the door. Nick followed on his heel.

"This better be it," Thomas said. "If we're wrong, Avira is dead."

Nick wanted to assure him that he wasn't wrong, but he couldn't. This was the best lead they had, but it wasn't a sure thing by a long shot.

They averaged a hundred and fifty miles an hour down I95. Nick was shocked they didn't see any flashing lights along the way. Finally, they turned off and made their way through rural forests and swamps.

The sky began to brighten as the sun approached the horizon. Nick glanced over at Thomas. He clutched the steering wheel so tight, there was blood dripping down his wrists. He hadn't retracted his claws since he noticed the first glimmer of sunlight on the horizon. He also hadn't said a word.

Nick was worried himself about Fae. He had no way of knowing if she were alive or dead. He only knew one thing: if Lafayette has killed her, Nick would rip him apart with his bare hands. He didn't care if it landed him in prison. If Lafayette had harmed her in any way, he would pay for what he did.

Nick glanced over when he heard a low rumbling growl coming from Thomas. Nick had a feeling Thomas was thinking along the same lines—though Thomas was more equipped to rip people to shreds than Nick was.

Finally, they came to an old, beat-up mailbox at the head of a dirt driveway. Thomas passed by the box, pulled into a hollow in the foliage, and parked. Reaching into the back seat, he grabbed a thick blanket under his arm.

"Our priority is search and rescue," Thomas said. "Vengeance will come later."

"Agreed," Nick said as he headed into the trees. They moved in silence for several minutes before Thomas grabbed Nick by the arm and pulled him to a stop.

"What?" Nick whispered harshly.

Thomas nodded toward the ground. In front of them in an unbroken line, sat a row of rocks going on as far as he could see. Thomas gestured to the left. Nick's gaze followed his. There was a small candle flickering in the wind. As brisk as the wind blew, it should have blown it out.

"That's a protection circle," Thomas said. "If we try to pass this..."

"What?" Nick said.

"Bad things will happen."

An especially hard gust of wind blew at Nick's back. Leaves fluttered around the candle, and it flickered out.

Thomas turned to Nick, his eyes wide. "That's not supposed to happen."

"What does that mean?"

"The protection spell is broken. The witch is inviting us in. Why? I have no idea, but we need to proceed with caution." Thomas pulled out his gun, and Nick followed suit.

They moved carefully, and quickly. The glow of a porch light beckoned them forward. They kept to the trees to see the layout. Nick could see the touch of direct sunlight lighten the leaves on the tops of the trees. They had little time before time ran out.

A low growl rumbled from Thomas's chest. "I need to change," he whispered. "This body is too slow."

Nick nodded. "You look for Avira, and I'll check the house."

Thomas nodded as he stripped out of his clothes. Nick's eyes were on the house as he moved forward. He stopped when Thomas began to transform, and his eyes locked on the strange sight. Thomas's whole body quivered. His face morphed and changed. Hairs sprouted over his body and he hunched over, hands turning to paws just before they touched the ground. In seconds, a large mountain lion stood before him. Thomas raised his head to scent the air and leaped back into the forest.

Nick shook off the awe and turned back to the house. A shout caused him to stop in his tracks. *That was a woman's cry.* It very well could be Fae. It seemed to come from behind—toward the barn.

Nick sprinted to the old barn and stopped at the door. He looked inside. By the light of a flickering lamp, he could see two women wrestling on the ground. The one on the bottom kicked her foot around and pinned the leg of the other woman, then lifted her hips. The woman on top—unable to move her foot—tumbled off to the side. Fae's frantic face surfaced and locked eyes with him. "Nick," she breathed as she scrambled away. He rushed forward just as she was yanked back. The other woman had caught her by the ankle.

Nick lifted his gun. "Let her go or I'll put a bullet in your head."

The other woman paused, her head down, her face covered by a mop of wild hair. She lifted her head, and he breathed out a curse. It was Morgan. Her face was covered in smears of blood, and her once vibrant eyes were now clouded over. If he didn't know better, he'd say it was the face of a dead woman.

"Morgan?" he said, stunned.

"Nick!" She smiled, her teeth tinged with red. "How's it going?" she asked, her words slightly slurred, and there was a gurgle deep in her throat.

"What are you doing to Fae?"

"Fae?" Morgan said. "Oh, she's being a terrible friend. She hates what I've become. But you know it's not like I asked for all this." Morgan yanked on Fae's leg.

"Let her go," Nick said.

Morgan frowned. "Fine." She let go and Fae scrambled to her feet. She rushed to his side and wrapped her arms around his waist. Even though they were not out of danger, he couldn't help the wave of relief that washed over him at having her so close.

"What happened to you?" he asked Morgan. He kept one hand tight around Fae's shoulders and the other grasping his gun, pointing it at Morgan.

337

"Lafayette killed me, and then he brought me back." She shrugged. "It's really not so bad."

"Not so bad?" Fae said. "You cracked open someone's skull."

"I was hungry," Morgan shrugged.

Nick's blood ran cold. His stomach twisted. Would he ever get used to this crazy new world?

"Besides, he had it coming," Morgan said. "He would have done the same to me."

"The question now is," Nick said. "What do I do with you? I can't just leave you like you are. You could hurt innocent people. But I've got to get Fae out of here."

A growl rumbled at Nick's back as heavy footsteps padded the ground behind him. Nick turned to see a massive grizzly bear raise up on its hind legs. Before he could turn his gun on him, the bear knocked him and Fae to the ground. The gun went flying as heavy paws slashed at him. Nick covered Fae with his body to shield her from the onslaught. Pain sliced across his back again and again as Nick roared.

"Hunter," a man shouted. "Stop before you kill him."

The bear ceased his attack. His warm breath blew the back of Nick's neck. Nick collapsed to the ground. The pain flared in his back, and darkness seeped into the edge of his vision. Through the darkness, he could see Lafayette standing in the doorway. His brows creased as he pursed his lips. He looked genuinely worried.

"We might need him alive." He turned to Morgan. "And what are you doing here, my dear?"

She didn't answer. She simply bolted out the other door.

"I'm afraid I'm going to have to put her down." Lafayette shook his head.

"She's not an animal," Fae said.

"I beg to differ," Lafayette said. "She's nothing more than a rabid dog." He turned to the bear. "Take Agent Chase to the cellar."

This bear must be highly trained—or Lafayette was certifiably crazy.

"You're not going to kill me?" Nick asked.

"Not yet," Lafayette answered.

"What are you going to do with Fae?" he asked, dreading the answer.

"She and I are going back to the house to get intimately acquainted before she goes into the well. That'll give her something to dream about for the next decade while she sleeps. Don't worry, I'll be gentle with her."

Adrenaline shot through Nick. His pain forgotten, he leaped to his feet and charged Lafayette. "I'll kill you," he snarled. Lafayette sidestepped him and threw a punch. Nick anticipated the move and blocked it. Nick let his training take over as he punched, parried, blocked, and then went on the attack again. They traded blows, both landing strikes determined to kill the other. Nick shook off the pain each time Lafayette's fist connected and fought back harder.

Lafayette stepped back, gasping for breath. Nick did the same. "You're a natural born fighter, Agent Chase. I can't tell you how good it is to finally go the rounds with someone close to my equal."

"You're equal? I don't think so, old man." Nick charged again, faking right and then coming at him from the left. He shouted as his fist flew. The punch landed, Nick could feel the bones crunch under his knuckles.

Lafayette roared in pain as dropped to his knees. His arms circled his head to block any further onslaught. Nick's next target wasn't his head, though. He gave his kick everything he had, but this time targeted Lafayette's groin as the villain's threat filled his thoughts. If he had anything to do with it, Lafayette would never touch another woman, ever again—especially Fae.

Lafayette crumpled to the ground, writhing in pain. "It's over, Lafayette," he said even as Fae shouted, "Look out!"

He turned his head just in time to see a massive paw flying towards his face. There was a flash of pain, and then everything went black.

Chapter 36

Fae's heart dropped when Nick fell unconscious to the ground. She had fists of fur in her hands, but her attempts to stop a full-grown grizzly bear had been about as effective as a fly trying to stop a speeding train.

Fae held her breath as she watched the bear sniff Nick as he lay face down on the ground. Lafayette moaned and grumbled profanities.

"I'm going to kill him. I swear I will tear him limb from limb." He attempted to stagger to his feet. His face was already so swollen Fae could barely recognize him.

Fae gasped as the bear stood on its hind legs and changed right in front of her, morphing into a man.

"I'd be happy to do that for you, boss."

Fae rushed forward, covering Nick's bloody body with hers. "You stay away from him." She glared at the man-bear and then at Lafayette. He narrowed his eyes as he stepped toward her. His open hand flew. She ducked. As soon as his back was turned, she threw a punch to his kidney. Lafayette roared. Strong arms pulled her back and locked her in a vice.

She fell back into her training, dropping her weight and throwing her head back, kicking her heels up behind her. Nothing worked. This man wasn't much smaller as a man than he was as a bear, and he seemed to anticipate her every move.

Lafayette shuffled into her line of vision. "You've made a big mistake, Fontaine. And Nick will pay for your error. I have half a mind to skin him alive and feed him to Morgan. I've done much worse for less than what you both have done to me."

"You do that, and I'll destroy your precious Fountain of Youth."

"And how, pray tell me, would you do that?" Lafayette asked.

"I'll kill myself."

"Ah, a suicide threat. How juvenile and shortsighted. Well, my dear, I won't give you the chance." He looked at Hunter. "Is the well ready?"

"It's ready, but it's still filling with water. It should be full very soon—I'd say about ten minutes."

"Put her in it now." Lafayette hobbled away, obviously still in pain. "And keep her from injuring herself," he shouted over his shoulder.

Hunter kept his arms around her and carried her away. "No, let me go," she shouted as she looked back at Nick, lying there helpless. Would this be the last time she saw him alive? Tears streamed down her face. "If you don't let me go, I swear I'll kill you."

"You're full of empty threats." He smirked.

Fae did everything her training taught her as she tried to break free. He simply countered her strikes, eventually wrenching both of her arms behind her back.

"You're a feisty one, aren't you?" He hauled her down the familiar path.

She could hear rushing water just before they reached the well. When it came into view, Fae's heart sank. There was a heavy steel cover over the well. A thick padlock lay on the ground beside it. Lafayette was right. There was no way she or her ghost helpers could open this.

"Let me go," she shouted. She squirmed and flailed her legs—anything to keep him from putting her down the well.

"Stop fighting me." He grabbed a fistful of hair and yanked it back, bringing her face to face with his livid expression. "If you don't go in there peacefully, I'll return to my bear form and rip your fiancé's throat out. I swear I'll do it."

Fae immediately went limp. "Please," she whispered. "Why are you doing this?"

"Lafayette is paying me handsomely."

"You really think he's going to pay you? Did he agree to pay Theon too?"

Doubt flickered in his eyes, and then he narrowed them. Using his one free hand, he heaved the door open. She could see a shimmer of water about two feet down from the top. "Get in," he growled. His tone let her know there would be no debate.

Fae's legs were shaking when she swung them over the side. Her feet went in the water first.

"Now," he said, "get in."

He pushed her, and she plunged into the blackness. Her breath stole away as the fear squeezed her chest. When she could finally breathe, she gasped.

She looked up to see Hunter frowning down on her. "Listen," he said. "I'm not completely heartless, so I'm going to do you a favor." He leaned down, and before she could guess what he was going to do, he pushed her head under the surface. Fae thrashed around as she tried desperately to get a breath of air. Through the panic and desperation, she felt something else—the same feeling she felt when Lafayette drank her blood. It was power, and she was giving it to him. The Lady of the fountain was right; they only needed to touch the water to gain youthfulness.

Those thoughts flew from her mind when her chest began to burn. She needed air! Finally, she couldn't fight it anymore. She took in a deep breath. Water filled her lungs. The burn in her chest stopped, and she felt such tremendous relief, she nearly cried.

And then she could focus again. Power was leaving her body, going to Hunter. She was giving him youth—the man who might kill Nick.

No! She wouldn't do it. Fae concentrated all her efforts on pulling that power away from him. And then something snapped. What was once flowing from and through her was sucked up deep inside.

Hunter swore and pulled his hand out like the water had suddenly burned him. Her face broke through the surface of the water.

He shook his head and took a deep breath. "So, you've learned to control your power. That might have helped you before, but now it's too late." He looked around at her prison. "Enjoy your stay. From now on, you're on your own." The metal cover slammed down, trapping Fae in a nightmare.

Nick's pulse pounded against his skull. He tried to take a deep breath and sucked something gritty into his mouth. Turning his head, he coughed and spat. It was dirt. He'd been lying facedown on the floor. He tried to get his bearings as he looked around. He was still in the barn. Daylight streamed through the door and spilled through the slats in the barn walls.

What happened? Brushing his hand across his head, he came away with blood.

It was the freakin' bear. He'd swiped him with his paw.

"What happened to you?" A familiar voice accompanied a figure entering the barn. Thomas was back.

"Got mauled by a bear," Nick said. "Avira?"

"There's no sign of her. I searched every inch of the property. She's not here, I can't even catch a hint of her scent. It must have been a ruse to draw us here."

"You're probably right, but I don't think it was Lafayette. He didn't seem too happy we showed up." He staggered to his feet. They needed to find Fae before something bad happened to her.

"He invited us here," Thomas said, following Nick to the door.

Nick stuck to the shadows as he peeked around the corner. He could see Lafayette's house just ahead. No one was in sight.

Nick turned back and whispered. "He invited us through a text. I don't think he was the one who sent the message."

"Interesting," Thomas said, frowning.

Nick moved to leave when the front door opened. A large, bare-chested man walked through. Nick sank back into the shadows.

"Hunter," Thomas growled.

"Who?"

"The bear," Thomas said. "Hunter is a shifter."

"I *thought* the bear was incredibly well trained." Nick scowled. "I should have known."

"I'll handle the bear," Thomas said and then stepped into the sunlight. He didn't take his eyes off Hunter when he said to Nick, "You find Fae."

347

Thomas raced toward the man and leaped into the air. Mid-flight, his body morphed and the cougar came down, tackling the man. They both rolled, tumbling off the porch. It looked like it would be a short fight as the cougar snarled and mauled. Less than a second later, he was thrown back. The grizzly recovered quickly and rose to stand on his hind legs.

Nick didn't waste a moment as he ran into the open door of the house. He passed through the main floor, searching for Fae. He moved quickly and silently. Though, with the animal's snarls and growls reverberating from the outside, Lafayette had to know that his hideout was under attack. Nick wished he still had his gun. He'd have to use hand-to-hand combat—if Lafayette didn't shoot him first.

Nick headed for the stairs and took the steps two at a time as he rushed forward. Room by room, he searched, coming up empty. Maybe Lafayette wasn't here.

When he came to the last door, he opened it.

Something silver whizzed toward him—a spinning blade. He knew he wouldn't have enough time to dodge it. He was about to be decapitated. A feeling of hopelessness filled his heart just before a cool breeze passed over him.

The blade's path curved. Pain slashed his neck and he heard a thud behind him. He slapped his hand against the wound. Shock and elation greeted him as he felt only a slight nick and drizzle of blood. He thought he'd lost his head.

Lafayette snarled as he threw another blade. Again, icy wind passed over Nick as the blade's path curved—this time it didn't touch him.

Nick could hear a woman's laughter in his ear as Lafayette cursed and charged him. Nick anticipated the move and stepped off to the side. But Lafayette must've had a backup plan. His hand shot out, silver glinting from the knife he clutched.

Pain exploded in Nick's stomach. He looked down. The handle of a knife was all he could see. The blade was embedded in his abdomen, and it burned like the deepest pits of hell. Nick's eyes widened when he noticed smoke rising from the wound. What did Lafayette do? Dip it in acid?

Nick moved to remove the knife, but Lafayette shoved it deeper. Nick roared in pain and dropped to his knee.

"Burns, doesn't it?" Lafayette sneered. "That's because this knife is made of iron."

Nick scrunched his brows. "Iron?" How could Lafayette know about his allergy?

Lafayette scoffed. "You know nothing about being a Fay, do you?"

Lafayette spun around. Nick knew he was preparing to kick him, but he was in too much pain to react fast enough. Lafayette's kick landed directly against the knife, driving the rest of it into Nick's body. Nick collapsed to the floor, writhing in agony.

Lafayette stepped over him to the doorway and pulled a blade from where it was embedded in the wood. He returned, grabbed Nick by the hair—exposing his neck, and held the blade against it.

"This is where you die, Agent Chase."

Beg him to take you to Fae.

Nick could hear an unfamiliar voice in his mind. He knew it wasn't his own or anyone else he knew. This was the voice of a stranger. And why should he listen to her? The last thing he wanted was for Fae to see him murdered right in front of her.

Do it!

The voice reverberated against his skull.

Despite serious doubts, he suddenly realized that this voice probably belonged to the same being that was responsible for keeping his head connected to his shoulders. Whoever it was, he decided to take a leap of faith and follow her instructions.

"Please," Nick said, gasping from the pain in his stomach. "Just let me see Fae one last time."

Lafayette's eyes narrowed. "You really want her to see you get your throat slit?"

No, he didn't. Regardless he said, "I just need to see her one last time."

Lafayette didn't answer right away. He seemed to mull it over in his mind. "Okay, I'll allow it, but only because I think it would be entertaining to watch Fae's heart get crushed and her hopes disintegrate. But you'll have to walk. There's no way I'm carrying you."

Nick nodded. His body screamed at him as he pushed himself off the floor. His stomach heaved, and he did his best not to vomit.

"I don't have all day for this." Lafayette pushed him forward. Nick stumbled, the agony stealing his breath away. Still, he managed to right himself again, and he moved forward.

They passed by the cougar and the bear—both of them bloody and barely able to stand. The cougar's concerned eyes flickered to Nick, and the bear took the advantage as he leaped forward and tackled him. Nick wished he could help, but he was in no better condition than Thomas.

Nick saw what looked like an old well with a steel lid bolted over the top. The sound of running water echoed off the metal trap. Lafayette pulled out a key, opened a thick padlock, and heaved the cover open.

Nick stumbled over to the well and peered down. At first, he saw nothing, and then his adrenaline spiked as Fae's ethereal face rose to just below the surface.

"Fae," he breathed.

Chapter 37

Nick's his heart raced. Fae looked from Nick's face down to the blood soaking his shirt and then over to Lafayette. Rage darkened her features.

Nick's heart skipped a beat when he heard Fae's voice in his head.

Bring Lafayette to me.

No! he screamed, answering her in his own head, not knowing if she could even hear him.

I know what to do, Nick, she answered. *I'll be fine. Trust me.*

Lafayette clamped his hand down on Nick's shoulder. "Say your goodbyes. I've got things to do."

Nick grabbed Lafayette's hand and pulled him forward. Lafayette must have anticipated the move. The next thing Nick knew, he lay on his back staring up at the blue sky.

"Nice try, agent. But I've heard that Fae has learned to control her power to give and take life. I won't be going near that well while she's still awake."

Lafayette knelt beside Nick, grabbed his hair, and wrenched his head back—exposing his neck. Lafayette pressed a blade against Nick's skin. He could feel the blade prick him as warm blood dripped down his neck. Water splashed in the background. "Now, Nick Chase, this time it reallyis time for you to die."

"Lafayette." A hollow voice spoke like a whisper of wind.

Nick looked up to see a glowing figure hovering in the air just above them. Her black dress floated like ghostly tendrils, and she glared in hatred at Lafayette.

"You thought killing me would be the end?" she said. "You're a fool, Lafayette."

"Lavinia," he gasped, his eyes wide as he dropped his blade. "No, it can't be."

Dark clouds billowed above and darkened the sun as she grew and expanded. She had to be at least fifteen feet tall! Her face transformed from beautiful to grotesque. Just the sight of her could give a grown man nightmares!

"You not only severed my head from my body," she continued, "you allowed my flesh to be devoured. While I was still alive!"

Nick covered his ears. Her voice bellowed so loud he thought his eardrums might burst.

"Now, you will get what you deserve. Death. But as the saying goes, 'Death is only the beginning.' For you, my dear Lafayette, I will make your eternal existence an unending nightmare from which there is no escape."

Lafayette turned and ran. He'd only made it two steps before he was swept off the ground by an unseen force. He screamed and flailed as he floated above the well. Fae pulled herself up and reached for him.

"Please," he wailed, "let me go!"

"As you wish," Lavinia said as she dropped him into Fae's arms. "See you on the other side."

Lafayette and Fae sank down. He surfaced again quickly, coughing and sputtering, clawing at the side of the well. He splashed down again.

Nick grabbed the knife still embedded in his stomach and yanked it out. He felt immediate relief. Ignoring the lingering pain, he rushed to the well and reached down to pull Lafayette from the water. He didn't want this man anywhere close to Fae. When Lafayette looked up, Nick was shocked to see his face. It aged right in front of his eyes—the twenty-two-year-old man who had faced him just moments before now looked deep into his forties, and growing older. Fifty. Sixty. Seventy. And then it stopped.

Lafayette gasped. "She stopped. Oh, please, Fontaine, no more."

Nick hauled him from the water as Lavinia screamed at their backs. He shoved Lafayette face down on the ground and slapped handcuffs on him.

"Finish him!" Lavinia snarled.

Fae's hand slapped over the side of the well as she pulled herself up from the water. Nick rushed to her and dragged her from the water. She coughed as she expelled the fluid from her lungs.

"Why won't you destroy this man? He would destroy you and everyone you love," Lavinia said, confusion on her face.

"Because," Fae said, her rasping voice barely above a whisper. "I'm not like him. I've taken back the youth he stole from me, and now he'll face the justice system for the lives he took."

Nick's heart swelled with pride.

"Well, I'm not like you either," Lavinia said. Nick saw a flash of movement from Lafayette. His head turned sharply, and Nick heard a snap. Lafayette slumped to the ground and lay still. Lavinia had broken his neck.

"I'll give the Order today to clean up this mess," Lavinia said. "But, after that, I will not tolerate anyone else on my land. Any human or supernatural creature that ventures here will face my wrath. I've lived a long life; I'm ready to rest. Do not let anyone disturb me. Is that clear?"

Nick nodded. "Yes."

"Oh, and keep Conall away."

Nick wondered what kind of history Conall had with Lavinia. Everyone was so tight-lipped about it. He dismissed the thought. He had much better things to focus on. He held Fae safely in his arms. Lafayette couldn't hurt her ever again.

"I can't believe it's over." Fae pressed her cheek against his chest. Nick kissed the top of her head. Fae looked up. Her face still glowed as she smiled. He blinked at her radiance as she pulled him down for a kiss.

Nick closed his eyes and savored the taste, the touch, and the feel of Fae. He could feel power surging through him and wiping away all the worry and the pain of his injuries. In moments, he felt completely whole again. But the most incredible thing—Fae was here, she was his, and he would never again let her go.

When they finally pulled away from each other, he couldn't contain his smile.

"You don't know how happy I am that this is over," she said.

Nick laughed. "I think I may have an idea."

Fae looked around, avoiding looking at Lafayette. "Did you come here alone?"

Nick swore. "I forgot. Thomas is here." He grabbed her hand, and they took off running.

When they came to the clearing around the house, they saw Thomas looking a bit worse for wear and holding Morgan by the throat. The bear lay dead at his feet. His throat had been ripped out.

"Please, Nick," Morgan said, her eyes frantic. "You have to save me."

Nick pursed his lips as he stepped toward her.

"She has no pulse," Thomas said. "And she reeks of decay."

"What's the protocol for this situation?" Nick asked.

"There's nothing we can do for her." Thomas shook his head.

The spinning of gravel caught their attention. They turned to see Avira's car speeding toward them. She braked and the car slid, stopping inches from them.

She opened the door and jumped out, stopping short when she saw there was no danger. Nick wondered about the danger of sunlight for a second until he saw she was completely covered in a wide-brimmed hat, trench coat, and gloves.

"I got your message, love," she said, looking at Thomas.

"I can't tell you how good it is to see you alive," Thomas said, relief evident on his face.

"Looks like I should have been more worried about you than I was," she said. "You look like you've been put through a shredder."

"Nope. Just had a run-in with an old friend." He glanced over at the dead bear.

"Is that Hunter?" she asked with surprise on her face.

"It was Hunter," he answered.

"And who's that you're holding?" She eyed Morgan.

"This was Fae's friend."

Avira's expression saddened as she approached.

"Is there anything you can do?" Fae asked, her voice shaky.

"I'm not sure," she answered. She stopped just out of reach as Morgan squirmed in Thomas's grip. "How did you die, Morgan?"

"I don't want to talk about it." She frowned.

"I may be able to help you, but I need to know how you died."

Morgan's eyes darted from face to face, distrust in her expression. Finally, her focus rested on Avira. "He got angry when I wouldn't stop talking. Then he..."

"Go on," Avira said.

"Suffocated me with a pillow."

Avira sighed with a hint of a smile. She turned to Fae. "I think we can help her."

"We?" Fae said with disbelief.

"Physical trauma would have made it hopeless, but suffocation...that we can work with."

"What do you want me to do?"

"You need to turn back the clock for her, so to speak, and then I can return her spirit to her body."

"You can do that?"

"If her spirit hasn't moved on."

"I don't think it has. I've seen her."

"Where?"

"By the well," Fae sighed. "She was there. She helped me. But I haven't seen her for a while. What if she's gone?"

"Let's just go back there and see," Avira said.

Fae led the way. They all followed her—including Thomas, who still had Morgan in his grip. Nick could tell Fae was worried. She squeezed his hand so tightly it cut off his circulation.

When they got to the well, Avira looked at the dead body.

"Looks like you handled Lafayette."

Nick shook his head. "That wasn't us, it was Lavinia. Well, her ghost, actually."

Avira raised her eyebrows. "That's convenient." She pressed her hands against the well. "Limestone. No wonder you could see her." She waved her hand in a circular motion and Morgan's transparent form appeared alongside a woman who looked eerily like Olivia Harris. Nick frowned. Looks like they were too late to save her sister.

"Morgan," Avira said, "it's good to meet you." She turned to the second ghost. "And I haven't met you either.

Thomas stepped forward. "You're Jenny, aren't you?"

The woman's eyes widened. "You know who I am?"

Thomas nodded. "Your sister is looking for you."

Jenny's face saddened. "I figured she was."

"Can we help Jenny too?" Fae asked.

"I'm not sure," Avira said, and then turned to Jenny. "Hello, Jenny. I'm Avira. I know it's painful to recall, but I need to ask you. Do you remember how you died?"

She nodded, her eyes haunted. "He broke my neck."

"I'm sorry to hear that," Avira said, looking truly saddened. "I'm afraid there's nothing we can do for her."

"But I healed Nick," Fae said.

"Nick is part Fae, and the power you healed him with is faery magic. Jenny is human."

"Why did you bring that?" Morgan's ghost asked as she gestured toward her corpse. She avoided looking directly at it. The sight of her body obviously unnerved her.

"We may not be able to help Jenny, but I think we can help you," Avira said.

"I'm dead," Morgan said. "There's nothing any of you can do."

"But, there is," Avira said. "Do you know why Lafayette wanted Fae?"

Morgan shook her head.

"She has the power to restore youth. She can turn back the clock. And me...I'm a succubus. I can send your spirit back into your body."

"Are you saying I can be brought back to life?" She turned to the woman at her side. "But you can't help Jenny?"

"I wish we could help her," Avira said, "but we can't. But I *can* help her move on."

"To heaven?" Jenny asked. "Would I be able to see my mother again?"

Avira nodded. "Yes."

Jenny smiled, looking truly happy, and then her face darkened again. "You'll need to tell Olivia."

"I'll tell her," Fae said.

"We'll tell her," Nick said, entwining his fingers with hers.

Fae looked over at him and nodded.

"Okay, Morgan, Fae," Avira said. "It's time."

Fae nodded and stepped toward the well. She sat at the side and dipped her hand into the water. Thomas moved Morgan's corpse to the water. She'd stopped struggling. Maybe she wanted to be restored.

Morgan reached her bloodied hand toward the water and dipped her fingertips in, clouding the water with red. The first thing Nick noticed was her skin flush with color, then her milky-white eyes cleared up and were bright again. In less than a minute, she looked like her old self.

"Okay, Morgan," Avira said, looking at the glowing figure floating nearby. Avira reached out her hand, and Morgan's image swirled into an unrecognizable mist. The mist swirled around Morgan's now-healthy looking body and disappeared.

Morgan took a deep breath and reached her hands up to touch her own face. "It worked!" She started jumping up and down and shrieking. "It worked, it worked, it worked!" She turned and threw her arms around Fae. "Thank you, thank you! Oh, my

361

gawd! I can't believe I'm alive." She looked from face to face, and then her expression fell when her eyes landed on Jenny. "I'm so sorry," she said with tears in her eyes.

Jenny shook her head. "Don't be. I knew it was hopeless for me. I'm just happy that monster didn't take everything from you."

"I'll never forget you," Morgan said, choking on her words.

"And I won't forget you," Jenny said.

"Are you ready?" Avira said, stepping up to Jenny.

Jenny nodded.

Avira reached out, and a bright light appeared just a few feet away from them.

"What do I do?" Jenny said.

"It's simple," Avira said. "Go toward the light."

Jenny nodded, with a smile lighting her face. She stepped toward it and then turned back. "Wish me luck."

Everyone nodded and said, "Good luck."

And then she started to glow. She brightened so much that they couldn't look directly at her. And then the light was gone.

Epilogue

Fae stood in front of the full-length mirror, amazed at her reflection. The wedding dress was perfect. Becca was right. With the capped sleeves, scalloped neck, fitted bodice, and full skirt, she looked like she had stepped out of a fairytale. She seriously felt like Cinderella after her wish was granted.

"Come on." Morgan took her by the arm and pulled her forward.

"Morgan's right," Becca said. "It's time to get that ball and chain shackled to your ankle."

Fae frowned. "That ball and chain is your brother."

"Yeah, so I should know what you're getting yourself into. Did you know that when Nick is feeling down, he likes to listen to Hall and Oats?"

"Who are Hall and Oats?" Fae asked.

"Believe me, you don't want to know!" Becca said with a sparkle in her eyes.

"Sorry, but nothing you say will change my mind." Fae tried to hold back her smile. She didn't succeed.

"Don't say I didn't warn you." Becca smirked.

Fae didn't know what she would have done without Becca or Morgan. She couldn't believe they pulled off this wedding so quickly. They were miracle workers.

Thomas and Mason stepped into the room. Her would-be guardian didn't even give her a passing glance. Mason's eyes were on Becca and he was actually smiling! Becca smiled in return as a blush touched her cheeks. He approached her, leaned down, and whispered something in her ear. Becca's face lit up as she nodded. Mason offered her his arm and they followed Morgan out the door. Fae wondered if Nick knew about this development in his sister's love life.

Probably not. She'll wait until after the honeymoon to enlighten him.

Everyone but Fae and Thomas filed out. Thomas stepped to her side, and she linked her arm in his. He grinned as he looked down at her. "You ready?"

Fae nodded and swallowed.

With Thomas on her arm and her bouquet clutched in her hand, Fae stepped into the cathedral. Light spilled in from the stained-glass window, blanketing the throng of guests—who were all looking at her. Her chest quivered in nervousness as she searched for the one person she wanted to see.

And there he was, smiling at her. Standing in his tux, Nick looked so handsome she could swear her heart stopped. Her nervousness evaporated as she focused only on him.

The music began, filling the cathedral, and Fae took her first step toward her new life.

The End

About the Author:

 Holly Kelly is a mom who writes books in her spare time. Translation—she hides in the bathroom with her laptop and locks the door while the kids destroy the house and smear peanut butter on the walls. She's married to a wonderful husband, James, and they are currently raising six rambunctious children. Her interests are reading, writing (of course), martial arts, visual arts, creating Halloween props, and spending time with family.

You can find all of Holly Kelly's books on her website:

AuthorHollyKelly.com

Coming 2017
The next installment in
The Unnatural States of America Series:

Beauty and the

Horseman's Head.

~A Sleepy Hollow Story

Made in the USA
San Bernardino, CA
12 January 2019